Magick's Pathway – A Haller Lake Series – Book 2

Lauren Marie

Copyright

Magick's Pathway
Books to Go Now Publication

ISBN-13:978-1985417892

ISBN-10:1985417898

Excerpt from
Magick's Pathway

"I want to try something else. Close your eyes. Can you hear me?" Roman asked.

"Yes, I can hear you." Kris smiled.

"Keep your eyes closed, babe," he said.

Kris heard his footsteps move away from her.

What about now, can you still hear me?

"Of course, Roman. You're beginning to sound like that telephone commercial. What are you doing?"

Which direction are you hearing me from?

Kris felt her eyebrows crease. What did he mean which direction?

Tell me, where am I coming to you from?

It suddenly occurred to her that he spoke to her mentally. *I know what you're doing,* she thought.

Can you find me?

Kris opened her eyes and glanced around the trees. *Are.*

we going to play hide and seek?

If you find me, I'll give you a treat.

In memory of my grandparents - Florence and Ray Davis. I miss you and know we'll meet again.

.

OTHER BOOKS BY LAUREN MARIE

Going to Another Place

One Touch at Cobb's Bar and Grill - Montana Ranch series,

short story

Loves Touch - Then and Now

Love's Embers - Canon City series book 1

Love on Ice - Canon City series book 2

I'm Not What You Think - short story

Golden Ribbons - The Miss Demeanor Detective Agency

series - short story

Big Mike, Little Mike - short story

The Haller Lake series - A Demon Scheme

YOU CAN FIND LAUREN MARIE HERE:

twitter- Lauren Marie @HallerLake11

https://www.facebook.com/lauren.marie.963

https://www.facebook.com/lauren.marie.books

laurenmariebooks.com

LAUREN MARIE

PREFACE

"You'll need to be careful, Pelonus. She still isn't aware of her powers and would be able to level you easily." Garda scratched his beard and looked at the demon.

Pelonus pushed his dark hair over his shoulder, flopping into a chair by Garda's fireplace. He wiggled his fingers and started a roaring blaze in the hole. "Your room is cold. Why do you insist on surrounding yourself with spirits?"

"They're helpful in watching the humans." Garda continued to sit by his seeing pool. He waited for a sign, but all he saw was the woman and the Lakeman celebrating their nuptials. It infuriated him that they'd married and she was now pregnant. "I wanted to send Guillermo in to turn the woman, but he is not available at this time."

Pelonus snorted and laughed. "Not available, you say? I heard he was having a wonderful time in Asia and not answering your summons."

"My oldest son does have a mind of his own. It is trying," Garda said. He didn't want to give too much information, but needed someone to go after the woman.

The demon stretched out his legs. "What do I get when I turn the woman?"

Garda sat back in his seat and smiled. "You could

have the child."

Pelonus made a disgusted face. "What would I want with her spawn? It would be years before it would be old enough to play the game. I haven't the time to deal with baby dung and snot."

The elder demon nodded his head and played his trump card. "There is another. The Lake Guard is bringing in a young one who has remarkable abilities." Garda twisted his hair between his fingers.

Pelonus stood and strolled around the room. "Tell me about this young one. What can I expect?"

"His powers are in their virgin state at the moment. He knows of his abilities, but is leery of using them. The Guard superiors have kept a tight hold on him knowing what he wields. He can open portals easily, which is unusual for one so young."

"What is his age?" Pelonus turned to the senior demon.

"One-hundred and twenty-nine."

Moving along the boundaries of the room with his back to Garda, Pelonus continued his circuit. "Interesting. Where does he originate from?"

"Somewhere from the North country; he's Canadian."

"Is he a native?"

"No, I believe he has a Scottish background, but I could do a bit more checking if you find acquiring him worthy," Garda said and knew he had Pelonus where he wanted him.

Finding his way back to his chair before the fire, Pelonus tented his fingers and looked into the flames.

"It's been a time since I've had an assistant with any powers. My minions are low in the demon pecking order, I don't believe they can see up. Fine, you have a deal. I'll take the Guard, you can have the woman and child," Pelonus said, and closed his eyes.

"Fine, fine, she's only just conceived. It will be best to wait until its birth before you get to work. I want the woman more than the child, really. It could stay with its father, but the woman, I believe, would make a perfect mate for Guillermo. He needs to settle down and start working on another seventh," Garda said. He turned his gaze back to the seeing pool. "Sebastian!"

Quick footfalls sounded from the hall outside Garda's seeing room. The three-foot troll turned a corner and walked up to his master's chair.

"Yes, my lord, how may I serve you?" the diminutive being asked and stared at the floor.

"Bring my guest a drink," Garda said.

The troll looked fearfully at the demon who sat by the fire. "What may I get you, sir?"

Pelonus opened his eyes, and watched the troll. "Kool-Aid, with extra sugar would do nicely. I want no ice, though."

****

The Oracle leaned over her bubbling cauldron. She looked into the holy water which was blessed by one of the priest's from the temple, traced her finger over the steam and put her palm down into the bubbles. She, too, waited for a sign or vision to show in the depths below, but nothing appeared. As she continued to be patient, she saw the water turn muddy and smiled.

Come to me, a voice echoed in her head.

She'd seen the birth of the child not long ago and knew this would be a momentous occurrence. They would have to watch this one. He would play an important role in the future of the world. Unless God changed his mind about this young one, he would go far.

I'm waiting for you, the voice continued.

As she gazed into the steam, she saw something move out of the murky water. She leaned farther over the pot, and felt the warmth surround her. Something pulled at her. In the darkness below, she saw the face of one of the Guardians. He'd been taken by an evil and turned. His black eyes creased in laughter as his blonde locks blew around his face.

She knew something wasn't right with what she saw and heard. The pool never looked this murky. For some reason unknown to her, the Oracle couldn't sort out what created the unbalance.

She straightened, knowing the new Guardian would have to be watched, too. For the first time in hundreds of years, she didn't know what action she should take.

****

"Roman, it's time."

"Wait. Now? Do you mean now?"

"Yes, babe. I mean now."

"I'd better get Cassie to drive us, I think I'd put the car in the ditch.

Chapter One

Kris looked down at her little three-month-old bundle and continued to hum. Otter slept, but she knew from experience, if she moved, he would stir and want more humming.

She thought about the way things settled over the last year and laughed. If you'd asked her a year and a half ago what she would be doing now, she never would have come up with this scenario.

In June, when her ankles swelled and the doctor insisted she slow down, Roman went into overdrive trying to keep her in bed. She did some work from her computer, but every time she sat at her desk for five minutes, Roman would begin to growl at her. He'd pick her up and carry her back into the bedroom, scolding her and threatening to report her to the doctor.

Kris desperately loved her handsome husband, but she wanted to bat him upside the head at times. She didn't like it when he growled.

They argued often about her desire to work. Roman spent almost five-hundred years as a Lake Guardian and was compensated for his work. Since he hadn't spent much of the money, Roman turned out quite wealthy and felt that Kris didn't need her job.

With the baby on the way, Roman decided they needed to enlarge their own house. He hired a contractor and spent a good amount of time adding on two rooms. After the framing was finished, Roman worked on the rooms by himself, although he did bring in an electrician to do the wiring. Kris almost went into a fit when he mentioned doing the electrical work himself and thought he'd get zapped. In the new part of the house, one room would be a nursery and the other an office for her.

Kris rocked the baby and did a self-evaluation. Right now her agent work for artists was put on hold so she could care for her son. Her self-healing, psychic and sometimes a spirit-splitting abilities were ignored for the last year and Elzabeth, her alter-ego, still appeared from time to time.

Her husband, Roman, retired from the Lake Guard, still insisted on protecting her even though nothing evil came there way for some time. Since retiring, he kept himself busy every day helping the neighbors with chores or being Kris's personal bodyguard and nurse.

The three Lake Guardians at Haller, Omar, the leader, and Marcus, his second, who'd both served with Roman for a couple hundred years and the newest arrival, Cedric, did their work daily and became uncles to her little boy.

Kris thought about her best friend, Cassie, and smiled. She still practiced her white witchcraft and did her art work. How she found the time was beyond Kris's realm of understanding. Cassie and Omar were involved. Very involved.

Her other friend, Lorrie, also a practicing witch, previously owned the lot where Cassie built her house. Lorrie's house got blown up last year and she chose to sell the lot and move to another part of the state. She said the magicks were getting too intense and because of being caught up in negative situations, she'd decided to leave. She'd broken up with Marcus, the quiet one of the Guardians. When she left, he said very little to anyone and seemed very sad and lonely.

In the eight years Kris lived by the lake, she'd never known about the Guardians. She'd drank that stupid glass of poisoned wine which caused her mind to open to other-worldly possibilities and she'd been able to see Roman. Her love for him grew fast and she worried many times that he would have doubts once her abilities were all exposed. Kris shook her head when she remembered her usual human hang-ups back then, particularly when their romance moved so quickly. In the end, none of her worries counted for much, and she felt happy.

During the last month of her pregnancy, an odd thing occurred which surprised both of them. As they lay in bed one night with Kris on her side so she could breathe and Roman behind her with his hand rubbing her big belly, suddenly, his hand stopped and she felt him push up to a sitting position, without moving his hand.

"What's the matter, babe?" Kris asked, half asleep.

"Oh my God," he whispered.

She opened her eyes and looked over her shoulder at him. He stared at her stomach and when she followed his arm down to his hand, realized his merge spot lit up brightly.

"Roman, what are you doing?" She watched him move his hand away and saw a small round light on the skin of her belly.

"Kris, put your palm there." He pointed at the spot.

She did as he said and found a connection with her

child. "Oh," was all she could say. The experience felt miraculous and the innocence incredible. Kris looked up at Roman. "Is this normal?"

"I have no idea." He smiled, and put his hand over hers.

Kris felt herself pulled into a vision, which hadn't happened once in the last year. She could see Haller Lake, with the green grass and trees surrounding it. Ducks, geese and other critters lazed around it, but that was all she saw.

"Kris, what's happening? Are you seeing something?" Roman asked.

"It's weird, as though the baby's trying to show me something, but I'm only seeing the lake. It looks peaceful," she said with her eyes closed.

The next day, Roman told Omar what happened and asked him to check with the Oracle about this. When Omar returned, he said the Oracle commented she'd never heard of such a thing, but they should be grateful and thank God for this blessing.

When the baby finally decided to appear in early July, Kris felt ready to have her body back and glad to make his acquaintance in person instead of magically. She spent the first few hours focusing only on him. She'd read in a baby book that the attachment formed between a mother and child is most important in the first few days. Kris took the advice to heart and almost refused a couple of times to let the nurse put him back in the bassinette.

She laughed when she remembered how they'd gone in circles for months about names. They finally agreed on Elliott Roman Lake. Elliott was her dad's middle name. Kris threatened no more sex if her husband wouldn't agree to his name as the middle. He was dead set against using his name at all, but finally gave in. Roman started calling him Otter from the last three letters of Elliott and that's what they'd called him since.

All the way through the pregnancy and, for a couple of months after, things around the lake were pretty calm. Kris only experienced the one vision when connected with the baby and her alter ego, Elzabeth, stayed quiet. Roman and Kris started to run in the morning and slowly her body got back into shape. Cassie enjoyed babysitting and told them to go.

Their one-year wedding anniversary approached and Roman tried to be sneaky, but she knew he was up to something. No matter how hard she worked at tripping him up, it made no difference. He wouldn't say a word.

Kris purchased a round, white gold piece about the size of a nickel. The word MERGE was engraved on it, and then zigzag cut in half. One side said ME the other RGE with the cut just by the R. It was a small thing, but she thought he would get a kick out of it. He would get the ME side.

Chapter Two

It was the middle of the night and Kris thought she'd heard Otter squeak in the baby monitor over on Roman's night stand. Carefully she pulled herself out of his hold and tip-toed across the living room to the door that led to the nursery. She found that sweet little face looking up at her. He'd pushed his blanket off and kicked his feet in and out.

"Are you getting some exercise, young man?" she asked. Kris leaned over the crib, pulled him out and sat in the rocker. She wasn't much of a singer, but she could hum and Otter seemed to like it. According to the pediatrician, he was ahead on the growth curve. He'd be a big boy.

Kris undid the top of her nightshirt and adjusted him so he could latch onto her breast to feed. Breast feeding turned out to be a great interest for Roman at first. Then, Kris thought, he'd seemed a bit jealous, but got over it and now watched with a smile on his face.

As she rocked and hummed, Kris realized the strange feeling of a vision came on and felt herself being pulled into the darkness. She thought, at first, that maybe she'd fallen asleep and dreamt, but felt too aware of what went on around her. It reminded her of a vision she'd experienced last year when she saw Rochelle and Shadrach in a mirror. Again, a woman walked around the shore of the lake. Kris stood some distance away and the difference between visions was so obvious, but strange. Kris saw the houses were there and the paved road that ran around it. In the prior vision with Rochelle, there were only trees and water. Now she could see the lawns and flowerbeds. The woman wore modern clothes and had blonde, short hair. She seemed familiar.

Kris jumped a little and opened her eyes. Otter stopped sucking and looked up at her. He gurgled and began to squirm a little. Kris started to move him up to her shoulder to be burped, but he seemed intent on not doing that. His arms flailed around and she finally caught his tiny little hand in hers. This seemed to calm him and he moved his palm toward her merge spot. The light flashed and she got thrown back into the vision, which looked more vibrant and focused than before.

The woman still walked by the water and Kris heard her say, "I miss this place very much." Kris saw a swirling start out in the water and dark, brown locks began to show as a head emerged. She thought Marcus might be coming up. The woman approached him and took his hand. Kris then realized the woman was Lorrie, her friend who gave up magicks and moved to Moses Lake. The only thing she could feel from the vision was that Lorrie might return to their little community from Eastern Washington. It would make Marcus happy. He'd been alone for the last year. It seemed like a good vision until Lorrie turned to look at Kris. Her eyes were black and her grin menacing. Kris heard her say, "You didn't think I'd give up, did you? I won't wait forever."

Kris snapped out of the other world and shook her head. Looking down at Otter, she found he'd fallen asleep. He amazed her, but she felt bewildered, too. She straightened his soft, dark brown hair and kissed his forehead.

Once he lay back in his crib, she buttoned her nightshirt and headed back to the master bedroom. She could hear Roman breathe deeply and debated if she should wake him. He'd kill her if she didn't tell him about the vision right away.

She crawled onto the bed and straddled his hips. "Roman, wake up." She grabbed his arm and shook him a little. "Babe, wake up," Kris said with more force.

He took in a deep breath and his eyes popped open. "Kris, what's wrong? What's happening?" he whispered and tried to sit up.

"Everything's okay, I think. Something really weird just happened," she said. He looked at her with a question in his eyes. "I went in to feed Otter, and started to have a vision. It was a little unfocused and I guess since I held him, I didn't want to be too drawn into it. The vision took place here at the lake and a woman walked along the shore. I opened my eyes and Otter stared up at me. He put his hand over my merge spot and I flashed back into the vision with full force. I think I saw Marcus come out of the water and go to the woman. It looked like Lorrie, but her eyes were black and she said, 'You didn't think I'd give up.' Roman, the important part right now is Otter. Do you think he's aware of the connection? Do you think he brought me back into the vision?" she asked.

He put his hands on her thighs. The warmth of his touch calmed her some. "Babe, I think he was aware before he was born."

"Did we pass it to him in our genes or whatever?"

"Yeah, I mean, how else could he have gotten it?" Roman shook his head and yawned. "I am concerned about this vision," he said. "In fact, I'm very concerned. What do you think she meant?"

"I don't know." Kris felt her eyes open wider. "Roman, what if it was Rochelle? What if she went after Lorrie and took her as her vessel before her time was up?"

Roman appeared to think about the idea. "I suppose it could be possible. Perhaps we shouldn't have trusted that she would just cross over when we abolished the three."

"We didn't really abolish three, only Abednego and Shadrach. Rochelle took care of Meshach for us." Kris reached over to her nightstand and grabbed her cell phone. She dialed Lorrie's number and hit Send. Listening to it ring, Kris looked at the clock and saw it was just before three o'clock in the morning. Lorrie's message picked up. She heard the beep. "Lorrie, this is Kris. I know it's the middle of the night, but we need to talk to you. It's very important, so the minute you get this message, call us back. We're up. Bye." Kris clicked the phone closed. She looked down at Roman pinned underneath her. "Babe, we need to warn Marcus, too. I didn't see his eyes, but I wonder."

"I don't believe he can be turned, Kris. Marcus is very strong-willed."

"True, but women can make men do the strangest things. He's been alone for almost a year." She put her hands down on his stomach. "Roman, I know it's late or early, but we need to let Marcus know."

He patted her thigh and she swung off of him so he could get up. He put on his sweatpants and walked out to the back deck. Kris followed and stood with him.

He leaned on the railing and closed his eyes. She

could see his lips move and knew he called to Marcus.

Although Roman was no longer a Lake Guard and the portal between there and the other realm of Parcel were closed to him, he could still contact the others mentally.

Kris watched the water and after several minutes, she saw a head come up and out. An obvious male figure jogged up the incline. It was Cedric, the new third of the Lakemen. As he ran, he shook his head, drying his blond hair. Kris never understood how they could be dripping wet one minute and then totally dry. It also confused her when she found out the Guard considered Cedric a youngster at the tender age of one-hundred-twenty-nine.

"Sir, what can I do for you?" he asked.

"Where is Marcus this day?" Roman frowned.

"He is in Parcel, playing Coopley at the inn."

"What of Omar?" Roman's brows creased.

"He is with Miss Cassandra, sir."

Roman glanced over at Cassie's dark house. "And you've been left on watch alone?"

"Yes, sir, but it is a quiet morning." The young man smiled. "All boundaries are clear, the water balances are equal."

Roman crossed his arms. "When Marcus decides to return back to work, tell him I need to speak with him urgently."

"Of course, sir. Would you like for me to wake Mr. Omar?" Cedric got a mischievous grin on his face.

"No, Cedric, you'd only make him angry. Just have them stop by in the morning."

"Yes, sir." Cedric turned and went back to the shore.

Kris walked up behind Roman and put her arms around his waist. He put his hands over hers.

"How come I have the insane feeling we are not going back to bed?" he asked.

She grinned. "Because you are a man who knows his wife all too well and I won't be able to relax until we speak to either Lorrie or Marcus. I'd also like Omar to ask the Oracle again about the merge spots. She has to know something."

Roman turned and put his hands on her waist. He started kissing her neck and ear. "Come back to bed, my wife. I need to get some sleep if I'm going to keep up with Otter today," he said and chuckled.

"Yeah, I suppose I should try to sleep. I need to do some work," she said and yawned.

Roman lifted Kris up and wrapped her legs around his waist. "I wish you wouldn't work yet. You're still building your strength and Otter will need you here, too."

"It's been three months Roman and now you're making me feeling guilty."

"Guilty? Why?"

"A friend could be in trouble and here I am just thinking about working. Doesn't it make me selfish?"

Roman arched his eyebrow and started to move toward the house. "Then I'm selfish, too. There's nothing we can do right now. No need to feel guilty, my love." He carried her back to bed.

Chapter Three

Marcus, the dark-haired, second-in-command Lake Guard, swam through the portal leaving Parcel. He skimmed the bottom of Haller Lake and checked the contents of the silt at this depth. Fish dashed around him, some catching the smaller amoebas brought up by Marcus. He checked the boundaries and found nothing amiss.

When his head came out of the water, he heard a call in his mind. It was Cedric, who carried a message from Mr. Lake. They met up half way across the lake, treading water easily.

"Marcus, Mr. Lake wishes to speak with you immediately," Cedric said.

"Thank you, brother." Marcus went under the water and picked up speed, heading to the north end of the lake. He saw the beach approach, slowed, and walked up the incline. He stopped on the shore, shook the water out of his hair and then moved across the grass toward Kris and Roman's back door. He tapped lightly on the window.

Roman opened the door and smiled. "Greetings, brother. Come in."

Marcus moved into the kitchen. He saw Kris at the table with the baby in her arms, cooing and playing with a rattle. She looked up at Marcus and smiled, saying hello as he walked toward her.

"Good morning. How's the little one today?" he

asked.

****

Kris felt Otter jerk in her arms when Marcus spoke. He turned his little head toward the sound and opened his eyes wide. Kris sensed the baby felt a bit disturbed by Marcus's presence and wondered if he'd witnessed the vision, too.

"He's fine today, Uncle Marcus. Did you win at Coopley last night?" she asked, while the baby squirmed away from the Lake Guard.

****

Roman noticed his son's behavior and felt his brows crease.

"No, just broke even." Marcus sat down across from her.

Roman saw the baby watch Marcus with a slight frown on his little face.

"I think I need to go change someone and get him down for a nap. I'll be right back." Kris stood and headed toward the nursery.

Roman sat at the table. "Tell me, Marcus, does Omar believe it's wise to have Cedric on watch alone at night?"

Marcus smiled. "You'd be surprised at just how clever Cedric is. Did you know he could open portals?" Roman shook his head. "It's a rare talent. It's been said he is reminding some of the old Guard of another young intern from many years ago." He arched his brow.

"Yes, well, those were different days and I've never been able to open portals." Roman folded his hands on the table. "He is young, but does seem very wily and able. I will have to speak to Omar about it."

"Brother, I know I don't need to remind you, but

23

you are retired."

Roman glanced at him. "Yes, yes, I know, and I should let Omar lead in his own way. Sometimes Omar can be a bit devilish in his decisions and I am just concerned."

"Of course," Marcus quieted.

Roman knew Omar kept an eye on Cedric to be sure he conformed to the Guardian regulations. With the abilities and talent Cedric possessed, it would be easy for him to be led astray.

Kris came back in. "Would you like some tea or coffee, Marcus?"

"No, I'm fine, thank you."

"Babe?" She held up the pot. Roman shook his head. She emptied the pot into her cup and turned to the table. "Have you told him?" she asked Roman as she sat down.

"No." Roman leaned back in his chair. "I wanted to wait for you since you experienced the vision."

"Thank you. Marcus, the reason...well,"—she took his hand—"Before we go into the details, let me ask if you have spoken to Lorrie in the last couple of weeks?"

He pressed his lips together. "I've heard nothing from her in some time. The Guards over at Moses Lake checked on her for me, but I couldn't keep asking them to do that. The last time, though, the house she'd been renting was empty and she'd left. I've heard nothing since."

Kris looked across the table at Roman. "Marcus, I had a vision early this morning. It's the first one in a long while. Lorrie walked by the lake and you met her."

"Are you saying Lorrie might be coming back?" He smiled.

Roman knew Marcus missed her so much over the last year. He'd tried to convince her to stay in Seattle, but she'd been determined to get away from the magicks. He'd spoken to Roman about it a little and felt he should have tried harder to keep Lorrie with him, but in the end she'd left Haller Lake.

Kris took Roman's hand. "Her eyes were black and she asked me if I thought she was going to give up."

Marcus sat back in his chair and shook his head. He looked back at Kris. "And me. Was I turned, too?"

She reached across the table and grasped his hand again. "I couldn't tell. Your head turned away. Marcus, you are very strong. Roman and I both feel it isn't possible for you to be swayed. You must believe that and protect yourself. I've been trying to reach Lorrie all morning, but have had no luck," Kris said. "I'll keep trying. Marcus, I know you saw Otter's reaction to you when you came in. I think he pulled me into the vision and he may be aware of what I saw. It doesn't mean anything, though. He's only three months old."

"Children are very intuitive, Kris. I don't believe anything evil could convince me to change sides, but...well, anything is possible, right?" he asked. "I will check with the Moses Lake Guards and see if they can find out anything."

"Good," Roman said. "We've speculated that perhaps we trusted Rochelle too quickly last year, and she may have taken Lorrie. It's the only explanation we have at this point, but we could be way off-base. It might be something else."

Marcus nodded his head. He stood up and silently left the kitchen.

****

Lorrie opened her eyes and looked around. She couldn't remember how she'd come to be in this place, but knew she'd been tricked into something. The room felt cold and very quiet. She felt as though her ears were stuffed with cotton. The walls were gray, that much she could tell. She looked at the manacles circling her wrists and pulled on the chain attached to the wall above her head.

Something moved across the room from her. Lorrie tried to focus her vision and thought she must be seeing things. There were four women sitting across from her, all bound the same way as she.

"Where am I?" she asked. Her throat was dry and sore, and she needed water. The women across from her said nothing and continued to watch her. "Who are you?" she asked and sighed.

One of the women, wearing a long dress, with hair falling over her shoulders, opened her mouth. "My name is Beatrice. Did Rochelle bring you here?"

****

Marcus flew back to the lake. He launched into a long dive and swam hard and fast back to the portal. Within minutes, he arrived on the other side. He moved directly to the Guards headquarters. Making his way out of the water, he went to the main hall. There were several communication booths available, where Lakemen could communicate with other waterways around the world. Marcus went to the one closest to him and shut the door. He mentally opened a line of contact with the Lakemen in Eastern Washington, asking them to please check on Lorrie, it was imperative. He told them he would wait for a reply.

It took about an hour. The answer came through

and wasn't good. The house still stood empty and she'd left the place where she'd worked. They didn't have a forwarding address for her.

Marcus began to feel helpless. He couldn't think what to do. If he were to take the channels over to the east side of the state, he'd need Omar's permission, but felt certain he wouldn't find anything. His heart broke. He loved Lorrie very much, but because of her status as a witch and the fact that she'd been easily turned by Shadrach, he couldn't get permission from the leadership to merge with her. He wanted her back, but feared he may have lost her for good.

He swallowed and left the booth. Marcus walked toward the temple attached to the Guards' quarters, went into the prayer hall, and got down on his knees. Opening his mind, he began to pray. "Dear Lord in heaven, give me the strength to follow Your path and not be tempted by the evil that could be approaching. Protect Lorrie, wherever she is, and keep her safe. She is very dear to me. Stay with me always and help me to protect those I love. Guard me with Your strength and power."

He felt the air around him shift and a light flashed. Marcus opened his eyes and found the Oracle standing before him. He admired her for a moment. Her blue eyes were hypnotizing. Marcus then bowed his head to her but felt something was very wrong with her. Just for a second, it seemed her light faded.

I'm sorry to interrupt your prayers, Lakeman, but I've had a vision which is very important and disturbing. You must relay this to your leader and see that plans are processed and carried out. You must protect the lake and the innocents involved.

Yes, Oracle. Marcus looked up at her.

There is an evil coming to your area. I am not certain what its intentions are, but it is focused and determined. Its eye is watching the young one and will try to turn him. You must protect him. He could be turned, as he has not yet gained his full strength. She peered at Marcus and got a strange look in her eyes. *Your heart is strong, Lakeman. You may feel weakened, but you will overcome.*

Thank you, Oracle. I will contact my leader at once. Marcus bowed his head again and waited for the air to clear. He looked back up and saw she still looked down at him.

Lakeman, I am unsure of what I should do next. My mind is not my own, she whispered.

Marcus could see fear in her eyes. *Oracle, how can I assist you?*

Her back straightened and she clasped her hands in front of her. *Do your duty. I need no assistance.*

Her brilliant light caused Marcus to close his eyes. When he opened them again, he saw she'd left the temple. He stood and looked up to the ceiling. "Thank you, Lord for sending us this vision. We will carry on Your way. Amen."

He moved back to the shore, dove into the water and swam to the portal. Marcus sent a mental message to Omar to meet him at the north end of Haller Lake. He passed Cedric on his way and signaled for him to follow. They skimmed the bottom and came up as the shoreline appeared. The group of ducks floating around the area split into two groups and created an opening for the two Lakemen.

****

Omar waited on the incline, his blond locks shining in the sun and his tanned, muscular body covered with clothing.

The Lakemen did their jobs stripped of all clothing, and didn't want to spend time in wet pants. Omar tried to stay dressed when he was out of the water. His mate, Cassie, didn't really care, but since he'd merged with her, he didn't want the neighbors to see his body.

Marcus and Cedric approached him.

"Omar, the Oracle appeared to me in the temple," Marcus said.

Cedric stopped in his tracks, his mouth hanging open.

"The Oracle came to you? How odd. What did she have to say?" Omar felt a bit amused.

"She said there is an evil heading our way. She isn't certain what its intentions are, but she said it is focused on the young one," Marcus continued.

"Otter?" Omar asked.

"She didn't give a name, but that was my understanding. Omar, there was something strange about her. For a moment her light seemed...how do I explain? She seemed dim, somehow. She also said her mind was not her own."

Omar's brows creased as he turned. All three began to walk toward Kris and Roman's house.

"One other thing, Kris experienced a vision this morning. She saw Lorrie walking by the lake with black eyes. I apparently came to Lorrie, but Kris couldn't tell if I'd been turned. Roman and Kris think Rochelle may have taken her."

"Marcus, please remember, Kris's visions are subjective and can change," Omar said. "I doubt very

29

much you would be turned, anyway. We need to remain calm until we have all of the facts."

Chapter Four

Roman sat on the end of the bed and watched Kris dress. She'd made an appointment with an Everett City Council member to discuss an upcoming street fair. The art council tried to be more giving to the various artists in the area. Tom MacAndrew, a gallery owner, gave them Kris's name and she'd agreed to help out in a limited capacity.

"Babe, I'll only be gone a couple of hours. I don't want my breasts to explode and I'm not going to use the damned pump in some public restroom." She slid on her light purple skirt, tucking her shirt in and zipping it.

Roman chuckled.

She put her hand on her hip, and stared at him. "And you can stop laughing. I'd like to see you carry a couple of extra pounds of fluid around on your chest."

"Sorry." He put his hands up. "That pump gizmo does seem rather barbaric."

"It is, and it looks good under the sink in the bathroom, where I hope it rots." She slipped her pumps on and turned to him. "You'll be monitoring, right?" she asked.

"Of course." He smiled.

Ever since Kris argued with him to not monitor her with their merge spots and then got her soul stolen, she insisted he keep an eye on her movements when they were apart.

"Good." She held out her arms. "How'd I do?"

"You look absolutely gorgeous." He walked over to her and put his hands on her waist.

She stood on her toes and kissed him. "Thank you, but I think if I wore a potato sack I'd still look good to you."

Roman glanced at the closet. "Do you even own a potato sack? I'd love to see you in it."

"You are such a goof. I suppose that's why I love you so much." Putting her hands around his neck, she felt his hands cup her rear. She kissed his lips and pulled back. "We'd better stop now. I'll see you soon." She turned to leave their bedroom after a pat on the rump from him and stopped backing into his arms. Looking over her shoulder at him, she added, "What are you doing tonight, good-looking?"

He put his hands around her waist. "I'm thinking I'll be all yours."

"Start your engines, dude, I may be back home in an hour." She turned around, kissed him and then pulled away reluctantly.

She grabbed her keys and purse and opened the back door where she found Omar with his hand up, ready to knock, and Marcus beside him.

He smiled. "Good morning, Kris."

"Hi guys. I have an appointment and will be back." She looked at Marcus. "I'm still trying to reach Lorrie."

"Kris, you can stop," Marcus said.

She wanted to protest, but saw the look on his face. "Oh, no."

"The Moses Lake Guards checked. The house is empty and she's left her job. She's gone."

Kris turned and walked back into the house. Taking her cell phone out of her purse, she punched in a number and hit Send.

"I thought you had an appointment," Omar said.

Kris huffed. "Yes. Can I leave a message for Herb Crowley? This is Kris Bennett-Lake and we have a meeting set for eleven o'clock this morning. I won't be able to make it. I've had an emergency come up. Please let Mr. Crowley know that I'm sorry and will get in touch later in the week to reschedule. Thank you." She clicked her phone off and set it on the counter. Roman stood next to her. She looked at Omar and Marcus. "This isn't good, is it?"

Omar looked at Marcus. "Tell them."

"I was in the temple at the Guards' headquarters this morning after receiving the news from Moses Lake. The Oracle appeared and told me she had a vision. She said an evil is coming and it has its eye on the young one."

When she heard those words, Kris moved quickly toward the nursery with Roman right behind her.

She flung the door opened and went straight to the crib. Otter lay on his back with his fist tucked under his chin, sleeping peacefully. Kris took in a deep breath and felt Roman's hands on her shoulders. "We need to move the crib out to where we can watch it," she whispered.

Roman squeezed her shoulders, and asked Omar to help him move the crib to the living room.

While she changed into a pair of jeans, Kris decided Otter would sleep with her and Roman for a while. She didn't need to have a vision to know there would be an argument with Roman about it. He didn't like the idea of Otter sleeping with them and starting bad habits, but this circumstance was different from a son just wanting attention. They needed to keep him close and safe.

When Kris returned to the kitchen, she saw that Cassie had joined the men and listened to their conversation. She checked the crib again and then walked toward them. "Have you decided if this is Rochelle or some other evil?" she asked.

"That is a hard one to nail down. Rochelle may or may not have taken over Lorrie," Omar replied. "Kris, does Lorrie have a next of kin we could try to contact?"

"She mentioned a brother here in town. Marcus, did you ever meet him?"

"No, her brother wasn't a believer. He couldn't see me."

"We have to keep our ears and eyes open and should get the reserves involved, too. They might be able to discover some information for us. We do need to find Lorrie one way or the other," Omar said.

"One way or the other? What is that supposed to mean?" Kris asked, and crossed her arms.

Roman walked up beside Kris and put his hand around her waist.

"Kris, if she is turned or possessed by Rochelle, we will have to abolish her," Omar said firmly. "She's been taken before by Shadrach, but wasn't completely turned."

"No way, Omar," Kris snapped. "I'm not agreeing to that plan, no way."

Cedric spoke up. "Ah, excuse me, but I'm sensing some tension in the room and I'm not certain why. Could someone please explain?"

Kris tipped her head. "Omar tends to go in with guns blazing and I don't," she said. "It's been a bone stuck in his throat for a while."

"That isn't it and you know it, Kris. We have to protect our area and the people we care for, from the evil. Our major concern is the environment. You know that."

"Yeah, I have to protect my family and friends." She stared at him. "They are more important to me than the lake. Sorry, Omar."

"It is always so strange when you two have a pissing contest," Cassie said.

"I'm not giving up on Lorrie. Even if she is turned, we're getting her back and that's all there is to it," Kris said, and ignored Cassie's comment.

"Okay, okay, before you two take each other's heads off, we need to look at the facts," Roman said, as he held onto Kris. "We don't know for certain that Lorrie was taken by Rochelle. For all we know, Lorrie just left Moses Lake and could be happily residing elsewhere. We also need to find out where and when this evil is coming. Why does it want Otter?"

The room went silent for a moment.

"Roman, let's go back one step. The Oracle said the young one. She didn't state a name specifically. I should have asked for a name," Marcus said.

Kris looked up at Roman and nodded. "It makes sense. Otter has some abilities developing."

The three Guardsmen straightened their posture. Omar was the only one who didn't look surprised.

Roman mentioned the night the light appeared on Kris's belly when she still carried Otter and asked him if the Oracle might be aware of these kinds of magicks. "Before Otter was born, we were able to merge with him," Roman said to Marcus and Cedric.

"This morning, Kris started to have a vision, but wasn't focused. Otter connected with her. He put his hand into hers and slammed her back into the vision."

"Everything looked so clear. It was an incredible, Technicolor vision," Kris added.

"You're sure Otter re-connected you to the vision?" Omar asked.

"No, we're not certain, but he brought us into his world when I still carried him. Anything's possible, right?" Kris tried to smile at Omar.

Marcus nodded. "He frowned pretty deeply at me this morning. If Otter saw me in the vision with Lorrie, it must have confused him."

"Marcus, we don't know for certain it was you. The man never turned. I love you dearly, but I don't recognize you from the back in visions," Kris said.

Omar let out a huff. "Okay, we'll get the animal reserves talking and see what they turn up. Roman, do you want a protection spell set up?"

"Yes, let's do it now." Roman nodded and let go of Kris.

Omar leaned over, whispered into Cassie's ear and kissed the back of her head. Then the four men left the house to begin a protection spell.

Kris looked at her friend. "Have you been painting?" She went into the living room to the crib and checked on Otter one more time.

Cassie came up alongside her and locked arms with Kris. "No, I've got a wonderful studio space set up in the house and can't get motivated. After the show last May, I've been exhausted."

Kris led her to the couch and they both sat down. "That wouldn't have anything to do with a certain

Lakeman and nighttime activities?"

"They do have incredible stamina, don't they?" Cassie smiled. "I don't like you and Omar arguing, though."

"We weren't arguing really, just discussing. You know how it is with two different opinions in the room. It's a good thing, even if I don't always agree with him."

"You know, he does have a point about Lorrie. If she's been taken, the only way out is abolishment."

"Cassie, I know you and Lorrie didn't see eye to eye and you're taking this position because you want to support Omar, but honey, I can't agree with you. I'm sorry."

"I'm not saying it because she and I annoyed each other. She wasn't a very strong witch and trying to dispossess her would be next to impossible. I do respect your opinion, Kris."

"We're starting to sound like an infomercial." Kris laughed.

"How's my little step-nephew doing?" Cassie tried to change the subject.

"Really well. We went to the doctor last Monday and he's gained weight and grown two inches. I think he's going to be built like his dad, which is a good thing."

"I still think you were brave having him. The thought of a baby growing in my belly scares the crap out of me." Cassie crossed her eyes.

"Have you and Omar discussed it?"

"One step at a time, sister. I don't think he realized the commitment involved with just the merge. There are times when I know he'd rather be in Parcel playing

Coopley with Marcus and there are times when I pat him on the rear, and tell him to go have fun. The merge seems to make us horny, though, and he never makes it out the door." Her face turned pink.

"It will simmer down, I promise. Even though I was pregnant, Roman and I still went at it like teenagers. We've slowed down some." Kris went quiet.

"How many nights a week are you active now?" Cassie asked and grinned.

"We stopped for six weeks after Otter was born. It was the doctor's orders. I guess now it's four or five nights, but getting up twice to feed the baby makes it difficult. And trying to work on top of it." Kris shook her head and took a breath. "I wouldn't change a thing."

"Is Roman ever pushy with you?"

"No, not at all. Sometimes I wish he would be and I know that's El talking. I've only been able to sneak attack him once."

"Sneak attack? What does that involve?" Cassie started to laugh.

"All I will say is it takes place in the shower. You will have to fill in your own blanks. Omar isn't pushy with you, is he?"

"Sometimes, yes, other times, no. I don't really think of it as pushy. He just gets really aggressive and wants control. It's okay, as long as I get to be on top sometimes, too."

"Ah yes, positional politics, been there. Roman and I talked about it. Once we were both out with our feelings, it went more smoothly," Kris said.

"I'm going to borrow the talking idea. Omar does need to grow up and express himself better." Cassie ran her hands through her hair.

"Roman said it would take some time for him to adjust into the leadership role. He does love you, Cass, never doubt that."

They both looked toward the backdoor as it opened. Roman and Omar came into the house and just as the door closed, Otter started to move in the crib and squeaked.

"Time for lunch it seems." Kris stood and went to the crib. Bending over, she picked up Otter. "I'll be back." She turned to the nursery with Roman following.

Sitting in the rocker, she adjusted Otter. He started to squeal louder. When her breast came out he zeroed in and latched on. She looked up at Roman, who smiled. "Babe, I think we're going to have to do a rain check tonight."

"Yeah, we wouldn't want to mess him up by having sex while he's in bed with us. The way you scream my name could scare him forever." Roman grinned down at them and ran his hand over the baby's head.

"Me screaming? What about you, Mr. Groaner?" Kris smiled, and knew he teased. "You don't mind him sleeping between us?"

Roman knelt in front of her and put his hand on her thigh. "No, we have to protect him, right?"

"Damn straight. I thought we might fight about it," she said, and looked into Roman's eyes.

"Nah. We'll have a make-up sex argument some other time." He leaned in and kissed her lips. Straightening his back, he stood and left the nursery.

Kris watched Otter feed. Humming, she rocked back and forth as his hand curled into a fist, then stretched out flat on her chest.

She started to feel angry. Why couldn't the evil forces of the world leave her and her family alone? She'd been relaxed and happy for almost a whole year.

Cassie nagged Kris to learn spells and casting, but she'd declined. She knew magicks were a part of her and the family, but if she could keep them down to a low simmer, she would. She wanted normal as much as possible. The thought of brewing potions on the stove in the kitchen didn't interest her at all. She wondered if she'd start to have more visions and liked only one a year.

Last year, when she'd met up with her mom and dad in the Between Realm, her mom told Kris about her telekinesis abilities as a child. She hadn't really thought about it until one afternoon, when she sat at the kitchen table reading the paper and Roman pointed out a pot of soup on the stove with the spoon spinning around, stirring the contents. She didn't realize she'd done it. Since then, she'd noticed things moving when she thought about them, but she didn't practice the ability. She really didn't want that power.

Kris and Roman spent many nights discussing this subject. They hadn't argued, but it created tension. When she went alone for appointments, she could sense him monitoring her with their merge spots. Her hand would be warm and tingling during meetings and openings. It did give her comfort, knowing he watched. After the events of last year, it kept her feeling safe. Her independent nature wanted freedom, though, and there were times she felt suffocated.

Kris loved Roman with her body and soul. He'd protected her during every weird thing that happened to her since drinking Abednego Brael's tainted wine and he would do his best to keep her and Otter safe. She did want to do her job and thought about asking him to stop the monitoring, but with the current events, she felt it would be better to leave that subject alone.

She also felt confident in the Haller Lake Guards. Her one concern was Lorrie. She missed her friend since she'd moved to the east side of the state. Kris worried that something bad happened to her. It bothered her that Omar and Cassie leaned toward abolishment even though they had no proof that Lorrie was taken by Rochelle. She knew Marcus wouldn't contradict Omar with others around, but Kris thought he would fight for Lorrie in the long run.

She finished feeding Otter and burped him. He fell to sleep and she took him to the crib in the living room. Looking up from her son, she saw Roman watching the yard from the back door. She walked up next to him and leaned against his arm, which made its way around her waist.

"What are we watching?" Kris asked.

"Not really watching, I'm listening. There's a ton of chatter out there." His eyes were closed. "There's no news about Lorrie, but everyone is still looking."

Kris saw his face pinch. "Babe, what is it?"

Roman's head tilted. "It's strange, there's a huge black...I don't know, a space out there. The silence around is weird. It seems to be a hum, but it's a silence."

Kris continued to watch him. "Where is this space, Roman?"

"It's just beyond," he whispered. "It's terribly violent in there." He sucked in his breath and stepped back. Opening his eyes, he looked down at her.

"What happened?" she whispered, concerned by the look on his face.

"I've never experienced anything like it." He looked back out the door. "Although there was silence, it sounded as if there were millions screaming in pain and agony. It was deafening."

"Are you okay?"

"Yes, I'm fine." He hugged her. "I didn't mean to worry you."

She hugged him back. "Do you want me to start lunch?"

"That sounds very good. I think I'm going to rock Otter. My arms feel a need to hold him."

They let each other go and Kris watched him walk to the crib, where he took their son in his arms and settled on the couch. As Roman closed his eyes and his lips moved, she knew he prayed.

Chapter Five

Pelonus felt frustrated. He sat in his realm, just milliseconds from the world where the humans existed, and worked on his plans. Black wisps of minions floated around him, and tried to claim his attention, but he focused elsewhere. A power in the human realm teased him unmercifully for weeks and continued to grow. Just as he thought he'd nailed it down, the power would disappear again. He growled and caused his minions to cower in fear. His search would continue. He wanted this power, and determined it would be his. With his fingers, he twisted his long, black hair and wanted to yank it out from the roots.

Two of his spies returned to the realm and walked before him with caution. They bowed their heads and waited for Pelonus to acknowledge them.

Fredrick and Seth were turned many years before by Pelonus and served him well, but did their best to protect themselves, too. Their lord could be very cruel when they tested his anger.

Pelonus turned his black eyes on them. "What say you, servants?"

"Lord, we have found the woman responsible for destroying Abednego, Shadrach and Meshach. She resides by one of the lakes in the other realm," Fredrick said and glanced up.

Pelonus' black eyes swam with flashes of yellow light. "This is already known to me, Fredrick. Could you tell me something I wasn't aware of now?"

"She is protected by a Lakeman and his brothers, master, but she also has a power about her. It is hard to tell if she is even aware of her own abilities. She uses them not," Seth added.

Pelonus grinned. "I also know about the Lakeman. It is interesting that she isn't using her abilities. Perhaps we could teach her about her magicks. Bring her to me." He leaned back in his seat and saw Fredrick and Seth exchanged frightened glances.

"Lord, the woman is protected by a spell cast by the Lakemen. Our low-level powers are too small and weak to break the enchantment. Please, forgive us for our weakness, great lord," Fredrick begged.

Pelonus' eyes turned bright red. "Must I do everything myself?" he hissed.

Seth fell to his knees and bowed lower. "Please lord, forgive us. We will help you all we can and our weaknesses are unforgiveable. What service can we do for you, great master?"

"Show me the woman." His eyes continue to glow red.

He felt the two minions open their minds and searched finding a memory of a woman with dark blonde hair and blue eyes. She walked around the shore of the lake, holding the hand of a tall, muscular man. "Is that him, the Lakeman?"

"Yes, my lord. They stay close to their home. He and the other Lakemen cast a protection spell this morning," Seth answered.

Pelonus arched a brow. "It would make it even more satisfying to steal her from that man. He would be crushed by it, I can tell. Garda would be very amused

with this. Where is the young one? I can't sense him."
As he watched, he saw the woman carry a baby. "That
must be the spawn. Keep that thing away from me, do
you hear me well enough?" he roared.

"I'm sorry, my lord, but I'm confused. I thought
you wanted the child. Isn't the child the young one?"
Sweat appeared on Frederick's upper lip.

"She is not a virgin...a shame. It does make me
wonder if the power I've been sensing has to do with
the child. Fredrick, the young one isn't the child, get
that straight," Pelonus snapped.   He   then   saw
something else of interest. The happy couple walked
with others. Another Lakeman and woman with long
blonde curls laughed and spoke to each other. There
was yet another Lakeman off in the distance. "Ah, there
you are. I've needed to get a look at you. He is radiating
with powers. I want him brought to me." He looked
young, tall, and muscular with blond hair and brown
eyes.

Pelonus glanced at his servants, shook his head
with disgust and released his hold on their vision.
"Leave my sight. I will call for you when I need my
shoes cleaned. As usual, I'll have to take care of this
myself."

Fredrick and Seth bowed and faded from view.

Pelonus ran his hands through his hair, and closed
his eyes to increase his focus. He couldn't latch onto
the aura of the woman and began to use his own
magicks to open the spell protecting her. Then he would
hand her over to Garda on a platter. The young one
though, he couldn't wait to see what this one could
conjure.

Chapter Six

As Kris and Roman finished eating lunch, they sat at the table in silence. Both mulled over all that could come. They'd talked some about all of the things that surrounded them magically, but Kris still held back from acknowledging any of her magicks. She accepted the merge spot and her connection to Roman and Otter, but nothing else.

"Roman, is there a way to do a partial binding spell? One where I'll remember you and Otter, but not the rest?" she asked, and poked at the remnants on her plate.

"Sorry, babe. It's all or nothing, I think," he answered.

Dropping the fork, she put her hand in her hair and scratched her scalp. "I guess I already knew that and I'm just frustrated. We went almost a year without evil plaguing us." She put her merge hand out palm up and found she could still make an electric ball. She played it around her fingers and looked at Roman, who watched her with pride in his eyes. "Some things are like riding a bike, you know?"

"Ah." He smiled and started to clear the table.

Kris closed her palm and shut off the ball. Roman took their plates to the sink, ran water over them, and put them into the dishwasher. He dried his hands and turned to her.

Leaning over the back of her chair, he wrapped his

arms around her. "Kris, I know it's a pain, but at some point you're going to have to accept this. You are a part of this world now, warts and all."

She leaned back into him. "I know, but I don't have to like it. I know without the magicks and tainted wine I would never have found you, but it is a pain in the ass when something dark and evil decides to come for a visit. Maybe I could get some of that wart removal stuff." She smiled up at him.

"Ha, ha, Mrs. Lake." He kissed her forehead.

There was a light knock on the back door. Kris felt Roman lurch and remove his hands from her shoulders. She looked at the window in the door and her jaw dropped. Standing out on the deck was Lorrie. Her short blonde hair shone in the sunlight.

Roman went to the door and opened it. Lorrie smiled up at him. "Hello, Lakeman."

"Roman, it's not Lorrie." Kris moved toward the crib, picked up Otter and held him tight.

"Rochelle?" Roman said and closed the door a little.

"How'd you guess?" she asked.

"You have no aura or light of any kind."

"Very good, you're smarter than I thought. Because of your protection spell, I cannot enter. I'm here to give you a warning." She smiled again, and looked at Kris and the baby. "Cute kid, sorry we missed the birth." She looked back up at Roman. "Since you saved me from Meshach last year, I believe I owe you. This will make us even."'

"I didn't save you, Rochelle. Kris did all the talking," Roman corrected her.

"Whatever."

"Well, what have you to say?" Roman asked.

"There is an evil heading this way," she stated.

"We've been told this from our own sources."

"It's Pelonus. He's very dangerous and will be more difficult to overcome than the last three. He has a multitude of minions and you are being watched. His spies are everywhere."

Roman crossed his arms. "I know that name, why?"

"Hello...Donner Party? Jamestown? Plague? Geez, Roman when did you stop paying attention? Pelonus has been around since before the Christians met the lions in the Coliseum and he's not to be trusted. Is there somewhere you could hide her? This paltry protection spell may keep me out, but it won't hold him back. Believe me."

Roman turned to look at Kris. She shook her head no. "We'll discuss it. Thank you for the information, Rochelle. We do appreciate your candor." He began to close the door.

"If he finds out I helped you, I'll be mud." She shook her head. "Please, keep your mouths free of my name for a while."

Both Kris and Roman nodded. Kris went to the window above the kitchen sink and watched Rochelle walk to the middle of the lawn and disappear. Closing the door, Roman turned to her and she met him half way. His arms enfolded her and the baby.

"Roman, we are going to have to tell the others. Poor Marcus, he's already so sad." Kris felt tears roll down her cheeks.

"Babe, I'll speak with him in private. We'll tell the rest after he knows."

He hugged her and she heard Otter squeak. "I believe we have woken our son up." Kris pulled back and saw Otter frown at her.

"I think he senses when we're upset," Roman said. He looked down at Kris and kissed her lips. "My love for you grows more every day."

"What made you say that?" she asked.

"Here we have disaster breathing down our necks and you worry about Marcus. I knew there was a reason I fell in love with your aura."

"I know what you're trying to do. It's a nice thing for you to say, but I don't want to run away and hide, Roman."

"I know."

"Who is this Pelonus anyway?" Kris sat at the table and looked at Otter. He seemed to listen to the conversation.

Roman sat at the head of the table. "He is very, very old. I'm not certain, but I believe he predates the Bible. I've never dealt with him, but I've heard he can be ruthless and very cruel."

"What Lorrie said about having a multitude of minions, what is that about?"

"He steals souls and they serve him forever." Roman ran his fingers over his eyes and put his chin in his hand.

"Forever?" Kris shook her head. "A dank dungeon would be better. If we burn sage and lavender would it help protect us?"

"It will help, yes, but the only way we will be safe is to get us to holy ground. We should take Cassie, too."

"Cassie? Why?" Kris started to feel more concerned.

"She's a powerful witch and would be tempting to Pelonus. If we leave her, she'd be vulnerable."

Kris put her hand on Roman's arm. "I love you. I guess we have to run."

He smiled. "Now what caused you to say that?"

"When we first met, you didn't trust Cassie at all. You were quite rude to her. But now you care. I'm very proud of you."

Roman nodded and chuckled. "Call Cassie, tell her to pack a bag for a couple of days, lock up her house, and get over here. I'll call the others." He stood and held out his hand.

She took his hand and rose next to him.

Roman went to the back window, and Kris to the cell phone. She speed-dialed Cassie and gave her the message. Kris then packed a canvas bag with clothes for her and Roman, and gathered up some baby things from the nursery. She never put Otter down and wasn't about to let him out of her sight.

When she walked out of the nursery with the bag slung over her shoulder, she saw Omar, Marcus and Cedric out on the back deck with Roman. She could tell that Roman must have told Marcus about Lorrie. It broke her heart for him. He looked upset and for Marcus, that said a lot. He very seldom showed much emotion.

They came back in as Cassie arrived carrying a duffle bag.

"All right, I'm here. Where are we going and why?" Cassie asked, and looked at them all as she put her bag on the floor.

"We've received word that the evil coming is Pelonus and he's on his way here to cause some trouble. I'm taking you and Kris to holy ground for protection. Then I'll come back here to help the others fight him," Roman said.

Kris frowned. "Wait just one second there, babe. You never said you were coming back."

"I'll have to come back and aid the men. You and Cassie will be safe, but the lake will still be at risk."

"Roman, I'm not separating from you for five seconds. No way. If you're coming back, then Otter and I might as well stay here. End of subject."

****

Roman could see that Kris meant it, but he wasn't about to let her stay.

"To be honest, Roman, I don't much like being apart from Omar, either," Cassie said and held Omar around the waist. "I also don't want my brand spanking new house blown to bits."

Roman looked at Omar, who shrugged. "Women can be very stubborn, brother."

Cedric's brows creased. "Who is Pelonus?"

Roman brought everyone up to speed on Pelonus and his history. He told about Rochelle taking over Lorrie and her visit.

"Pelonus will be much more difficult to abolish. He's not likely to fall into the traps we used last year. He's very wise and I'm sure has seen every trick in the book by now."

"How do we abolish him then?" Omar asked.

"We're going to have to put our heads together on it and come up with a plan," Roman said. He watched Kris pick up the baby bag, walk toward the nursery and slam the door. He knew he was in hot water.

"I'll head down to Parcel and see if the Oracle will

meet with me. She may have a spell up her sleeve we could use," Omar said and left the house.

Cassie sat in a chair. "So, we're not leaving, I take it?"

"Yes, we're heading out. Just give me a minute," Roman said. He went to the nursery and stuck his head inside the door.

Kris sat in the rocker with Otter gazing up at her. Roman closed the door behind him.

"I'm not talking to you right now, Roman. I'm so very angry and I don't want to say something hurtful," Kris said in hushed tones. Otter put his hand up. Kris took it in hers and kissed his little palm. He gurgled and smiled.

Roman knelt in front of her with his hands on her thighs. "Babe, I'm not doing this to make you angry. I want you and Otter safe. There's nothing on the planet with more meaning to me than you two, and I won't let Pelonus anywhere near you."

"Sorry, but I'm not leaving without you. I also wish you would have told me earlier. It could have saved me time in packing. I'm not big on surprises and we could have had a discussion about it." She shook her head. "There are times, Roman, when you don't give me all the details. It makes me look stupid and I don't like secrets." She looked at him.

He looked back at her and frowned. "I knew this would be your attitude and I didn't want to argue with you." He put his hand up to hers and Otter's. "Babe..."

Roman and Kris were both thrown into darkness. He could hear Kris call for him and felt his hand in hers, but couldn't see her. The area became warm and very bright. The light was so intense that Roman closed his eyes and felt comforted with warmth, but he stayed on Guard, desperate to protect his wife and child.

When he opened his eyes, he stood on the lawn outside their house, and held Kris's hand.

She looked up at him and smiled. "Okay, this is weird," she said.

They both watched as a tall young man with dark hair and brown eyes walked toward them. He wore jeans and a T-shirt with his hands pushed into the pockets on his pants.

"You know, I really don't like it when you two fight." He stopped in front of them. "It messes with my brain worse than my name does."

Kris's mouth dropped open. "Otter?" she whispered.

"Hi, Mom. I know this is a bit strange, but I've needed to talk with you and it's really difficult when you're only three months old."

Roman put his hand up on his son's shoulder and gazed at him. "How is this possible?"

"It has to do with the merge spots, but we don't have time for explanations now. Dad," he said and looked at Roman. "Mom is right. We can't separate. It would weaken our strength against Pelonus."

"I'm worried you two will get hurt or worse. I won't let that happen, Son," Roman said and couldn't work out that he spoke to his son.

"I know, but we must stay together. Our strengths lie within our love for one another and nothing can overcome us." Otter pulled his hand out of his pocket and put it on his father's arm. "Mom." He looked at her. "I know it's been difficult for you to accept your abilities, but if there ever was a time to change your thinking, now is it. You are strong and you need to open your mind and move forward. Some changes are good, you know?"

"I'm finding that out slowly." She smiled.

"Dad, if you take Mom and me to the holy place, you must stay with us. It will do no good for you to return to the lake. The Guardians will protect the lake, but if you are here, Pelonus will have a way of taking you as a hostage. He'll try to trade you for Mom. There's also someone else, something stronger, standing behind him. I haven't been shown everything, but I've seen what Pelonus will try to do and it must not happen."

"Otter, are your visions subjective, like your mom's?" Roman asked.

"Yes, I believe they are and can be changed. Pelonus is very powerful and it will take something we don't have yet to abolish him."

"What's that, Son?" Roman's brow creased.

Otter looked at Kris and took her hand, holding it to his chest. "Mom, you have to come to terms with your position in this realm. You have got to open your mind and let your powers develop."

Kris took in a deep breath and squeezed Otter's hand. "I'll do my best, sweetie. It's difficult, though, and sometimes very overwhelming."

"I know, but you can handle it. Look what you've accomplished so far. You can do anything you set your mind to, Mom."

"Your faith in me is very comforting. Thank you for the pep talk." She smiled again.

"Anytime." He looked at them both. "Don't argue anymore. It gives me a headache. I love you both very much, know that." He put his hand out, palm up.

Kris put hers in it and Roman put his on top. They were pulled back into the nursery and stared at one another in silence. Otter squeaked and grinned in Kris' arms.

"That was amazing," Roman whispered.

Kris looked down at the baby. "My brilliant son." She hugged him. "Roman, how was that possible? I mean"—she looked at Otter, who pulled on her fingers—"how can he know this stuff?"

Roman raised his eyebrows and shook his head. "I'm stumped, babe. Once we get to the safe place, we'll talk to Cassie. She might know of something. There's someone else we can talk to about this. I'm willing to bet he'll know something."

"Who?" she asked.

"Father Rupert."

Chapter Seven

When they left the house by the lake, Kris tried very hard not to have any negative thoughts. She wanted to believe they would be home soon and not worrying about evil demons coming after them. There would always be evil in the world. Since Otter could sense emotions from his parents, Kris wanted to send as many positive vibes as possible. She sat in the back with Otter, who was strapped into his baby seat. Roman drove and she could tell he tried not to speed.

Cassie sat in the passenger seat and sulked. She didn't want to leave the lake. Omar spoke to her and somehow convinced her that doing so would keep her safe. Cassie could be more stubborn than Kris at times. They all knew if she'd stayed, Pelonus would go after her, too.

They headed north on I-5. Roman said he knew exactly where to go, but didn't tell them and Kris began to feel antsy. She unfastened her seatbelt and leaned between the seats.

"Roman, where are we going?" Kris asked.

"Sedro Woolley," he said over his shoulder.

Both Cassie and Kris looked at him as though he'd spoken French. "Why there?" she asked.

"There's an old monastery outside the town. We'll be protected there. It's where Fathers Rupert and Greg practice."

"There's a monastery in Washington State?

Weird," Cassie said.

"There are a few monasteries and convents in the state, Cass." Roman smiled. "The two monks at this one have helped us out from time to time over the years. They mostly work with ghost hunters and demonologists, but have opened their doors as a refuge many times in the past and are highly regarded. You have both met Father Rupert."

"You said, 'over the years.' How long have these monks been around?" Kris asked.

"Let me think. The monastery was built in the late 1800s. Father Rupert came sometime in the 1950s. Father Greg...I can't remember when he arrived, but it was after Rupert."

Cassie raised her eyebrows. "This should be interesting. I hope they won't mind being on a first name basis. I refuse to call them Father."

Roman laughed. "First names are fine, Cass. They understand."

Silence came over the car for a few minutes. Kris checked on her sleeping son. Sitting back, she saw Roman look at her in the rearview mirror. She crossed her eyes at him, and saw his lips curl into a smile.

"Hey Cass, I just thought of something we need to ask you." Kris pulled herself back up. Cassie turned in her seat to face the back. Puffing out her checks, Kris blew out a breath. "Wow, how do I explain this one? Remember us telling you about Otter somehow merging with me to boost my vision of Lorrie?"

"Right," Cassie answered.

"This afternoon we experienced another strange thing. Otter held my hand, Roman put his on top, and we were pulled into another realm where Otter appeared to us."

"That is strange." Cassie sat up straighter.

"Cass, when he appeared, he was about twenty years old, and spoke like an adult." Kris watched her. "He looked an awful lot like Roman—"

"But had your beautiful ash-blonde hair color," Roman interrupted.

"No he didn't. He had brown hair and your brown eyes. What do you think, Cass? Have you heard anything about this kind of thing?"

Cassie righted herself in the seat and looked out the window. "I suppose it's like the split you and Elzabeth did last year, but how on earth do you appear twenty years older? I'll have to call my group leader on this one and see if he knows of anything. Amazing." She looked back at Kris. "What did he tell you?"

"He asked us to stop arguing. He said it gives him headaches." She looked in the rearview mirror again, seeing Roman peering at her. "He also said I need to come to grips with my powers and accept them."

"Smart kid," Cassie said and chuckled.

"That's what I said, except I used the word 'brilliant.'"

"Are you going to start training?" Cassie actually sounded excited.

"Training? You make it sound like I'm preparing for the Olympics. When I have time, I'll work on expanding my knowledge." Kris heard Otter squeak and saw he'd woken up and frowned. "Oh, dear, by the look on Otter's face, I guess I have the time now."

He grew fussy. Kris threw a blanket over her shoulder and opened the buttons on her blouse. She thought it would be a good idea to get him to nurse before they arrived at the monastery. He'd be less grumpy.

Cassie brought her hand up to her face. "It's amazing. Incredible that he has such a strong consciousness," she said.

Roman took an exit off the freeway and followed the signs into Sedro Woolley. It wasn't very far from the exit to the town. They bypassed the small central area and headed east on an old two-lane road.

The trees were tall and thick through this part of the countryside. It became dark under the trees and Roman turned on the headlights. After heading into the mountains for several miles, they came to a turn-off. If you didn't know about it, you wouldn't have seen the street. Roman eased the car onto a poorly paved road heading north. They bounced a little which caused Otter to squeal with delight. He seemed to enjoy bouncing around in his car seat.

They went a couple more miles into the forest and then came to a large wrought-iron gate attached to a huge concrete brick wall. The black and gray of the fencing was hard to miss amongst the lush greens and browns of the woodland.

Roman pulled his cell phone out and tried to get a signal, but couldn't find anything. He got out of the car and held the phone up with no luck. Laying on the car horn, he blasted it off and on for some time.

Finally, they saw an older man in a brown robe approach the gate. Roman jumped out of the car and waved. The monk waved back and smiled. He pulled at the gate until it opened all the way and then walked out to the vehicle. He and Roman shook hands and spoke for a moment.

Then Roman moved the car through the gates and followed the drive uphill around a couple of curves and came out in front of a large, almost gothic, building. After he parked the car and they got out and stretched, Kris really looked at the church. It was built with the same type of gray stone used in the wall surrounding it. There was a tall spire in front with a bell in the tower. The area around the drive had a lawn with beautiful flower gardens randomly placed. It looked stunning, but because of the woods bordering it, Kris didn't think they got much direct sunshine. She wondered how they managed to get the flowers to do so well.

****

Roman took Otter out of his car seat and held him up, showing him around. Their son looked very curious and would point his little fingers in a direction, getting him to turn.

Father Greg, who opened the gate, came up the drive. "You've arrived just in time for dinner."

Roman introduced him to the ladies and his son. He guessed the monk must be around sixty years old with gray hair cut short and very warm, kind blue eyes.

"Come, come inside and meet Father Rupert. He's waited patiently for your arrival and prepared a hearty dinner for us." He took Kris's hand and put it around his arm. "I've been looking forward to meeting you, Mrs. Lake. Roman has spoken very highly of you and now I see why. You have a lovely aura, as do you, Miss Nelle."

Cassie looked at him, a bit surprised. "How do you know my name?"

Kris grabbed the baby's bag from the back seat, but Father Greg took it off her shoulder and insisted on carrying it. Roman got the duffels out of the trunk and put the straps over his free shoulder. In his other arm, Otter still looked in every direction at once.

Father Greg smiled at Cassie. "We've heard of you, too."

"Heard what? From whom?" she asked and sounded a bit paranoid.

"Oh, we have connections." He smiled a bit shyly.

"Connections?" She huffed and shook her head. "Go figure."

They all walked into the church. Roman pointed out the stained glass windows in the main hall, but since it was late in the day, he found it difficult to tell what the colors depicted. He leaned toward Kris and said with her art consultant's eye, he knew she'd find them beautiful. She said she wanted to see them in brighter light.

Father Greg escorted them to the back of the building where there were rooms for guests. They were decorated in an old-fashioned style. The beds were huge four posters with fluffy, thick comforters. Both rooms had large fireplaces with overstuffed chairs in front.

"We put a crib in here for the little one." He pointed out the little bed in the corner. He folded his hands and smiled at Otter. "Hello there, young man."

Otter grinned and wiggled in Roman's arms.

Setting down the baby's bag, Father Greg showed Cassie to another guest room. Roman saw Kris look at the large claw foot tub in the bathroom with desire.

"My love, do you want to take a bath before dinner?" he asked.

Kris smiled. "If I were to crawl in there, I think I'd

fall asleep and probably drown."

"Not if I'm in there with you." He wiggled his eyebrows.

"Horn-dog."

Father Greg knocked on the door and looked solemnly at Kris. "You look very weary, Mrs. Lake."

"Please, call me Kris. I am tired. It's been a long day and not quite what I expected when I woke up this morning."

"Why don't we go to the kitchen and have some dinner? Then you can get some rest. Nothing can enter here to bother you." He led them down a hallway.

****

Roman and Kris traded off with Otter, eating in short shifts. Father Greg opened a bottle of wine, which Kris passed on, and asked for water. Ever since last year when she'd drank the tainted Brael Mist wine, she'd been unable to stomach it.

While they ate, Father Rupert came into the room. He stood very tall, somewhere around six foot six, with gray hair and twinkling blue eyes. His smile comforted her. He'd done such a nice job with the wedding service for her and Roman.

Both priests sat with them and they spoke about subjects unrelated to the current situation. Kris noticed Otter fell asleep in Roman's arms. She envied her son and wanted to do the same.

"I think you all should get a good night's rest. In the morning, we can discuss your next steps in dealing with Pelonus," Father Rupert said.

"Thank you, Father. I believe I agree. We've had a day, haven't we?" Roman looked at Kris and smiled.

She raised her eyebrows. "You said it." She stood,

and held out her arms. "I better get him to bed, too."

Roman shifted and handed over the youngster. "I'll be there in a minute," he said.

Cassie stood and said goodnight to the priests, and then walked with Kris back to the guest quarters. Kris felt as though she slogged around in mud. Cassie helped her get Otter ready for bed and changed his diaper after Kris fed him.

"You do look really whipped, Kris," she said.

"I was supposed to meet with Herb Crowley from the arts council this morning. Lord, things did a flip somewhere along the way." Kris sat on the edge of the bed and kicked off her shoes. "This is an interesting bed and breakfast, though." She looked around the room.

Cassie laughed. "Do you suppose they have tea and croissants in the morning?" She sat next to Kris.

"Probably with lots of butter and jam," she said and leaned against her friend.

"I'm going to be missing Omar something fierce tonight. I've gotten pretty used to his warm buns under the sheets.

"I'm feeling a little guilty having Roman here, but only a little." Kris nudged her arm.

"I know. I promise not to try and snuggle up with you two tonight, but I may get lost coming from the bathroom."

They started to laugh and Kris thought they were both tired because they couldn't stop. Roman came through the door and they laughed so hard tears ran down their cheeks.

He crossed his arms over his chest and watched them, which made them laugh even harder. Kris held her sides they hurt so bad.

After a few minutes, they calmed down and were breathing normally, but it threatened to start again if Kris looked at Cass. She checked the crib and found they hadn't woken Otter.

"If the hysterics are over, I think we should get some rest," Roman said.

"Rest. Right," Cassie stood up. "Goodnight then." She turned and went across the hall.

Roman shut the door. "Okay, what was so funny?"

Kris turned from the crib and tip toed over to him. "It was a girl thing, babe." She put her arms around his waist.

"I have nothing to worry about?" He rubbed her shoulders.

"No, Cassie is already missing Omar." Kris looked up at his warm brown eyes. "You know, I haven't had much of a kiss today. I'm feeling very neglected."

"I'm sorry. Have I been shirking my duties again? I'm all yours." He leaned over and brushed his lips over hers. She felt his tongue flick at her mouth. Kris opened and let his warm cinnamon flavor flood her system. She thought that would be something he'd lose when he retired from the Guardians, but he still tasted juicy and warm.

Kris pulled back and looked at him. "Roman, is it a sin to want to make love to you in a church?"

"I don't think so. We *are* married." He smiled. "We'll have to be quiet though." He looked over at the crib.

"No merge spot then. It makes me moan too loud. Want to take a bath?" She put her arms around his neck.

"It won't be like the shower at home." He arched a brow.

"So?"

Roman ran the warm water in the tub and undressed. Kris took her clothes off, checked Otter and then joined him. He'd already stretched out and she worked her way into his arms, lying half on his chest. They both decided to forego making love. She didn't feel comfortable leaving their son alone and even though Roman assured her they would be safe, she couldn't let go of an uneasy feeling.

Weighing their options, Roman said they didn't need to worry about getting in the monks' way. Father Rupert told him they could stay as long as they needed.

"We can't hide here forever, babe," Kris said, and rested her head on his shoulder. "We'll have to go home. In fact, I want to go home. This is a nice, peaceful place, but it isn't ours."

"We just need to gather up our strength and work out a plan." Roman held her close.

"You know, it's funny." She put her chin on his chest. "I never imagined our first vacation together would be to a church."

"I'm such a romantic, don't you think?" He chuckled which caused a vibration in her chin.

"If we're still here on our anniversary, I'm going to be very angry."

"I'm sure Father Rupert would be happy to make a cake."

"Roman, it's not the cake. I have something very special planned for us and I don't want it messed up, evil demons be dammed," she said.

"What have you got going?"

Kris could hear a smile in his voice. "It's a surprise and I'm not saying a word." She still hadn't planned anything, but didn't want to tell him.

"We have a week to go, and hopefully this will be settled by then," Roman whispered.

They were quiet for a few minutes and although her mind raced around trying to come up with an anniversary plan, Kris started to drift off.

Roman tapped her on the shoulder. "Let's dry off and get under the sheets, babe," he said.

They finished getting ready for bed and crawled onto the huge bed. Although it wasn't the one she'd slept on for a million years, it felt comfortable. The pillows were fluffy and soft, as was the comforter. Within a few minutes, Kris could hear Roman's deep breathing which meant he'd zonked out. She envied him a bit. She couldn't get her brain to quiet down.

Chapter Eight

Around two o'clock in the morning, Kris got up to feed Otter. After he went back to sleep, she slipped on her jeans and a sweatshirt and wandered the halls. She couldn't settle down. Something rode around in her brain and caused an uneasy feeling deep in her stomach.

Kris thought about what Otter said in the vision. She needed to accept her abilities and work with them. She walked into the main part of the church and sat in one of the pews. There were candles burning and a giant cross in the chancel, which gave the room a warm, calm feel.

She leaned forward, and clasped her hands. "Dear Lord in heaven, I know I don't talk to You much, but I need Your help. Please protect my family and keep them safe. They are so precious and I don't want them hurt because of my own stupidity and stubborn streak. Please help me find the right path." She sat back in the seat and continued to look at the cross.

"The Lord will hear your prayers, Kris."

She heard a voice behind her and turned. Father Rupert walked down the aisle. She slid over, making room for him and watched as he sat down.

"Sometimes He's a little slow in the answering, but He does hear you," Father Rupert said.

"I hope I didn't disturb you, Father."

"No, no. I tend to sleep only a few hours. Sometimes I wake up trying to remember a thing and spend the next few hours working my brain. The diocese checked me over once to see if my brain was still fit to be here. I worried they'd discover my memory deficit, but I passed with flying colors. Then I read in a magazine that sometimes we forget things because we are distracted or they have no meaning. It wouldn't seem like there would be much distraction here, but there can be."

"I sometimes have information overload. It's as though my brain says stop, can't process anymore." Kris held up her hands on the word *stop*.

Father Rupert chuckled. "Yes, I've experienced that before." His face took on a thoughtful look. "My dear, Roman told me some of what happened earlier with young Otter. I'm also aware of the things which went on last summer. He said you were able to conjure the electrical balls?"

"I don't really think it's conjuring. It's more a byproduct of the merge spot."

Father Rupert crossed his arms. "How do you mean?"

"Well, I understand the merge spot is part of mating." Kris felt her cheeks turn hot and knew her face got red.

"It's all right, dear. You don't need to be embarrassed." He smiled. "Does it surprise you, Kris, to learn the spot does have other uses? You can spread the field out and use it to protect yourself like a shield. Or if you're in a dark place you can use it to light the way. I'm surprised Roman hasn't told you these things."

"He's tried, Father, but I've denied my abilities and shut him out. They aren't something I asked for, and I keep hoping to have a normal life."

"Ah, who can define what is normal? For one person it may be normal, but for another just a boring existence," he said.

"I know what is normal for me. There have been a few times... I don't know. I haven't understood half of what I've experienced... It all seems too big." She realized she'd begun to ramble and felt unsure of what she wanted to say. "It would be nice to worry about critters eating my plants or getting something in the house fixed, rather than about who might be possessed this week."

"Yes, the rhythms of life certainly can keep us on our toes." He smiled. "It's what keeps our brains working and creates such daily challenges."

"Father, I'm not Catholic," Kris confessed.

"Neither are we, dear girl."

"But the monastery...I thought this was a Catholic church." She got more confused.

He answered her with a surprised look on his face, but smiled. "The Lord doesn't require a name for faith in Him, Kris. If you believe with your heart, it is all He asks for."

"I guess I wasn't much of a believer before. If you'd told me about all of the magicks and demons a year ago, I would have laughed and gone about my business. I just wasn't open to it." She looked away from him. "Roman told you about our son coming to us in a vision?"

"Yes, a little."

"Do you have any idea where it's coming from, or how it's possible for him to appear to us as a twenty-year-old?"

"I'm going to need to do some checking on this

topic. There are some books I want to look at in our library before I make any comments," he answered.

"Otter told me that I needed to accept the power and learn to work with it." Kris looked at her hands. "It scares me some." She glanced back at him.

"All of life's trials can be scary. Once you've learned to work with your abilities, your confidence will grow. Trust Roman, he is a very good teacher." Father Rupert patted her hand.

"I do trust him, Father. It's me I don't trust." Kris saw Father Greg come down the aisle.

"It's time for our prayers, Kris. We'll discuss this further tomorrow. Goodnight." He stood and went up to the stand in the front of the hall.

Kris didn't want to get in their way and left, making her way back to the guest rooms. She checked on Otter and found he slept soundly. His sweet, perfect face was relaxed and peaceful. Roman lay on his back and his breathing wasn't deep. She realized he watched her.

"Hello, husband." She peeled off her clothes and slid under the covers into his waiting embrace.

"Hello, wife. Are you having a hard time falling to sleep?" He wrapped his warm arms around her tightly.

"A little, yep. I had a very nice chat with Father Rupert." She felt Roman's hand move into her hair.

"What did you talk about?"

"Oh, just this and that. He said I should trust you as a teacher. Apparently, he feels you're very good at instructing." She kissed his chest. "He didn't really have to tell me that. I already knew, but I'm just a really bad student."

"I'll have to crack the whip and spank you if you

don't concentrate on the instruction more," he said and chuckled.

"Spank me? Roman, I thought we weren't into corporal punishment?"

"As parents, yes." He rolled her onto her back and looked down at her. "You know it will only be love pats." His lips brushed her collarbone and ran up her neck. His warm breath caused her to shiver.

"Oh... well, love pats can be tolerated." Kris whispered.

He lowered his lips down to hers and she opened her mouth. Waiting for his tongue to begin exploring, she thought of her husband as one of the best kissers on the planet. It caused her body to warm and her breathing to deepen.

He pulled his lips away and went for her ear lobe. "You know what this will lead to if we continue."

"Yeah," she said and sighed. "Not with Otter in the room."

"What can I do to help you sleep?" he asked.

"Just hold me, babe. Never let me go," Kris murmured back.

"That's on my bucket list of things to do. I'll always be here, always." He kissed her again and then tightened his grip around her which made her feel safe and at ease.

Chapter Nine

The next morning, Roman took Kris by the hand and walked her out of the guest quarters to the back gardens. They went to the tree line and found a spot to do some work. They'd arranged for Cassie to watch Otter.

When they came to a small open area in the woods, Roman stood Kris on one side and then he moved to the other and looked across at her. He put his hand out and formed an electrical ball. Kris did the same.

"Now in your mind, visualize a shield in front of you. The shield is impenetrable and nothing can reach you. Feel the idea of it move through your system into the merge spot. It is warm and it should feel as though it's a part of you. Do you sense it?" Kris nodded. "Remember to breathe, babe. You're holding your breath."

Kris took in a deep breath and stared at her hand. She could feel the warmth spread through her. She saw the shield in her mind and remembered this feeling when Roman first taught her to form the balls and it felt gratifying, but also exhausting.

"Roman, has Omar taught Cassie to do this?" she asked.

"I'm not sure, we haven't discussed it."

"I'll have to ask her." She closed her palm and shook her hand.

"Try again, Kris, and concentrate. I know you can

do it."

"Task master," she mumbled and opened her palm. After a few minutes, Kris felt the warmth push out of her palm and saw the ball of light widen. It looked like a three-foot by one-foot block in front of her.

"That's great, babe, you're getting it." Roman smiled.

"Yeah, it's great if I want to protect my boobs," Kris whispered and felt a bead of sweat run down the side of her face.

"Stretch it out. Feel the warmth widen even further."

"Husband, you're making me horny, all that stretching and feeling." She grinned.

Roman chuckled and continued to watch her. "I see sweat on your upper lip and want to lick it off. Keep concentrating, Kris."

The shield grew longer and covered her completely.

"You got it, now keep holding it. Get used to the feeling of it."

"This is so weird," she said. "I can feel the electricity zapping me."

"It doesn't hurt, does it?"

"No, not at all." She shifted her feet.

Roman brought his shield back down to a ball. "Kris, my love, I normally wouldn't do this, but I'm going to launch a ball at you. Just block it with the shield."

"Okay." She braced herself.

"Here we go." Roman shot the ball straight at her. Kris backed up a couple of steps. The ball hit the shield and crackled, throwing sparks.

"Wow, I barely felt that." She smiled at him.

"Want to do it again?" he asked.

"Yep, hit me with your best shot."

Roman wound up and launched the ball. This time Kris didn't back up. The light hit the shield and broke apart.

"All right, bring the shield back down to a ball. I want to show you something else." He started toward her as the shield came down. Roman stood next to her and put his hand out, bringing up his own ball. "Arch your wrist like this." He pushed his palm out with his fingers pointing down.

Kris mimicked the position. The electrical ball shot out of her palm, but seemed to elongate, looking like a bolt of lightning. She looked up at Roman. "Oh my God... babe, what was that?"

"It's just a different way of shooting out the current. I knew you could do it, beautiful lady."

"Yeah, but how do I do it again?" Kris looked at her palm, and then brought up the ball again.

They worked side-by-side for a couple of hours, and then stopped to take a break. Roman went into the church and brought out two water bottles. Kris didn't realize she'd gotten so thirsty and drank half down in a few swallows. She dripped with sweat. They sat down and leaned against a tree.

"I want to try something else. Close your eyes," Roman said.

Kris closed her eyes and could feel him stand up next to her.

"Can you hear me?" he asked.

"Yes, I can hear you." She smiled.

"Keep your eyes closed, babe," he said.

Kris heard his footsteps move away from her.

What about now, can you still hear me?

"Of course, Roman. You're beginning to sound like that telephone commercial. What are you doing?" She laughed.

Which direction are you hearing me from?

Kris felt her eyebrows crease. What did he mean, which direction?

Tell me, where am I coming to you from?

It suddenly occurred to her that he spoke to her mentally. When Kris communicated with the Oracle last year it was through some sort of telepathy. The woman spoke without moving her lips. Kris could hear him in her mind, not in her ears.

I know what you're doing, she thought.

Can you find me?

Kris opened her eyes and stood. *Are we going to play hide and seek?* She glanced around the trees.

If you find me, I'll give you a treat.

She felt him start to laugh. *What kind of treat?* She looked behind some bushes and went back to the tree she'd sat under. She closed her eyes again. Kris reached for him with her mind.

What kind of treat do you want?

Hmm... let me think. Your tongue on my nipples would be a treat. Or my mouth sucking your... she stopped and heard something crack. *It's been a while since we've been in the shower together.*

That would be a treat for you, not for me, babe.

I thought you liked the shower sneak attacks, she thought.

Oh, I do, but you came up with that one. I still need to figure out one for me.

Like what?

I'm going to have to think about it. I'll get back with you on it soon.

She opened her eyes and looked up into the branches of the trees. *I see you, how'd you get up there?*

You know you've given me a hard on?

Oh dear, come down and I'll see if I can take care of it.

Roman stood about fifty feet up on a limb in a cedar tree. He launched himself off the branch, came down to the ground and landed feet first. He stood up straight and smiled at her.

"Husband, you totally amaze me," she said.

"Show me how much." He stood his ground.

She walked up to him, put her hand on his chest, and stood on her tiptoes to kiss his lips. Her hand moved down his chest, past his stomach to the zipper on his jeans. Clasping the tag, she moved the zipper down and noticed he indeed got excited.

"Babe, you know, we've never made love outside in nature." She pressed her hand on his bulging slacks. Working her hand in, she felt his hard erection twitch. She put her fingers on it and felt ready to kneel down to suck the warm hardness.

"And," he said as he picked her up and pressed her back against the trunk of the tree. "As much as I want your lips on my penis, it desires to be somewhere else in you just at this moment." He pulled back, put his fingers on the waist of her jeans to unbutton them and pushed her zipper down. "Open sesame," he whispered.

It caused Kris to giggle.

Roman had used this line before and it always

made her laugh. He slid one leg of her pants down and off and then moved his own jeans down. Wrapping his arm around Kris's leg, he pulled it up and opened her sweet, hot folds to him.

"I'm not in any hurry, babe. I just need to be in you now," he whispered in her ear and pressed his shaft into her with one swift movement. "I've been about to die since the tub last night."

"I can't allow that." Kris put her hands around his shoulders. "Roman. " She sucked in her breath. "We're not doing this enough."

He held the position and licked her neck. "We'll get back to business soon." He pulled out and rammed back in. "When Otter is through with your breasts, just try to keep me away." He pressed in and gave her another pump.

"You feel so good. I wish we could do this twenty-four/seven." She blew out a breath. Wrapping her other leg around his waist, she kissed his earlobe, and bit it lightly.

"Kris, I want to devour you, do you mind? I may get a little crazy."

"I'm yours, body and soul. Do me hard, my love." She felt him ram her and she tightened her walls to feel the whole length of his shaft. "Oh, yes, bring it home, babe."

Roman began to pump with an intensity he hadn't felt for some time. He wanted to connect their merge spots to increase the tension. He pulled her hand from his neck and made the connection with her soul. The light beamed out and both shouted and moaned.

Kris felt the warmth flood her system fast and saw sparks behind her eye lids. After several minutes, they both climaxed. Roman roared and trembled, and held her tight.

"I love you so much, Kris. My life belongs to you, only you." He kissed her and let her leg down.

"I'm yours, too, always, always." She reached up and put her hand on his check. "You know, you just put me on the moon."

Chapter Ten

Kris and Roman walked back to the church hand in hand. Hoping they didn't look too disheveled, she stopped Roman in the hallway, kissed him, and whispered how much she loved him.

When they finally made it back to their room, they found Cassie sitting in the rocker reading a book. Otter just woke up for lunch. Cassie started to excuse herself, but Kris asked her to hold up a minute. Roman disappeared into the bathroom.

Kris picked Otter up out of the crib and sat in the vacated rocker. Putting a blanket over her chest and the baby, she unbuttoned her top and let Otter find his way.

"Cass, has Omar shown you how to manipulate the merge spot electric balls into a shield?" she asked.

"No, I've just learned how to do the electric balls. I know there's more, but Omar's busy training Cedric and all of the lake job. He hasn't had time to show me."

Roman stepped through the doorway from the bathroom, drying his hands.

"Babe, could you work with Cassie a little, too, and show her the shield? Omar hasn't the time and I think she should know it," Kris said.

"I agree. Why don't we go do it now? Then we can get some lunch." He smiled.

"Sure, okay," Cassie said. She waved at Kris and left the room.

"I'll be right there, Cass." Roman turned to Kris

and leaned over the rocker to kiss her. "I love you, my beautiful wife."

"Love you, too, husband. Thanks for the lesson in the trees." She arched her eyebrow. "Father Rupert was right. You are the best teacher."

Roman's mouth covered hers, tongue and all. "I'll be back very soon."

"I think when Otter finishes chowing down, we'll come out and watch. It's a nice day and he could use some fresh air."

"Meet you outside then." He kissed her again and turned to leave.

Kris pulled the blanket off her shoulder and Otter looked up at her with a grin.

"What are you doing?" she whispered. He giggled and gave a huge toothless grin. "You're supposed to be eating your lunch, sweet pea."

"Blaf," he squealed, and kicked his feet.

"If that's the way you're going to be about it." Kris straightened her top and took him to the bed to change his diaper.

Once finished, they went out the back door and sat in the shade to watch Roman and Cassie work on the shield. He acted very patient and gentle with her. Otter sat with Kris and watched closely, or seemed to watch the lesson. When Cassie brought the shield up and held off Roman's electric shots, Otter grinned and clapped his hands. Cassie curtsied to him, saying thank you.

Roman walked up to Kris and Otter, and gathered his son up in his arms. Otter cooed, and grabbed his dad's nose.

Cassie and Kris practiced bringing up their shields together and after a while, it became easier and more comfortable.

Kris walked up to Roman. "Babe, Lorrie...or Rochelle said the protection spell wouldn't work to keep Pelonus out. Is the shield strong enough?"

Roman started to answer, but Father Rupert came around a corner and interrupted. "Let me answer this question for you, Kris. The shield will protect you and whatever you may cover with it. However, Pelonus can break through. It would give you time to conjure a spell or perhaps call on a good wizard for assistance." He clasped his hands and smiled.

Cassie walked up beside Kris. "I wonder if good wizards are listed in the Yellow Pages?" she asked.

Roman started to laugh. Kris looked at him. "Okay, what's so funny?"

"Oh, nothing." He settled down. "It's just that Father Rupert here and Father Greg are both grand master wizards."

Cassie started to back up, but tripped, and landed on her butt. Father Rupert walked over to her and offered a hand up. Cassie stared up at him with her mouth hanging open.

"My dear. It's nothing to be in awe of."

Cassie took his hand and stood. "But you're a grand master... I never dreamed I'd ever meet anyone with your abilities. The spells I could learn from you... this is amazing." She continued to stare.

"Okay, not a magicks geek here. Are grand master wizards like gold medalists in the Olympics or something?" Kris asked.

"Or something, yes." Father Rupert continued to smile.

"Do grand wizards rank above evil demons?" Kris

looked at him with different eyes.

"There are no rankings as such. You have good and evil. In my book good always prevails, it's just a matter of beating the evil. Pelonus has a reputation as being very strong, but what it comes down to really is he can intimidate weak-hearted humans into submission. If you refuse to play his games, he should have no influences over you, but it will anger him and that's when you have to be careful." Father Rupert looked into her eyes.

Kris sat down next to Roman and put her head on his shoulder. "I'm suddenly feeling very tired," she said, and continued to look at Father Rupert. "Mentally, more than physically. I've spent the last year ignoring all of this. I should have been learning."

"Don't be hard on yourself, my dear. I think you were busy with something much more important." He leaned over and tweaked Otter's cheek, which caused the baby to giggle.

"You know, we can't hide out here forever." She looked up at Roman.

"No, as I said last night, we're just getting our ducks in a row. Building up your abilities being our number one priority," Roman said.

"Have I mentioned that I miss Omar?" Cassie asked, and put her hand on her cheek.

They all looked at her as though she'd recited the Gettysburg address from memory. Roman seemed to pick up on her mood first.

"Cass, you haven't even been apart for twenty-four hours," he said.

"I know, but I miss him. That bed felt so empty last night." She crossed her arms and frowned.

Kris stood up and grabbed Cassie's arm, before she could continue. "We're going for a walk," she said, and pulled her friend toward the tree line. Looking over her shoulder, Kris could see that both men wore questions on their faces.

"Cassie, Father Rupert is a...a monk, I guess," she whispered. "We can't be talking bedroom stuff with him around, it's embarrassing."

"Oh crap. I forgot how you can be such a prude sometimes." Cassie walked ahead of her and turned down a path.

"Cassie, please, don't become dramatic. I pulled you away so you could talk about Omar with someone who'd understand where you were coming from. Father Rupert wouldn't understand any of this stuff, I'm sure. Besides he's a boy." Kris caught up and hooked her arm with Cassie's, who stopped. "Look, the night before the wedding last year, Roman stayed over with Sylvia and Fred. I hated it. It's the only night we've been apart since we met. So believe me, I know where you're coming from."

Cassie started to walk again, but slowed her pace. "I know you do. It's really hard watching you and Roman being all lovey-dovey, which I know sounds silly, but it makes me miss Omar all the more."

"Roman and I will just have to behave."

"No, no, I'm just being all weird and whiny and I want my man," she said and pouted.

"I just want to be in my own home and bed. Not that the monks aren't nice and all, but that bed just sucks," Kris said as they rounded another corner.

"I thought the bed was all right. The comforter is so soft." Cassie laughed. "If we don't sound like a couple of bitches having a pity party, I don't know what."

"You know, Roman taught me something. He communicated with me without talking, the way the Oracle does. That mind thing with telepathy," Kris said.

"You mean you two can communicate telepathically?"

"Yeah, I think it's the merge which ties us together. Why don't you try to talk to Omar?" Kris asked.

Cassie looked at the palm of her hand and rubbed the spot. She closed her eyes and went into deep concentration. Kris leaned against a tree and watched her.

After a couple of minutes, Cassie grinned. "Oh crap. I think I just scared the begeebbers out of him."

"Did you reach him?"

"Yeah, he hears me." She continued to grin. "He missed me last night, too. Maybe he appreciates me a little more now."

"He should, you're one in a million," Kris said.

"Thanks," she said and frowned. "Oh wow, Pelonus is at the lake." Cassie opened her eyes. "We have to find Roman."

They both moved toward the back of the church. When they broke through the tree line and were on the grass, Kris saw Roman move to them.

"I heard. Omar shared his communication with you, Cass," Roman said as he got nearer.

"Sheesh, great. We have a party line," she huffed.

"I didn't hear anything else. Now, this is the *ducks-in-a-row* part. I should head back to the lake and assist Omar. At this point, they're hiding out in the boundaries, but it won't last for long. Cedric is too young and his strengths aren't developed enough. Omar sent him back to Parcel. He and Marcus are alone and I can't abide this," Roman said in almost one sentence.

"Babe, remember what Otter told us. You can't go back there. It's too dangerous for you." Kris looked at him. "Cassie, I believe we have an argument coming on. Would you take Otter inside? I'll just be a minute," Kris asked.

Roman handed the baby off to Cassie. Otter became fussy, but settled down when he realized he wasn't going to get his way. Cassie moved to the guest quarters.

"Kris, those men are my brothers. I can't just desert them." Roman crossed his arms.

"I don't want to ask you to choose. I'm your wife. Otter is your son. He told us it would be safer for us to stay together. We're stronger together. You can't do this." Kris felt her throat start to tighten and her eyes burned. "I know you care for them, I know they were your family for a very long time—a lot longer than you've known me—but what Otter said scares me and I don't want to risk losing you. I'm not a risk-taker, babe. I'm not planning on jumping out of planes anytime soon."

"You once said you weren't brave, but that turned out to be wrong," he said and she knew he was trying to sidetrack her.

"Roman, please stay on subject. You are retired from the Guardians. Let them deal with it and—"

"And what?" he cut her off. "Babe, we're on holy ground here. Pelonus can't reach you or Otter. He can't come to this place. You'll be safe. I have to go help the others. If I don't, I won't be able to respect myself. I'd lose my ability to stand tall and proud."

"Now you're sounding like a military commercial. Roman, how is it belittling you to stay and defend your family?" A tear rolled down her check. It made her madder and she did feel guilty for hurting him, but didn't want him to go. Every time they fought, she'd end up crying while she tried to defend her position. She stepped back from him. "Roman, go. Just go and do whatever." Kris started to walk away from him. "If something bad should happen and you didn't go, you'd resent me forever," she said and cleared her throat.

He caught her wrist and turned her around. "And if I go and something bad happens, you'll resent me. We're on a fence, Kris. Either way we fall, one of us is pissed off."

Kris pulled her wrist from his hand and moved to the back door of the guest quarters. She got to the room and found Cassie and Otter playing on the floor.

Cassie looked up as she entered the room. "Uh-oh."

Kris walked past her into the bathroom, shut the door and leaned against it. She locked herself in, which she knew wouldn't keep Roman out. He was good with locks. If she knew him, he'd be right behind her and she needed to think. What could she do or say to keep him from going to Haller Lake? She stared at herself in the mirror over the sink and suddenly had a thought. It would make Roman mad at her, but it would keep him safe. She hated the idea of putting herself on the front line, but would think of some way to erase the line later.

Kris heard the knob turn, but the lock held and then came a light knock.

"Babe, we need to talk, please, let me in."

She dried her eyes, opened the door, and walked past him to the bed. "Young man, you didn't eat much earlier, what do you think?" She leaned over and picked Otter up from the floor. "Thanks, Cassie." She moved to the rocker and unbuttoned her shirt.

"Kris, are you not talking to me now?" Roman asked.

"Maybe I should leave." Cassie stood up.

"No Cass, it's okay." She looked up at Roman. "I'm going to feed our son. You know, he doesn't like it when we argue, so we'll have to continue this later." She looked down at Otter who latched on and got his nourishment. "Why don't you go talk to one of the monks and calm down?"

"I am calm." Roman frowned.

"Good." Kris looked up at him again. She knew he would be so angry with her.

He did as she asked and left the room. Kris motioned for Cassie to shut the door, which she did and sat down on the bed.

Kris looked down at her sweet little boy. "Cass, I'm going to do something that's going to annoy Roman very much," she said as quietly as possible. She didn't want to upset Otter. "In the baby's bag are a couple of cans of formula. Roman doesn't have the first clue what to do with it. I think he felt there would be time." Kris smiled at her. Cassie looked at Kris with her head tilted and one eyebrow up. "I may need you to help Roman a little."

"Kris, what are you thinking?" Cassie asked.

"Nothing major." Kris rocked back and forth.

"Nothing major, my ass. What are you thinking?"

"I don't want Roman to lose his pride or honor. He said he couldn't respect himself…" Kris closed her mouth and didn't say another word. She felt as though she'd start to cry again.

Otter began to drift off and fell to sleep. She put him into the crib and straightened her shirt. "Cass, I know you want to run out of here right now to let Roman know I'm planning something." She touched Otter's soft hair, and then looked at her friend. "Please, give me a few minutes head start."

"Be careful, okay?" Cassie hugged her.

Kris went to the chest of drawers and picked up the car keys. She then left the room and didn't look back.

Chapter Eleven

Roman spent a half hour in the main nave of the church. He communicated with Omar and listened to what he reported. Pelonus walked up and down the shoreline. Omar and Marcus watched him go through both houses and sent out his minion when he found nothing he wanted in either of the homes. Pelonus shouted at the Lakemen and made several threats, but there were no developments yet.

Father Greg came out of the back of the church and when he saw Roman, his jaw dropped.

"Father Greg, what's wrong?" Roman stood and hurried to him.

"Oh Lord, forgive me, Roman. I saw your car pull out. I thought it was you as you said earlier you were going back to the lake," Father Greg replied in an anxious voice.

Roman heard what he said and looked over his shoulder. "Sweet Jesus," he whispered as he took off for the guest quarters.

He reached the room, opened the door with a bang and found Cassie in the rocker with her knees pulled up. She looked up at him.

"Where is she?" Roman barked, and she jumped. Otter woke up and started to cry.

"She left about fifteen minutes ago." She stood up and leaned over the crib trying to calm the baby.

Roman ran his hands through his hair and started

pacing. "What was she thinking?"

Cassie straightened up and glared at him. "She was thinking of protecting your sorry ass, Roman. You and your stupid honor. How dare you put that above your love for Kris and Otter? What were you thinking?"

Roman stood, frozen. He heard her words in his head and heart. "Oh God, I screwed up," he mumbled.

"What was your first clue?" Cassie asked with a lighter tone. "You can talk to her, Roman. Do the mental connection thing, reach her and tell her to come back. And be sure you apologize for being such an idiot."

Roman sat down on the end of the bed, put his fingers on his temples and tried to concentrate. His mind raced all over the place. He needed to settle down or he would never get through to her.

Kris, Kris. listen to me, please. Turn around and come back to me and Otter. I wasn't thinking. Please, I need you here. Otter needs you here. I'm an idiot. I should never have put my needs and selfishness before our love. My pride went nuts, babe, and I should have paid more attention to you. Please forgive me...Kris, can you...

Roman, be quiet. I'm trying to drive, he heard her say.

Babe, come back. I'm sorry I didn't listen to you, he thought.

Roman, it doesn't matter now. I'm going. Please get out of my brain.

No, talk to me, Kris, he pleaded.

No.

Kris, I know you're trying to protect me because of what Otter said, but if his visions are subjective like yours, they can be changed. You're already changing it. Please, talk to me. What are you planning? Let me help. He could feel her cry and pull away from him. *Turn around and come back,* he thought.

Roman, I love you, he heard her say and then the connection went black.

He opened his eyes and sat up straight. "Damn it, she's being stubborn." He stood up and grabbed Cassie's hand. "Let Omar know she's on her way to the lake and—"

"I know, I'll watch over Otter. Go, go now," she said and took her hand from his.

Roman turned to the door just as Father Rupert walked. The monk held a set of keys. "Father Greg explained what happened. There's a truck in the barn. It's old, but reliable and should get you to the lake." He handed the keys to Roman, who moved out of the room, but stopped and looked at Father Rupert. "Follow the path outside the kitchen door into the woods. You can't miss it."

Roman nodded and bolted for the kitchen. He went out the back, found the path and raced past the tree line. As his feet pounded the dirt, it caused dust to fly up. He continued to try and reestablish the link with Kris. He could feel her pushing him away, but tried everything he could think of to work his way around the block.

He found the barn at the end of the path and opened the large doors. Sitting in the middle of a poorly-kept space was an old Ford pickup. The body looked rusted and he couldn't tell the original color. He put the key in the ignition and prayed. The engine roared to life with only one twist and he shifted to Drive and hit the gas.

He followed the dirt road to the gates, which Father Greg stood by as he flew past the wrought iron and stone wall and honked. He saw the monk wave in the rearview mirror.

As he maneuvered the truck around curves, he talked to Kris in his mind. *Hey babe, you're never going to believe this. I'm driving a truck, an old rusted out Ford. If you'd slow down a bit, I can catch up to you. I'm about twenty minutes behind and I want you to see this truck. It's amazing.*

Damn it, Roman. Go back. You need to protect Otter! she yelled at him.

Thought that might get your attention. He grinned and looked through the windshield. *Listen, since I'm being such a big, thoughtless idiot today, I'm going to take it a step further and meet you at the lake.*

No, Roman, turn around and go back to our son.

What are you planning, Kris? How are you going to deal with Pelonus?

I'm not sure yet. Her voice quieted.

Are you going to wing it?

Roman, please, just shut up. I can't think with you rummaging around in my head.

"Hmm... *Maybe I should try to tickle your erotic zones.* His eyebrows furrowed. *Hey Kris, do you think we might be able to climax this way?* He continued to push his way into her mind and tried to distract her.

Roman, stop it. You are making me really angry and I will block you again, she growled.

Roman rethought his position. *There's a rest stop just before Arlington. Why don't you pull over and let me catch up? We need to talk and you can hit me. It's in your voice that you want to beat on something. I volunteer.*

I don't want to hit you. She sighed.

But you are mad at me?

I don't know what I am anymore. I'm not even sure I care.

He could hear her voice start to sound tired and it stabbed his heart. *Babe, don't say that. I know it isn't true. You have a big, caring heart and the most beautiful light,* Roman frowned. *Kris, are you listening to me? Kris?* He realized that she blocked him again. He growled low in his chest.

He came to a light and slowed down. When it turned green, he made a left turn onto the freeway ramp. He sent out his thoughts to Omar, but got Marcus instead.

Marcus, is Pelonus still milling around or has he given up? he asked.

Nope, he's still here. He's got his rats running around. We're still monitoring from the boundary, Marcus's thoughts came back.

Kris is on her way.

What? Marcus sounded shocked.

We argued and she grabbed the keys and left. She's on her way toward you. I borrowed Rupert's truck and I'm about twenty minutes behind. Keep an eye out, okay?

Will do. I'll let Omar know, although I think he's hearing from Cassie. We'll see what we can do. Maybe we need a distraction.

Thanks Marcus. Roman closed his thoughts to the lakeman and began trying to reach Kris one more time.

Chapter Twelve

Kris looked at the odometer and saw it read eighty miles-per-hour. She thought about slowing down, but decided not to and pulled into the carpool lane. Roman still tried to grab her brain and she felt so upset with him, it was easy to block him out.

It wasn't his pride that overpowered him, she thought. She didn't think he'd any faith in her, which killed her own self-confidence. He also didn't pay attention to his son's vision, subjective or not. Roman wanted to be the alpha male and she wanted him to stay safe. If she'd stayed at the church, they would have continued butting heads and, in the end, he would have left to return to Haller.

Roman wanted her to be a docile woman, but then wanted her training to do magicks. *So much for a docile female,* she thought. He seemed to forget that she took care of herself long before he arrived, and one of their main arguments centered around his need to be overbearing and protective.

Oh, wahhh! Kris heard a voice in her head and jumped.

El? Is that you? she thought.

Yeah, it's me. I'm gone for a while and you turn all whiny. What gives?

Kris's alter ego decided to put in an appearance. She tended to act like a spoiled brat sometimes, which annoyed Kris to no end.

Where have you been? I thought you and I merged and you were gone for good.

I've been here all along, sister. The baby stole some energy and I had to hibernate for a while. Why are you and Lake Boy fighting so much? I've caught some of it, but what? Did the honeymoon end, sweetie?

I guess that's about the best way to put it. We're having a power struggle of sorts. Oh crap... Kris looked in the rearview mirror.

What's wrong?

Cops. I've been speeding along and now we have a cop with the lights on. Crap, crap, crap, I left my purse back at the church, which means no driver's license, Kris mumbled in her head.

Want me to take over? El giggled.

Kris pulled the car over three lanes to the emergency pull-off. The cop followed and parked behind her. A tall officer with a blond crew cut unfolded from the car and walked up to the driver's side of her car.

Rolling the window down, Kris looked up and smiled at the tall man. "Hello, sir, I know I was speeding. I'm in too much of a hurry today." She tried to sound apologetic.

"You were also driving in the carpool lane, Miss Bennett," the officer said "I'll need your driver's license and registration."

"See, that's the funny thing, officer. I left my purse back in Sedro Woolley and..." Kris saw his eyes and felt stunned by the black orbs shining from his eye sockets. They were swimming with electric flashes. She wondered how he'd known her name, but now it made sense.

When she froze, El pushed her way forward. Kris felt her eyebrows fold, but then they smiled at him.

****

"Officer, be a darling and tell Pelonus we're on our way." She flicked their tongue around their lips. "Damn, but you are good-looking. If I didn't think a delay would annoy Pelonus, I'd say let's find us a room. I'd love to see what your…uh…*equipment* could do to me." El smiled.

Hey, no distractions. Besides this body is married and belongs to Roman, Kris thought as hard as she could.

Yeah, right, you get to have all the fun. Maybe sometime we could switch with Roman and...

No. Now concentrate, Kris demanded.

They looked at the policeman. "I guess we don't want to anger him, do we, officer?"

The man smirked. "Just stay out of the carpool lane. I'm going to follow you to be sure you arrive safely for the lord." He turned and walked back to his vehicle.

El put the car into drive and swung them back into the traffic. *Did you see the bulge in his pants, Kris? I bet he could have fucked us silly.* El laughed.

El, do you know how to drive?

Nope, never drove, never ever. Only been along for the ride.

****

Move over and let me take the wheel before you get us killed, Kris hissed and pushed her way forward.

Control freak, El sighed, letting her back in front. *You do know that Roman is trying to talk to us?*

Yep, I know. Kris checked the rearview mirror and

96

saw the cop behind her.

And why aren't we conversing with tall, dark, and gorgeous?

He wants me to go back to the monastery and hide from Pelonus, while he goes to the lake and gets himself killed.

Run-on sentence, sweetie.

Shut up. If you're not going to contribute something helpful, then be quiet, Kris snarled at her.

Okay, okay. Let's see now. Pelonus is a powerful demon. We haven't faced anything this strong. The only way to vanquish him is with at least a four-way and you and I don't count as two. Have you learned the vanquishing spell yet? El asked.

No, not all of it. Kris kept looking in the mirror.

Then why are we going on a suicide mission?

To protect Roman, Kris replied.

Oh, this has got to be good. Tell me.

Otter had a vision. Roman went back to the lake and was taken hostage by Pelonus to use as a trade.

Trade for what?

Otter said Pelonus would try to trade for me. The Oracle told Marcus that the evil was after the young one. I'm... we're protecting our family. Kris gripped the wheel and waited for a smart aleck remark to come back from El.

Otter said? Wait a minute, Kris. Otter's like, what, three months old?

Yeah, he can manipulate alternate realms using the merge spot. In the other realm he's about twenty years old.

Wow, cool kid, El thought. *Kris, we need Roman.*

No, not if he could be hurt.

What he said about changing the vision that Otter had makes sense. I hate to admit it, sweetie, but we need him.

Kris looked once more in the rearview and saw the same thing. She couldn't figure out how to get rid of the police vehicle and opened her brain cells to reach for Roman.

Babe, are you there? Kris thought.

Yes, I'm here.

I'm just passing the Stanwood exit. I'll meet you at the rest stop. I've got a cop following me. He's been turned, has black eyes and knows my name. Do you have any idea how to get rid of him? There was silence. *Roman?*

Just thinking. Pull off at the rest stop and go into the bathroom and stall. I'm about fifteen minutes behind. I'll let you know when I'm close.

Got it. I'm in the slow lane now and doing the speed limit.

You could even go do fifty miles-per-hour, but that might make him wonder. Just hold steady, babe, Kris heard him.

Roman, I should warn you, El's back.

You're kidding? When did she show back up? Are you wearing the black dress?

She resurfaced a few minutes ago. No, I'm still in my jeans.

Hmm...those are good, too.

Roman, I'm nervous and I know you're trying to distract me, but stop it, Kris scolded him.

Sorry. I just enjoyed a nice visual, he thought and chuckled.

I'm coming up to the rest area.

Please, keep the communications open with me. I want to know the cop isn't hurting you.

I'll do my best. I'm on the exit now. I can see the restrooms up ahead. I'm parking and Mr. Cop passed me and parked three spaces down.

Kris got out of the car and headed to the ladies' room.

"Miss Bennett, just what are you doing?" She heard the cop's voice behind her.

Turning, she saw he followed her up the walkway. "Officer." She crossed her arms and leaned on her hip. "My name is Lake. Mrs. Roman Lake. I think you need to update your records. I have to go to the restroom and hope there isn't a problem."

"I'll escort you." He put his hand on her shoulder and pointed with the other.

"No, see, I'm an adult. I pee all by myself. Why don't you wait here? You'll see me come out if you just keep an eye on that door."

Kris saw his black eyes watch her. He didn't say anything further, so she turned and headed toward the door. She went in and locked herself into a stall.

*Roman, how far out are you? S*he leaned against the stall door.

I'm just passing Stanwood. I hope by going sixty-five I don't blow the body off of Father Rupert's truck. Hey, I loved it when you told the cop you were Mrs. Lake. That sounded cool.

Glad you liked that one.

Loved it. What are you doing now?

I'm in the stall in the restroom, reading the graffiti on the walls. Kris looked up and around.

Tell me what it says.

Roman, she sighed, but heard him grumble. *Okay, let's see, there are a lot of 'for a good time' calls and 'Jennifer is pissed at John because he couldn't keep his dick in his pants.' And 'Karen loves...hmmm...Sue forever.' Damn, now I wish I had a pen.* Kris could hear Roman laugh.

What would you write? he asked.

I love my husband very much, except when he annoys the hell out of me. She grinned.

Ah...I don't annoy you all that much, do I?

Sometimes, yes.

"Mrs. Lake, what's taking you so long?" Kris heard the officer move inside the restroom.

"Officer, this is a ladies' room, please get out. I'll be with you in a few minutes," Kris said with as much anger as she could muster. She heard the outside door open and close.

Did he leave? Roman asked.

Yep.

I'm about a mile from you.

What do you want me to do next?

Flush and wash your hands, but give me a minute and don't come out until I say.

The communication line went quiet. Kris leaned over to flush the toilet, let it run, and then opened the stall door. She looked around and found the officer gone. Walking up to the sink, she turned the water on and put her hands under the tap. She almost jumped out of her skin. The water felt ice cold and she pulled her hands out, but left the water running. She counted to thirty, turned the water off and hit the button on the hand dryer. The warm air felt good after the icy water.

Okay Kris. When you come out, you'll need to

break away from the cop. I can see him lurking by the bathroom. Pervert. I'm parked right behind our car. When you come out, run...your door will be open.

I'm on my way. Kris opened the outside door and saw the cop. "You know, standing around out here makes you look like a stalker," she said.

"Mrs. Lake, please, no more stalling. I could give you a ride to Pelonus." He started to walk alongside of her.

"No thanks. I don't want to leave my car," Kris said, and then started to move fast down the walk. She saw her car ahead and an old truck with both doors open, behind it.

A blur flew past her and she heard what sounded like a punch. Roman came out of nowhere and flattened the policeman by hitting him in the nose. The tall blond man sat on the walk with blood running down his chin. Roman appeared behind her. Kris ran around the truck and jumped in. Roman put it into gear and got them moving by the time she got the door closed.

Chapter Thirteen

Pelonus was getting angry. How was it possible for one slight woman to cause him so much annoyance? There'd been a lot of chatter going on amongst his minions and it gave him a headache.

He looked up at his two slaves. Frederick and Seth returned several minutes ago, but he hadn't acknowledged them yet. "What information do you bring me?" They exchanged glances and remained silent. "Are you two connected at the hip or something?"

"No lord, it's just...we are fearful to answer your question," Frederick said and bowed his head.

"As well you should be. Don't try my patience. What information do you have?" He leaned toward them.

The tall, thin one, Frederick, looked to shake in his boots. "Lord, the woman has escaped."

Pelonus moved quickly into Frederick's face. "What?" he hissed.

"The minion up north, who watched her, got attacked by the Lakeman and two of the tires on his vehicle were punctured. They escaped, my Lord."

Pelonus snarled. "Where is this servant? This is outrageous."

"Yes, Lord, we do agree." Frederick kept his head down.

"Where is this shirker?" Pelonus roared and his

eyes turned red. Heat radiated from his body and the two minions stepped back.

"He fled the body he possessed and returned to the underworld, Lord. He fears you greatly," Frederick continued to speak.

"Bring him to me at once. He will be dealt with." Pelonus stared at him. "What are you waiting for? Go. Bring him to me now."

Frederick and Seth vanished. Pelonus continued to fume. He paced back and forth along the lake shore and thought about making the lake water boil. Nothing went the way he wanted it, which he couldn't wrap his mind around. His flunkies were in need of more whip cracking. The Lakemen were nowhere to be found and that woman and the witch disappeared.

Within a few minutes, Frederick and Seth returned and dragged a demon, who they threw at Pelonus's feet. The two minions then vanished.

"What is your name," Pelonus said and breathed hot, heavy air at him.

"Roberto, my Lord." The demon bowed and got on his knees.

Pelonus studied the dark-haired demon. "Why did you leave your human, Roberto?"

"The body was damaged..."

"Damaged?" Pelonus shrieked. "So what? Since you've given it up it is now lost to you. You are an idiot and I have no time to waste on you." He waved his hand over the demon. "Return to the underworld and pay for your stupidity," he commanded.

The demon crouched in fear, burst into flames and disappeared with a pop.

Pelonus turned away from the black smoke.

Standing a few feet behind him was a blonde woman, wearing a black cape that scraped the grass. "Hello, Rochelle, what brings you out today?"

****

"I'm here to find out your intentions for Kris." She smiled and stared at him.

"Who's Kris?" he asked.

She looked at him and tilted her head. "Kris is the body Abednego tried to steal for me to possess. She is very tricky and protected by a Lakeman."

"That's old news, my dear. Why are you so interested in this one?"

"No reason. She is quite attractive and I would enjoy working with the body. If you're not here to take her, why are you here?" Rochelle walked up close to him.

"I'm going to acquire her for Garda. I get the young one in exchange. There is a great power source waiting to be tapped there." Pelonus smiled. "I think he'll be easy to turn; the woman, I'm not so sure."

"Turning a baby should be easy," Rochelle said.

"Baby? What is it with the baby?" he asked. "I'm here for the young Lakeman. What would I want with a baby?"

Rochelle grinned. "Oh, I see. I got misdirected. Tell me why this young one interests you."

"I'm not going to tempt you, my dear. He's mine and you'll keep your mildewed fingers off." Pelonus turned serious.

"I'm not in the least bit tempted, Pelonus. I have my sights set on another prize."

"I'm serious woman, hands off," he hissed at her.

"We're good, Pelonus. I promise I'm not

touching." Rochelle began to walk away when she saw a familiar face out in the lake. A part of her heart wrenched, and caught her unawares. Her throat tightened and she felt her eyes well. It was him, the one this human, Lorrie, slept with before Rochelle took possession of her body. She could tell there were still feelings for him and a longing sank into her mind.

She looked at the face and shook her head. Rochelle wanted to touch him, but now just wasn't the right time.

****

Garda leaned over his watching pool and growled. Pelonus planned a double-cross and he didn't like it. The stupid demon worked with that trouble-making ghost. Garda hoped for more from Pelonus than he should have.

The elder demon sat up. "Sebastian!" he shouted.

"Yes, master. How may I serve you," the three foot troll said and stood by the side of Garda's chair.

The demon's eyebrows creased and he frowned. "How did you get here so fast? You're supposed to be finding my son."

"I have word on that, master. I was waiting for you to acknowledge me." Sebastian bowed his head.

Garda sighed. "Tell me what you have heard?"

"I have contacted Guillermo, my Lord," the troll started, but went silent and looked at the floor.

"And?"

"Please, don't beat me, master. Your son is very stubborn," Sebastian said.

"Troll, if you don't tell me what Guillermo said, I will beat you."

Sebastian lifted his large round head and glanced at

the elder demon. "He is afraid to come here. He knows you're very angry with him for not answering your summons immediately as he is supposed to. He said he will know when he should appear to you."

"That wasn't so hard, was it?" Garda looked back into his pool. "My son can be very strong-willed and it is getting annoying. Tell him to come to me and I will give him a great gift. Tell him, if he doesn't come here soon, I will send the harpies after him. That threat should wake him up."

"I will tell him, master. Thank you for not beating me," Sebastian said and moved from the room.

Garda shook his head. *The insolence I have to tolerate can be taxing.*

Chapter Fourteen

Once Roman got the truck onto the freeway, Kris looked out the back window and saw the cop didn't follow. She started to calm down and just realized how wound up she'd become.

As she started to put on the seatbelt, Roman grabbed her arm and pulled her next to him. He wrapped his arm around her shoulders and kissed her forehead.

"We need to talk. I'm pulling off up ahead and we're getting coffee." He kissed her again. "Please don't give me a heart attack ever again."

"Sorry, I don't want you hurt, Roman," she said and looked at her hands.

"I know." He pulled the truck off the exit and they went to a drive-by espresso stand. Next door to the establishment, they found a parking space that couldn't be seen from the road. Roman thought they would be okay for a time. He turned off the engine and leaned against her.

Kris looked up at him. "I get to go first. You have taken really great care of me and I always feel safe and protected. There have been times I've complained about being suffocated, but really I cherish your care, I really do. However, I'm not going to agree with you now or ever about you being in danger for me. It makes me feel guilty. I love you too much and I'm not letting you get into harm's way." She pressed her lips together and frowned.

Roman nodded and let out a breath. "I understand what you're saying, but your big-Neanderthal husband isn't going to let you be in harm's way for him, either. We need to put our heads together and come up with a plan. I understand why you left Father Rupert's. I'm not sure what you planned to do once you were up against Pelonus, but, babe, you can't do it alone. He's too strong. You're going to need some backup." He took her hand and kissed the palm. "You are my life, Kris, and I refuse to let you get swallowed up by some inhuman evil. I know you're angry with me because I wasn't listening. You're right. I didn't hear you. Will you forgive me for that foolishness?"

Kris pulled his hand to her chest. "Of course I forgive you. It was the heat of the moment and neither one of us paid any attention," she whispered. "I'm not sure what I would do against Pelonus. El says it's a suicide mission."

"I'd love to say El's wrong, but...does El know the abolishing spell?"

Kris went silent for minute. "She says yes, in Latin."

"We can probably use it. How do you feel about using the electric balls and the shield?"

Kris looked at her palm and made it light up. "Even though I learned it only this morning, I think I can do it."

"Good, you'll need them. I've been in touch with Omar. Pelonus continues to lurk around the grass at the shoreline. He went through both houses and eliminated one of his minions. Omar says he's acting pissed off."

"Why would he go through Cassie's house?" Kris asked.

"Power is power, babe. He'll take whatever he can get."

Kris put her head against Roman's shoulder. "I forgot how exhausting all of this can be."

He hugged her tight as she looked out the windshield. Her eyes got bigger and she sat up straight.

"Roman, I think we've been found."

He saw two wisps of smoke stop at the front of the truck and look in at them.

"Shit," Roman hissed, started the engine, and handed his cup to Kris. "Here we go, hold on," he said, and backed the truck out of the spot.

****

"Roman, can Omar and Marcus do the other realm stuff?"

"What do you mean?"

"You know the *beam-me-over* split?" Kris thought she might have come up with an idea.

"I'm not sure. What are you thinking?"

"The minions have found us for Pelonus. We need to get a plan together with the guys. If we met them in another plane, we could speak privately and when we come back, circle around Pelonus and abolish him."

"If they could, it might work, but I can't drive and split at the same time. I'd wreck the truck," Roman said.

Kris put on her seatbelt this time. Roman flew onto the freeway and headed south to Seattle.

Any ideas, El? Kris thought.

I'm thinking.

Kris looked through the back window and saw the

black smoke trail behind the truck. She squinted when she saw something else by the side of the road.

"Roman, contact Omar. Tell him to call in the crows. We need a distraction." She smiled at him.

"Such a beautiful, bright woman," he said. "My wife." He pointed at her and raised a brow.

"All yours, babe." Kris could hear El make a gagging noise in her head.

Kris saw him look out the front window and think to Omar. She kept looking between the front and the back windows. After several minutes, she saw about ten crows dive at the smoke. Their aerial acrobatics were amazing to watch. They distracted the smokies long enough for Roman to pull the truck off the freeway and lose them. He said they'd have to side-street it the rest of the way back to Haller Lake.

"I told Omar we'd meet him and Marcus at the boat ramp on the south end. It will take longer this way, but at least Pelonus won't know when we arrive," Roman said.

"That was too cool the way the crows went after those two smokies," Kris said and found something to laugh about.

"Yeah, it was. I've been thinking we could get the raccoons involved. They are pretty good fighters."

"It seems strange to think about teaming with raccoons."

"Hey, I've even seen the ducks create havoc. We could use them, too." Roman chuckled.

They became quiet for a few miles. Kris knew that a hot topic bored a hole in both of them and needed to be discussed, but wasn't sure this would be the best time. She could tell Roman felt miffed with her for leaving the holy ground at the church without him. She didn't want to go into this business with Pelonus with anger between them. It could be used against them if discovered.

"Roman?" she said.

"Yes, babe."

"I am sorry for being a bitch earlier. I shouldn't have left the church without you, but you did plan to leave me behind, didn't you?"

"I don't like you being in this situation, but face it together we will. Otter is safe with Cassie, so we have one less thing to worry about."

Kris unhooked her seatbelt and slid over next to him. "Roman, I don't want us to go into this with any anger issues. We need to sort some things out. We're so good together, except for one small thing—your wanting to protect me so much I can't move. It does tend to make me act irrationally. I know you were born during a different time when women were subservient, and let the men make all the decisions. You know I'm not like that. I need my own thoughts, too." She put her hand on his arm as he steered and saw his eyes well up.

Roman looked out the side window. "I understand what you're saying, I do. It's hard though. There's so much evil in the world today and I don't want to allow any of it near you or Otter. I have to be able to defend my family."

"How do we stop driving each other crazy?" she asked.

Roman shrugged as he steered the truck. "Do you think we should do marriage counseling?"

"Oh right, my husband comes from the lake and I can shoot fireballs from the palms of my hands. That will go over big." Kris pushed against him. "We can work this out, right? I mean we're both adult enough to deal, aren't we?"

"Two sex maniacs, with a three-month-old who appears to us in visions as an adult. I guess we need to work it out and keep the interesting stuff under wraps." He stopped the truck at a red light and looked at Kris. "How do I keep you from wanting to go into situations without a plan?"

"Good question. How do I keep you from acting like a He-Man, take control dude?" Kris smiled at him and batted her eyelashes.

Roman started to laugh. "We do have some work ahead of us, don't we?"

"Yep, we do."

They agreed to wait until after the business with Pelonus got cleared up. Taking side streets to the lake from the north, doubled their travel time. They finally reached the boat ramp. Omar and Marcus and a couple of raccoons waited for them.

The sun set and Roman left the headlights on in the truck. They got out and moved toward the others.

Kris felt El come back into her head. Her alternate itched for a fight and wanted to hear the plan being discussed.

"So, how are we handling this one?" Omar asked.

Silence fell over the group and they eyed one another.

Chapter Fifteen

"I saw Lorrie talking to Pelonus," Marcus said and looked at Kris. "I guess it was Rochelle not Lorrie, but she motioned me off. She didn't want me to come ashore."

"What?" she asked.

"Even though Rochelle took the body, Lorrie's still there." He looked at his hands.

"We've been discussing a disassociation spell. It could work," Omar said.

Marcus looked back up at them. "I know the Oracle will never approve of a merge between Lorrie and me, but we could still marry. I'm not sure she'd have me, but when I saw her today, I could tell she still felt something. She gave me a warning."

Roman scratched his chin. "I don't want to get your hopes up, Marcus. It could be difficult getting her back."

"Okay, so El is jumping up and down in my head," Kris said and closed her eyes. "She wants me to tell you it's not a disassociation spell, you idiot." She opened her eyes and felt El move forward.

****

"Hey, El," Roman said. Both Marcus and Omar looked stunned at how fast the transfer had taken place.

El smirked at Roman. "It's a dispossession spell, sort of like an exorcism. It would clean Lorrie's pipes out and we'd have to do an abolishing spell on Rochelle once she's out." She turned to Roman. "Hi, gorgeous, I've been in hibernation for twelve long months due to your son stealing some of my energy. Want to play?"

"Kris told me and sorry, only the missus gets to have those experiences." He smiled.

"Pfft, you're no fun." She looked at the others. "Now, what are we going to do about Pelonus? How are we going to deal with him?"

Omar shook his head. "Amazing," he whispered.

El rolled her eyes. "Brother, you guys are so weird sometimes. Okay, my nephew stole my power for a while and I got some vacation time. Now that he's out of the womb and working on his own, I've been able to build myself back up. Believe me when I say I'm ready to kick some demon ass. Now focus, Omar, we need a plan."

"We'll need to do an abolishing spell," Omar said.

"Been there, said that. Move forward, dude." El crossed her arms.

Omar raised his eyebrows. "The question is how to get Pelonus and his minion to play into it. He won't just let us circle around him."

"You know he'd be aware of any tricks. Even if we tried to distract him with the raccoons and ducks, he'd know something was up. He's surrounded himself with his groupies. Getting past won't be easy," Roman commented. "Two of them found us when were up in Arlington. The crows were able to divert them...hey, we need to call in the crows. If they could create havoc for a few minutes, we could get past the minion and circle Pelonus."

"All I know is that we have to get moving soon. Kris says these"—El grabbed her breasts—"are going to leak soon. I really don't like the idea of smelling like sour milk. And that should answer your question about the black dress." She looked at Roman. "We have one other problem. I can't do the electric balls. Kris can't do the grab and hold. Also, I know the abolishing spell, Kris doesn't. If I go in there against Pelonus, we won't have the fireballs."

"Wrong, El," Roman said and flattened his hand, bringing up an electric ball. Omar held his up, too.

"Okay, good, we have fireballs." She closed her eyes and winced. "Kris wants to know what we're going to do to save Lorrie."

"Do you know the dispossession spell?" Roman asked.

"No, we'd need your priest to do it," El answered.

"El, can I get Kris back for a minute, please?" Roman sighed.

"Okay, since you said please." She closed her eyes.

****

"We have to save her, Roman," Kris said as she opened her eyes and grabbed his arm.

"We'll do our best, babe. Right now, we have to vanquish Pelonus. I want our house back," Roman grumbled. He looked across the lake. "Do we still have contact with the cats?"

"Sort of, you know how temperamental they can be." Omar crossed his arms. "They tend to not converse with us until they want something."

"We'll need everyone on board, so try to contact them. Kris and I will come in from the east, you two from the west. If the animals can distract Pelonus long enough, we can get him surrounded and do the vanquish." Roman turned to Kris. "You'll need to start out as you. We may need you to shoot fireballs. Once we have him circled, let El take over. Is she listening?"

"Oh, yeah, she heard." Kris watched Omar send out mental signals to the animals. Marcus went into the water and some ducks surrounded him. Kris found this talent for talking to the animals astounding.

Omar turned. "Okay, the night creatures are on alert and waiting for our signal."

"Good. We'll get into position and then signal everyone." Roman smiled.

Omar nodded, then turned and with Marcus, headed into the water and dived under.

Roman and Kris got into the truck and headed to the other side of the lake.

Chapter Sixteen

Something didn't feel right to Pelonus. The air felt heavy somehow and wet. Humidity moved in and it felt thick.

He'd gone through the drawers and closets in the house and tried to find some clues to where the woman and her Lakeman were hiding. Rochelle wanted the woman to be a vessel and he'd told her that he wasn't interested in Kris. He only tried to turn her for the demon Garda.   In the house, he felt an enormous residual energy and found it very tempting. If he could turn her and get control of that power, there would be no stopping him. The young Lakeman, Cedric, emitted the same power and the source felt great.

Pelonus wanted to control them and leech that power from them. Garda would be angry, but would just have to get over it. If Rochelle, the ghost, thought she would get the woman, she had another think coming. He'd see to it that she spent the rest of eternity in oblivion if she got in his way.

If his stupid flunkies could just find out where that woman disappeared to, there would be no problem, but as usual, Pelonus had to do all the work himself. *If, if, if,* he thought, and bellowed inside his mind. That woman became an annoyance, as had the young Lakeman. He couldn't pass into the other realm and would have to wait for the boy to reappear. Or perhaps he could take the woman and offer her as a trade for the young one.

Pelonus left the deck of the woman's house and walked to the middle of the lawn. He looked out at the water and saw the ducks and geese staring at him. He could hear voices in his head. They spoke in some sort of code and he didn't have time to listen to a lot of drivel. After a time, the voices silenced and the water fowl still watched him.

"What do you want?" he hissed. One goose stretched its neck and honked. Pelonus felt something move against his leg. When he looked down, he found a black cat with golden eyes peering up at him.

"This is starting to get rather dull," he said to the cat and glanced around, trying to find the source of his unease. He couldn't put his finger on it.

The cat still rubbed against him. He moved his foot and pushed the animal away, causing it to hiss and arch it's back.

"Pelonus, I want my house back," he heard a female voice say from the hedge. He grinned. Things were picking up.

****

Half way around the lake, on foot, Roman and Kris split off. She followed the shore and he went up to the road so he could come in from behind Pelonus. Cutting through the neighbors' yards, she nearly broke her neck on a tricycle that was parked on the lawn.

She and Roman were in mental contact the whole way and at one point he started to whistle in her head.

Babe, I love it when you whistle, but right now it's making me feel like a teapot. Please, stop, she thought.

Yes, ma'am. She heard him chuckle. She wondered

if he tried to drive her crazy, but decided he probably didn't even realize he did it. He concentrated pretty hard and communicated not only with her, but also with Omar and Marcus.

Kris found her way around the lake and came to the hedge of bushes that separated her yard from the neighbor, Sylvia. The house looked dark, as she and her husband, Fred, left to spend the winter in Arizona.

She squatted behind the bushes, and waddled to the center. Peering through them, she saw Pelonus pace back and forth on the lawn. It made her angry. She wanted him out of their lives.

Hi, Mom. She heard a voice in her head. She turned so fast that she lost her balance and landed on her rear in the grass. She found herself looking into the brown eyes of the adult version of her baby son-who squatted next to her.

Kris' jaw dropped and she couldn't speak her questions, but needed to think them.

Otter, what are you doing here?

Hopefully helping. He looked through the bushes. *I think I might be able to get near Pelonus and sidetrack him a little.*

Otter, how did you get here? Kris felt confused. Roman listened in and started to ask questions at the same time Otter explained. Two strong male voices boomed in her brain. She put her hand on Otter's arm and held her finger to her lips.

Roman, let him explain. Hush.

There's no reason to worry, Mom. I'm still a baby being cared for by Aunt Cassie. She thinks I'm asleep, which I am in a way. I'm able to do the alternate reality split thing you and Dad can do. I must have some strong genes from you two. I'm also blocking Pelonus from hearing us. He listened in earlier and I really don't want him to hear us now.

Kris didn't know what to say. Otter was so well-versed in these magicks. He'd been born a wizard and Kris felt so proud, she almost started to cry.

Dad, are you and the others in place? Otter sent out his thoughts.

Yes, we're good, she heard Roman think back.

It seems strange that the minions are nowhere around. Dad, do you or the others sense any of Pelonus' pals? Otter asked and looked through the bushes, again.

Kris heard Roman and the other two Lakemen say no.

"Okay, I'm going to cause a little disturbance, then mentally grab Pelonus. Mom, you'll need to turn over to El since she knows the vanquishing spell, Otter said.

Got it. Kris reached out to him and readied herself. She started to let El forward, but stopped when she watched her son transform into a black cat. "Oh my God," she whispered and looked at the golden-eyed feline. Otter looked up at her and winked. She felt glad she sat in the grass or her legs would have gone out from under her.

Kris heard Roman ask what was wrong. When she didn't answer right away, he grew concerned.

Babe, answer me, what's the matter? she heard in her head.

You're never going to believe this, Roman. Our son is a shape-shifter. Keep an eye out for a black cat with gold eyes. It's Otter. She looked out at the yard. Otter walked up to Pelonus, and swished his tail back and forth. Kris smiled and tried not to laugh out loud.

She closed her eyes and let El come forward. Together, they watched Otter walk around Pelonus' legs. The evil demon didn't score any points when he tried to kick the cat. Otter slashed at him with claws out and hissed.

After a couple of passes, Otter pretended to start away from Pelonus, who turned his back on the cat and looked out at the lake.

The cat form stretched and the adult Otter soon stood behind Pelonus. He reached out his hand and held the demon by the back of the neck. Roman, Omar, and Marcus all ran from their positions. El parted the bushes and made her way to the gathering. They covered the four directions and Kris heard the chanting for the vanquishing spell begin.

Pelonus started to scream and tried to begin a chant of his own. Kris could see Otter tighten his hold on the demon's throat and cut off his ability to speak.

When the four reached a certain point in the chant, Pelonus screamed louder. Otter released his hold and backed out of the circle as the four finished the vanquishing. Pelonus went up in flames and disappeared in a puff of black smoke.

Kris watched from the back of her brain while the chant finished, but abruptly felt herself being pulled farther back. She couldn't see anything around her. The gathering disappeared, as did the lake, her home, the sky. Everything around her faded from existence. The silence consumed her.

****

Roman looked at everyone and then saw a strange look come over Otter's face. "Son, what is it?"

They all turned to him and waited. Otter stared at El, who stood with her hands out in front of her body. Her eyes were closed tightly.

"Something is wrong," Otter said and looked frightened. "Where is she? Where is my mother!" he shouted. He grabbed El's shoulders and shook her.

Chapter Seventeen

El's brows creased as she tried to find Kris. There appeared a huge black hole in her head and she felt very much alone. Her knees buckled and she landed on her butt.

She closed her eyes again and started to yell. *Kris, this isn't funny, where are you? Where are you hiding? Answer me, you slut, where are you?* She put her hand in her hair and rocked back and forth. Looking up at Roman and then Otter, she whispered, "I don't know where she is. It's empty."

Roman knelt in front of her. "El, this is no time for joking around. Let her go."

"Roman, I swear to you, she's not here. I can't—"

"Shut up, El. You've disappeared from Kris on more than one occasion and come back. Look in the places you went. You find her and bring her back, do you understand me?" Roman's gripped her arms tight.

El started to cry, which was unusual for her tough girl act. The tears rolled down her cheeks. It hurt her that he thought she lied.

"Roman, you're hurting her, let go," Omar said and pulled on his brother's arm.

"El, where is she?" Roman shouted.

"I don't know, she's not here!" El cried, and shook loose from his hold. "She's my sister and she's not here!" she shouted in Roman's face.

Omar turned back to Marcus, who held the boy

back. "Otter, go back to the church. We'll be out in the morning to pick up you and Cassie. Don't worry, we'll get this worked out and get your mom back."

"Uncle Omar, watch over Dad."

"I will," Omar said. He and Marcus watched as Otter's light shimmered and he faded from view.

"Roman, it's not like before when Meshach stole her soul. I could tell she was still in a realm. I can't sense her at all now." El sobbed.

"Shut up, El," Roman barked.

El pulled her knees up to her chin and wrapped her arms around her legs. She tried to cry quietly, but found herself sobbing in great huffs.

****

Roman began to walk in circles. He stopped and looked at Marcus. "You said you saw Lorrie here. We know she's been taken by Rochelle. Did you hear anything she and Pelonus spoke about?"

"No, I was too far out to hear them." Marcus looked out at the water. "Let me see if the animals heard anything." He walked to the shore and started to converse with the ducks and geese.

Roman looked at Omar. "We have to get Cassie down here. We'll need her help," he said and turned to El. He knelt back down in front of her. "El, I'm sorry I yelled at you. I need you to come with me. We'll get the car from the rest stop and then pick up Cassie and Otter."

"Dude, don't yell at me, but I can't drive. I don't know how," she said between sobs.

"Roman, it's late. We should wait until morning," Omar said.

"No, we go now or I go. Otter has to be going

124

crazy and Cassie doesn't even know what's happened."

"She does know, I've communicated with her." Omar frowned.

"Fine, tell her I'm on my way and to be ready to leave in an hour. We'll need Father Rupert, too." Roman turned and ran to the other side of the lake where the truck was parked.

****

El watched him leave through a blur. Omar put his hand down to help her stand.

"Omar, I've been trying to raise my powers. I wanted different shoes. These sneakers are killing my feet, but it's not working. I can't even get a little fizzle going. I think I'm tapped out,"
El said, as her chin quivered.

"It's a good thing they held while we were vanquishing Pelonus," Omar answered.

"Yeah, I guess so." She looked at her hands.

Omar reached out, and took one of them. "El, don't worry. We'll get Kris back. You know how Roman is, he'll never give up."

"I know. It's just so empty without her." She looked up at him.

Marcus walked back up from the shoreline. "One of the geese says he heard them. Pelonus is after Cedric only, but the goose doesn't know why. Rochelle acted disinterested in Kris, but the animals think she may have lied to Pelonus. She may be after Otter, too, but it's unclear."

"We can consider Cedric safe for now, but why on earth would Pelonus want him?" Omar asked.

Marcus shook his head. "It has something to do with a huge untapped source of power. That's what the goose heard, anyway."

"We'll have to keep an eye on him and help find his source." Omar arched a brow and shook his head.

El didn't find any of this interesting. She turned to Kris and Roman's house and walked toward it. She felt tired and empty and her breasts were sore and bloated, filled with unused milk. Hopefully Roman would get back soon, so she could get rid of some of it. How Kris put up with this was beyond her realm of understanding.

She went into the house and kicked off the sneakers, freeing her feet. Looking around the kitchen, she discovered Pelonus made quite a mess. She started to pick up things that weren't broken, and stepped carefully, not wanting to cut up her feet. Roman would kill her if she damaged this body.

She found a picture of Kris, Roman, and Otter just after the baby was born. The glass fell out onto the floor. Running her fingers over the picture, she began to cry again. Then she stopped, and took in a deep breath. She put the picture down, went to the kitchen closet and pulled out a broom and dust pan. It felt necessary to get things straightened up before Roman got back with Otter. Her nephew wouldn't be safe in this mess and she wouldn't allow him near it.

El put things away as best she could and got the furniture back in place. She sat down at the kitchen table and stared. Rummaging around in her head, she tried to find out where Kris went. She called out to her sister, but there was nothing. Only silence met her and would drive her nuts if she listened very long. Getting up from the table, she went to Otter's room to pick up and then to Kris and Roman's.

As she finished, she saw a light dance across the wall and realized a car pulled up past the window. She looked out and saw Roman unfolding himself from the car. A truck pulled up behind the car and she saw Father Rupert turn off the lights and open the door.

Roman bent through the back door and unbuckled Otter, who'd sacked out. Omar ran up to the car and helped Cassie out. El watched as he hugged his woman and kept a tight hold. El wondered if she'd ever know this feeling of being wanted and held. Right now, there wasn't a person out by the car or truck who cared one way or another if she existed.

She carried the broom and dustpan back to the closet in the kitchen and put them away. The back door opened. Roman brought Otter into the house and went straight to the nursery. He glanced at her as he passed, but that was all. It didn't surprise her that she got no "hello" or "thank you for getting the house straightened out." She would get nothing here.

El walked into the living room, sat on the couch and folded her hands on her lap. Cassie, Omar, Marcus, and Father Rupert came in and found their way to her. Cassie sat next to El and squeezed her hand.

"Cass, when did Otter last eat?" El asked.

"About two hours ago, but it was formula, which he doesn't like very well."

Roman came out of the nursery. El stood and walked toward the door.

"Where are you going?" he asked.

"To feed Otter." She looked up at him.

"I don't think so." He grabbed her arm and stopped her.

El sighed. "Roman, I may not be Kris, but this is

her body and I really don't want these"—she palmed the engorged breasts—"to explode or start leaking."

Roman stared at her and frowned. "Fine." He let her go.

****

"Roman Lake." Cassie looked at him and shook her head. "You have got to be one of the meanest and cruelest men I've ever met."

He stopped, turned to her and felt hurt. "I'm not cruel, Cassie."

She softened. "You can be, Roman. I know from firsthand experience, and you did admit that you were acting like an ass earlier today. This is not El's fault. She tried to help, if you recall. I think she's been a bit side-swiped, too. Try to remember that, okay?"

Roman ran his hand through his hair and nodded. "I know." He let out a huff. "Does anyone have an idea where Kris could have been taken? When Shadrach took her soul, we could still sense her. Even if Rochelle is holding her in another realm, we should still be able to locate her."

"Is the merge spot working at all, Roman?" Omar asked.

He looked at his hand. "No."

Omar held out his hands. "Have you checked with Kris's body?"

"No, I haven't checked."

"Well, no time like the present, brother." Omar stared at him.

He felt reluctant to move.

"Roman you must check," Omar said with more force.

He pinched his lips together and nodded. Turning

toward the nursery, he opened the door and stepped through.

Chapter Eighteen

El sat in the rocker with Otter. Her breasts were exposed and although Roman had seen them, he felt embarrassed. He looked away from the chair.

"El, perhaps you could cover yourself when feeding Otter," he suggested.

She shook her head and rolled her eyes. "Roman, if I'd known you were such a prude, I might have talked to Kris about giving her relationship with you a second thought. Didn't you use to swim around the lake naked all the time, for crap's sake?" She reached to the crib and pulled a blanket to her. Covering herself and the baby, she smirked back up at Roman. "Okay, it's safe to look now."

"Thank you." He looked at her. "El, I don't want you to think I don't appreciate what you're doing. It must be difficult." He knelt in front of her.

"When did you stop trusting me, Roman? Did I miss something while I was away?"

"No, according to Cassie I'm being mean and cruel. I guess I am being a jerk. I'm sorry, but I want my wife back."

"I know. I want her back, too. This breast milk stuff is really gross. I'm praying Otter doesn't decide to spit up on me," she said.

Roman laughed. "You'd get used to it, believe me. Kris adjusted pretty quick. Listen, I don't want to change subjects, but"—he held up his merge hand—"I want to check the merge and see if we can sense where Kris is being held."

El put her hand up. "Roman, you didn't merge with me. I don't have the spot, remember?"

"We can try." He put his hand in hers and began to concentrate. He got pulled into a black wall and he couldn't see or hear anything. He saw El wearing the black dress and three inch spike heels, and stared at the blackness. "El, are you sensing anything?"

"No, as I said, it's empty." She didn't even turn to face him.

Empty put it lightly. Roman never experienced a place like this before. The despair he felt in his own mind was intense and he pulled back, shaking his head. He let go of her hand and scratched his chin.

"Nothing, right?" she asked and shifted in the rocker.

"Right."

"I've had a thought. As soon as Otter's finished, I'll come out and discuss it with you and the rest. Omar may need to talk to his Oracle. We're going to need some guidance."

Roman straightened up. He wanted El to say what she thought about, but knew it would be best for Otter if she wasn't upset. "Okay, we'll be waiting." He stood and left the nursery.

****

El pulled the blanket off her shoulder and found Otter sound asleep with her nipple firmly in his mouth. If she moved he started to suck again. "Nephew, it's amazing you haven't worn your mother out completely."

When she finished nursing Otter, El stepped

through the door into the living room. She sat on the couch and looked at Cassie.

"I don't recommend that to the faint of heart. It's weird." She rubbed her eyes and saw Cassie smile, Omar frown and look at Marcus, who shrugged. El figured the boys didn't know what she was talking about.

Roman came in from the kitchen. "What were you thinking, El?" He sat in a straight back chair.

She sighed and sat up. "We know Rochelle's been lurking around and wanting something. It sounds like from what the goose heard," she said and looked at Marcus, "that she's still after Kris. If she did take Kris, this body wouldn't be here. The ghost would be in possession of it. If Rochelle took Kris's spirit somehow, what I'd like to know is if it would be possible for a ghost to steal the essence and soul together? Omar, can you ask the Oracle if she's aware of ghosts wielding this kind of power?" Omar nodded. "Good. If Rochelle can do that, we'll need instructions. I don't know the first thing about getting essences back," El said directly to Cassie.

"Don't look at me. I have nothing on that," Cassie said with her hands up. "I can talk to my group leader and see if he knows anything about it."

"I remember George from last year. He's smart," El said. She looked up at Roman. "Since my head seems to be empty, I have no powers and no defenses. Can a protection spell be done around the house? I'm not sure about the connection with Otter, but he needs to be protected."

"Of course," Roman answered.

El started to feel weary.

"Father Rupert, you've been very quiet. Have you any thoughts?" Roman asked the priest, who stood in a corner of the room.

"I've just been thinking and I don't believe I've ever heard of a ghost having the abilities this one seems to have. Taking souls and essences isn't really in a ghost's bag of tricks." He put his hands together. "Roman, your lady from the last century, Beatrice, did she have any abilities you were aware of?" Father Rupert asked.

"No, none that I ever saw her wield."

"Do we have any idea how long Rochelle has been collecting bodies?" El wondered aloud and continued to look at him.

The silence in the room sounded as bad as the nothingness in her head. "It would seem we have our work cut out for us. Right now though, I'm tired and going to get some sleep." She stood and started to the master bedroom, but stopped. Shaking her head, she continued in and closed the door. She fell asleep the minute her head hit the pillow.

Chapter Nineteen

Kris couldn't see anything but black. There were no weird flashes of light, like when you have your eyes closed. There was only darkness and it felt cold and there were no sounds. She tried to move, but couldn't feel her body.

She couldn't tell how long this went on for. It seemed like an eternity. Every now and then, she heard voices whisper, but thought her imagination came up with a way to entertain itself. She knew who she was and where she'd come from. She knew she had a husband and a child waiting for her. She knew there were friends.

What Kris didn't know and couldn't figure out, was she taken or in some type of accident? She didn't remember being in a car crash or fall, but if she'd gone to the next life, she didn't like it.

She tried not to dwell on the dead idea for very long. It made her feel sad and the thought that she might not see Roman or Otter again, became too much to comprehend.

It occurred to her that she did feel. The air felt cold on her skin. The more she thought about it, she realized that the air felt moist. She hooked onto this line of thinking and pulled herself forward. After a time, she became aware of parts of her body and she vaguely remembered opening her eyes.

Kris heard a voice say her name over and over.

Things around her started to clear and she worked at focusing her eyes. She saw something very dirty in her line of vision and when she leaned her head back, discovered a gray brick wall with black soot covering it. She glanced up and felt grit in her eyes which made them water. She hoped she'd be able to wash them out soon. They burned. She turned her head and tried to focus on the location. She didn't see much except the manacles chaining her to the wall. She felt herself frown. This happened with Abednego and he'd chained her to a wall, hadn't he?

She kept hearing the whispers and heard her name being repeated. She kept trying to see where it came from, but gave up and closed her eyes, leaning her head on her arm.

Time passed. It could have been five minutes or five hours. Kris didn't have a clue as to how long she'd laid on the filthy floor. She thought she might have slept, but wasn't sure. She opened her eyes and could see a little more clearly. The room appeared dim. She saw other shapes near the walls and some movement. She blinked a couple of times, and tried to focus her vision. She heard her name again. Turning her head, she looked between her arms down the wall. Chained in irons was a woman whose face seemed familiar.

She tried to speak, but her mouth was so dry and she couldn't say any words and ended up coughing.

"Kris, don't try to talk. It gets better if you make your salivary glands work," the familiar voice said.

She thought about this and tried to think of something that would make her mouth water. Food, cheesecake, and anything chocolate, didn't work. She pictured Roman standing naked in the shower. It worked and she felt some spit come into her mouth.

Kris looked at the other figure. "Where are we?" she whispered.

"I have no idea, although I think it has something to do with Rochelle," the blonde woman said. "In fact, I'm sure it does."

"Lorrie, we miss you so much," Kris said.

"I miss you, too. I thought about coming back over to Seattle from Moses Lake for good, but Rochelle did something to me. It was so long ago, I barely remember."

"Long ago? What do you mean? You've only been gone a year."

Lorrie looked at her with innocent eyes. "Kris, I've been here going on thirty years. Time is different in this realm," she whispered back.

"How long have I been here?" Kris felt almost afraid to ask.

"I'm not sure of exact numbers, but around eight or nine years."

Kris thought if she could hear her heart beating, she would make it stop. Being gone eight or nine years, meant she'd missed so much of her son's life. She'd wanted to see him go to his first day of school, play sports, and horse around with his father. She'd missed his first steps and words. She could feel tears well up in her eyes. It made her wonder and think she wasn't completely dried out.

"Kris, it's okay. Rochelle let me see Marcus and he hadn't changed at all. I don't think much time has passed on that side."

Kris shook her head, and tried to think. She felt that Roman would find them and bring them back. Holding up her hand, she looked at the merge spot, and hoped for a connection with him, but found the place on her palm, which usually lit up, was only skin. "Lorrie, Lakemen don't age. Marcus might look the same in thirty years."

"Did you have the baby?" Lorrie asked.

"Yes."

"I heard Rochelle talk to someone about a baby. It was the same time I saw Marcus. That happened only a week or two ago."

Kris glanced around the room they were being held in and saw four other woman chained to various parts of the wall. "Lorrie, who are they?" she whispered.

"I'm Rena," one of them answered.

"Sarah."

"Françoise."

"Beatrice."

Kris looked at her friend, who nodded. "Kris, these are some of the other woman Rochelle has stolen."

"I've been here over 500 years," the one called Francoise said.

"I'm a short-timer, according to Lorrie. I've only been here 200 years."

Kris looked at the one who said this. "You're Beatrice, right?"

"Yes, I am."

She couldn't believe it. This was the woman Roman almost merged with back in the 1800s. Beatrice got taken from him by the demon Abednego. If he and Beatrice joined, Kris never would have met him and given birth to her little son. She also wouldn't be in this predicament.

"Do I know you, ma'am?" Beatrice asked.

"No, no," Kris said and looked back at Lorrie.

"I know, weird huh?" Lorrie whispered.

"You are Roman's woman?" Beatrice inquired.

Kris looked back at her. She was pretty, in a natural way. She wore no makeup and didn't have a trendy haircut. Those things wouldn't change the fact that Beatrice appeared attractive for her time.

"Yes, I am. My name is Kris."

"I heard you say you gave Roman a son. What is his name?" Beatrice asked.

"His name is Elliott, but we call him Otter."

"Do you carry a likeness of him?"

Kris thought about this one. Lorrie mouthed the word *photograph*. "Oh no, not on me, sorry."

"Does he resemble Roman?"

"Yes. His hair is dark and his eye are brownish-amber. When he was first born, he had blond hair, but it all fell out a week or so later. It's dark now," Kris said.

"With you and Roman as his parents, I imagine he is very beautiful." Beatrice smiled.

Kris looked back at Lorrie. "How do we get out of here?"

"You don't think I haven't tried? I've tried for years, but finally gave up."

"Sweetie, we're not giving up. We're going to get out of this, so help me...." Kris looked at the other woman and tried to give her some hope.

Chapter Twenty

"Roman, we don't know for sure that Rochelle took Kris," Father Rupert said as he sipped a cup of tea.

"I understand your argument, Rupert, but it makes the most sense. Pelonus's minion split once we'd vanquished him and I don't think any of them would be clever enough to carry this out," Roman said as he sat across the dining room table from the priest.

Cassie, Omar, and Marcus left and were getting some rest. It was late in the day and Roman felt exhausted, but couldn't settle down.

"I'm interested to see what Cassie's group leader thinks about all this." Roman cupped his chin with his hand.

"Is there any possibility that this alter ego, El, might have something to do with it?" Father Rupert asked.

Roman thought for a moment. "I suppose anything is possible, but I doubt it. El's gone out of her way to save and protect Kris more than once. As much as she grouses about her place in the world, I don't think El can exist long without Kris. She said her mind was empty and that it would drive her mad. I know it would affect me that way."

"Roman, you look done in. Why don't you get some rest? I see Marcus and Cedric walking the shore out there. I'll take a watch in the morning."

"Thank you, Rupert. I'm not sure if I could sleep,

but I am tired. I'll be in the nursery for a bit." He stood and stretched. Putting his cup in the sink, Roman turned and headed for the nursery.

Roman closed the door and walked over to the crib. He found Otter playing with his blanket and kicking his feet.

"What are you up to, rascal?" He leaned over and pulled the baby up into his arms. They sat in the rocker and Roman adjusted Otter in his lap. The baby looked up at him and gurgled, and then held up his hand for Roman to take. He put his hand up and Otter moved his hand to Roman's palm

The connection lit up and Roman got pulled into the other realm with his son. When Roman could focus again, he found himself sitting in the grass by the lake with his adult son.

"Dad, I've been doing some checking. Mom can't be found in any realm," Otter said and looked upset.

"We'll find her, Son. I promise. We're pretty sure the ghost, Rochelle, took her. Your mom is smart and has gotten out of some sticky situations in the past."

"I know, Dad. I just don't like not knowing where she is." Otter looked out at the water. "I wish we'd hear something from Uncle Omar. Has he talked to the Oracle yet?"

"I don't think he could get an audience until this morning."

"Figures," Otter grumbled.

"We have to be patient, Son. It's hard and, believe me, I'm one of the least patient people I know next to your mom, but we do need information. It would be crazy to do spells or find a way to bring in Rochelle without a good plan," Roman said and hoped to help the boy not worry so much.

"I know. I'm just really concerned. I want her back." Otter looked directly at Roman. "I like Aunt El okay, but..."

"She's not your mom at all." Roman nodded.

"Yeah, and she's kind of sour, too." Otter explained, "I know I should be grateful I'm getting any milk. It is better than that canned stuff in the plastic bottles, but Aunt El tastes sour."

When Roman realized what Otter said, he started to laugh and wrapped his arm around the boy's shoulders. "You'd better not tell your mom that. She'll have a fit."

"You know what I mean, Dad?" Otter asked.

"Not really, but I get the gist of it." Roman felt his mind being pulled back and closed his eyes. He'd apparently slept for a bit with his arms around Otter, who also dozed off. When he opened his eyes, El stood over him with her hands on her hips. "What?" he asked and pushed up straight in the rocking chair.

"The baby book says we have to keep a routine going. No sooner than every two hours and no later than every four hours."

Roman looked down at his sleeping son. "Kris decided to ignore some of what the books say. She feeds him when he wakes up and is fussing. Why don't you get some more rest?"

"I'm not tired, and these"—she grabbed her breasts—"are starting to throb, again."

"There's a breast pump in the bathroom, but Kris hates that thing," he said.

El leaned against the wall. "I'm starting to feel like a fucking cow."

"Watch the language, El." Roman looked at her

seriously.

"Sorry, but he is asleep and I've heard you use that word before," she hissed.

"I don't think he would feed right now anyway. He'd be cranky and refuse to nurse if you woke him up."

"Fine, whatever." She waved her arms and left the nursery. "But if he wakes me up, I'll be cranky," she said on her way out.

Roman shook his head. He lifted Otter and put him back in the crib. He watched his son settle and then went out to the kitchen to make coffee. He needed to be more alert. He saw Omar on the back deck and went out to join him.

"I sent Cedric and Marcus to get some rest, although knowing Marcus, he's in the library trying to find a way to save Lorrie. Father Rupert is in his truck smoking a cigar and reading some book. He's watching the area, too," Omar said and looked at the water. "I'm supposed to meet with the Oracle in an hour. I'll get to Parcel and back as quickly as I can. With the protection spell up, there should be no problem. Hopefully, Kris will be back in time for lunch." Omar leaned against the deck railing.

Roman nodded. "That would be excellent."

"You know, I haven't mentioned this to Marcus, but I doubt we can save Lorrie," Omar said.

"Brother, you'd best not say that around Kris. She'll fight you tooth and nail about it," Roman warned.

"A good shouting match with your wife is always entertaining, Roman."

"Glutton for punishment, aren't you? Just

remember who she takes it out on." Roman looked at him.

"You love it, admit it." Omar frowned and turned serious. "I'm concerned about Marcus. He's doing all kinds of research about saving Lorrie. He's even put in a petition with the Oracle for a merge. I doubt very much he'll get it." Omar crossed his arms.

"Lorrie's history as a witch won't count for much, he must know that. Now that she's been taken again, I don't see it happening either." Roman turned and looked in the back window. He saw El walk from the nursery across the living room and go into the master bedroom. He watched the light go on in the bathroom and for a moment, got lost in his memories of times spent with Kris in the shower or tub. He felt his throat tighten. Turning back around, he leaned on the rail with his head down.

"Are you all right, brother?" Omar asked.

Roman pressed his lips together and cleared his throat. "Just worried."

Omar put his hand on Roman's shoulder and squeezed. "I'll be back very soon." He left the deck and ran toward the lake. When he reached the shore, he launched into a long dive. Roman remembered seeing Omar execute these dives before, but this time it was so smooth that the water barely rippled.

He turned and walked into the house and then went to the coffee pot by the stove. As he poured a cup, he saw a light from the bedroom shining into the living room. He went in and found the bed empty. Looking around the room, he saw El crouched down in the closet and heard rustling.

"El, what are you looking for?" he asked.

She sat up and looked over her shoulder. "Why does Kris have nineteen pairs of Sketchers?"

Roman thought a moment. "She likes them and thinks they're comfortable."

El held up a cream-colored loafer. "This pair, maybe. The rest look like track shoes. Doesn't she own at least one pair of heels?"

"She doesn't wear heels much, they hurt her feet." He leaned against the doorjamb and sipped his coffee.

El shook her head, sat on the floor and removed her slippers. She put on the loafer and stuck her foot out. "I suppose these will have to do." She looked over her shoulder again. "What's going on?"

"Omar just went to meet with the Oracle. Everyone else is resting."

"I thought of a way to draw Rochelle here." El stood up and walked out of the closet.

"Do tell," Roman said.

"We use Cedric as bait." She sat on the edge of the bed and put on the other shoe.

"Why Cedric?"

"Well, there's something there that Pelonus wanted. If he's got some strong source of power, it could make him very desirable. I think we could tempt Rochelle with it to draw her out." El looked up at him. "Roman, would you fuck me?"

"What?" Roman frowned, stood up straight and almost spilled his coffee.

"Look, I'm not going to be around forever and I'd like to just once experience what it feels like to be touched. I've never been there, done that, and I want to try it."

"No. No way." Roman turned out of the room with

El following him.

"It's still Kris's body," she whined.

"No, El, I won't cheat on her." He looked out the back window, and set his cup on the counter.

"It wouldn't really be cheating."

Roman shook his head.

"Fine, I'll ask one of the others, maybe the youngster Cedric, since he's not attached to anyone," El said and walked to the back door.

Roman moved toward her fast, grabbed her arms and pushed her against the wall. "Don't even think about it, El. The only way you'll have anything happen is if you play with yourself, period."

"You will not tell me what I can and cannot do," she hissed and poked him in the chest.

"No, but since you are in my wife's body, I'm going to insist you maintain some amount of dignity. If you don't, I will lock you in the closet with the shoes you hate until we get this sorted out." He wrapped his hand around her wrist and started to pull her to the bedroom.

"You wouldn't dare."

"Just try me. If anyone touches you, they will pay. Do you understand me?" he said directly into her face.

El stamped her foot and pouted. "You are not a very nice man, do you know that? No caring or warmth at all. Roman, you suck!" she yelled and pulled her wrist out of his grip. She stormed into the bedroom and slammed the door.

This caused Otter to start crying. Roman went into the nursery and held the baby for a while. He fell back to sleep and Roman changed his diaper and put him into the crib.

When he finally came out of the nursery, he saw the bedroom and back door open. El wasn't in the house.

Chapter Twenty-one

When Kris opened her eyes again, she found nothing changed. Lorrie still sat down the wall. Kris tried to move a little.

"Kris, are you in there?" she heard Lorrie ask.

"Yeah, how long have I been out?" Kris looked up.

"A couple of months. You'll be awake longer as time goes by." Lorrie rested her head on her arm.

"How do I get the feeling back into my hands?"

"It will be hard, but if you stand up for a while, you'll get the blood flow going the right way. Give it a try," Lorrie said with encouragement.

Kris looked up and tried to get her fingers wrapped around the chains. Moving her feet, she felt so weak and every joint in her body screamed in pain. It took several tries and she broke into a sweat, but finally she got to the balls of her feet and straightened up. She felt exhausted and so stiff that she leaned against the wall and closed her eyes.

"Kris, stay with us. If you go back to sleep, it could be months again before you're alert. Open your eyes," Lorrie ordered.

She forced them open and looked at her friend. Lorrie stood up, too. Smiling to her left, Kris heard the other voices cheer her on to stay up and keep focused.

"Lorrie, who's talking?" Kris mumbled.

"It's the other women. You met them the last time

you woke up. It's four of the others Rochelle stole. We think there are more, but we can't see them."

Kris looked to the right and saw four other women. Two stood, one squatted, and one sat with her back against the wall. Kris wanted to sit back down in the worst way. Her legs shook and threatened to buckle.

"Kris, kick your feet out and move them around. It helps, believe me," Lorrie said and moved her legs to show Kris how to do it.

She did this for a while, and almost fell a couple of times. It did help and she began to feel more alert.

Kris leaned her back against the wall and looked at the other women. She did remember speaking to one named Beatrice. She was blonde and blue-eyed, and wore a long, old-fashioned dress. It buttoned up the neck, but she'd opened it to the top of her undergarments. Two of the other women were brunettes, also wearing long dresses, but from a different time. The one with red hair, Françoise, wore a long gown without the corsets and looked like someone from the days of Caesar.

Listening to their stories, Kris tried to file what they said in her brain, but it was difficult. She kept thinking that they should be working at getting out of there, but didn't want to interrupt. Francoise asked Kris when her body got taken. She answered that as far as she knew, her body wasn't taken. This caused a bit of a stir amongst the women and they stared at her as though she might be the second coming.

"Kris, think, what happened?" Lorrie asked.

She tried to remember what happened when things changed. "There was a demon named Pelonus after my son. We got him in the circle and I turned over to El since she knows the vanquishing spell," she said and looked at the women. "It's a long story about El and I don't think we have time today. I remember something pulled at my senses. As hard as I tried to ignore it, I couldn't get rid of the feeling. Then everything around me went black."

"Rochelle didn't possess you?" the one called Rena asked.

"Not as far as I know. I think she's still got your body, Lorrie," Kris answered.

"Then why are you here?" Beatrice wondered.

Kris looked at Lorrie and shook her head slightly. "I have no idea why. When Rochelle first came after me, Roman and Omar speculated that she wanted my abilities. I never really found out what interested her so."

"Maybe she stole your spirit and separated you from El, or is she with you now?" Lorrie asked.

"No, I'm alone." Kris squatted down and leaned against the wall.

"Kris," Lorrie sat next to her. "Is Marcus okay?"

"No, he's miserable without you. Were you aware he'd asked the Lakemen over at Moses Lake to check up on you?" Kris felt her brow furrow. "In fact, I wonder why they didn't alert Marcus you were gone. That really seems odd."

"I miss him, too. I had such a good thing with him and I kick myself all the time for tossing it away because of fear."

"Well, once we're out of here and back in our own space and time, you can make it up to him." Kris tried to smile.

"I wonder if there are any houses for sale around

Haller. I'd love to be back by the lake. Maybe Cassie would sell me hers." Lorrie laughed.

"Yeah, right. Remember the one about ice skating in hell, when you think that Cassie will ever give up that house."

"I suppose I'll have to start over." Lorrie looked down at her hands.

"Kris, may I ask you a question?" Beatrice asked.

"Sure."

"Is Roman happy?"

"Yes, I believe so. He retired from the Lake Guards and works during the day helping folks around the lake. He's very pleased with Otter and spends every spare minute playing with him."

Beatrice nodded. "Roman is a good man."

"He was broken-hearted when you were taken, Beatrice. It left him sad for a very long time," Kris spoke to her.

"But you have made him happy. That's a blessing. Did you get to merge with him?"

"Yes."

"When he told me about merging, it scared me and I think it was my being so frightened which opened a door for Rochelle. She played on it to steal my body."

"If I have anything to say about it, we're going to get out of here," Kris said and looked back at Lorrie. "I think you said I've been here eight years. That means I'm thirty-nine years old now. I want my thirties back and I want to hear Otter speak his first words. We have to figure out how to get back to our own realm."

"Marcus once said you acquired special abilities with the merge spot. What did he mean?" Lorrie asked.

Kris looked at her palm and tried to feel the

warmth that she'd experienced since the merge with Roman. Her hands were cold. "Roman started to teach me how to form lightning bolts and shoot them. I can also make a shield." She started to rub the spot and tried to warm it. "If I can get the heat back, maybe I can get these chains off of us." She tried blowing warm breaths on her palms and moved them together. She concentrated on bringing up the light and pictured Roman's face in her head. She thought about the last time he made love to her in the woods by the church. She could almost feel his warmth build slowly somewhere inside of her.

Suddenly, there was a very bright flash of light from one of the walls and what looked like a doorway opened. A tall, red-haired woman walked through and Kris recognized the red dress. The woman looked very peeved about something.

"I should have known you'd cause trouble," she hissed. "If you don't behave, I will put you into a solitary realm. You could spend eternity on your own." She smirked down at Kris.

"Rochelle, I thought we'd parted ways in peace. I did save you from Meshach's game. Why have you brought me here?" Kris looked up into her fierce red eyes.

"We're even, remember? You still have something I want and the young one is very, very desirable." She seemed to glow. "I will get my hands on that one."

"Rochelle, I swear to God, if you touch my son I'll find a way to vanquish you to Hell. Your wish of being with Abednego will come true," Kris growled.

"Why on earth would I want your child? A squalling baby around would be too much to bear." She laughed.

"Then what is it you're after?" Kris asked.

"The young lakeman is very delicious, don't you think?" Rochelle leered.

"Cedric?" Kris felt floored. She'd never seen this coming. "What does Cedric have that could be of any interest to you?"

"Sweet, innocent, idiot Kris. Wouldn't you like to know? Now be still, it won't be long. Your alter ego is playing right where I want her and then you'll be mine," she whispered and grinned. She straightened up and arched her brows. "I've waited a whole year for this moment. Once I have you and the Lakeman, I'll be able to pull Abednego out of Hell. It's very lonely without him." She started sounding whinny.

"Oh, boo-hoo, Rochelle. That doesn't give you the right to mess with others' lives," Kris snarled. "I thought you were going to move on, anyway."

"You heard my message, Kris. How long did you expect me to wait? Let me guess, you thought I'd just give up and go to the light? As I said, you are being an idiot."

"Leave my family alone, Rochelle and let us go. You know, this is a no-win situation." Kris started rubbing her hand again.

"You're the one chained to the wall, Kris."

"You'll never get past Roman and his brothers. I guarantee it, Rochelle, one-hundred percent." Kris smiled at the woman.

"Willing to bet your soul on it, Kris?" She smirked. When Kris didn't answer, she walked back to the lighted doorway. "I didn't think so."

Chapter Twenty-two

Roman walked out on the back deck and looked around the yard. He couldn't see El anywhere around their area and felt anger start to build in his neck. Marcus came up out of the water and looked at him with a question in his eyes.

El took off. I don't think she's gone far. I don't want to leave the baby alone and it's too early to disturb Cassie. Would you see if she's somewhere around the lake? Roman thought.

Marcus nodded and started back to the shoreline. He'd only gone a couple of steps when he stopped and looked into the bushes between Kris and Roman's house and the one next door. He turned back to Roman and pointed.

Roman rolled his eyes and waved Marcus away. He walked over to the hedge and looked over the side. El sat on the grass with her chin on her knees. She looked up at him with anger in her eyes.

"How'd you know I was here?" Roman asked.

"You're not exactly a silent walker. Your sneakers squeak and your legs make jean noises." El sneered up at him.

"Ah, well, so much for stealth." He reached a hand over.

"You are a bastard, you know? How does Kris put up with you and your moral values?" She shook her head.

"I think she agrees with them," Roman said.

El looked up at him with tears in her eyes. "Please, let me have sex."

Roman sighed. "Sorry, but no."

"This is just not fair." She huffed and pushed his hand away. "Don't touch me or I might get the wrong idea." She stood, pushed her way through the bushes and headed back to the house.

Roman watched her move and thought he heard her say she hated him. *Can't be loved by everyone,* he thought.

It amazed him how different she acted from Kris. Even her stride wasn't anywhere near the same. He followed her into the house.

"Would you like some coffee, El?"

She sat at the dining room table and put her head in her hands. "Sure, sounds great." She sniffed.

He poured two cups, sat across from her and handed a cup over. They sat in silence for a while.

El looked at him. "I hate you. If I had my powers, I'd be pissy and attack you."

"Fair enough, but you're already acting pissy and you've been verbally attacking me for a while today." He sipped from his cup and watched her over the rim.

He heard a light rap on the back door and Cassie came into the kitchen.

"Hey guys," she said and walked over to the cabinet, got a cup, and poured coffee. When she turned around and looked at them, she frowned. "Ah, is everything okay?" She moved to the table and looked from one to the other.

"Roman won't fuck me," El hissed.

"Well, that's a good thing. Who wants more

complications?" Cassie said, and sat at the head of the table.

"Thank you, Cassie," Roman said. He thought for a moment that it seemed strange that she agreed with him.

"Sure," she said. "Omar should be back soon from the Oracle. Do we have any kind of a plan, yet?"

Roman glanced at Cassie then back at El. "Not really," he said.

"I think we should try to exorcise the ghost from this woman, Lorrie."

He heard another male voice and they all turned toward the doorway.

"Where are the coffee cups, Roman?" Father Rupert asked as he came into the kitchen.

"Sit, Rupert, I'll get one for you." Roman stood.

The priest moved to the table and sat next to El. "I've been thinking about the current situation and I believe that if we could exorcise the ghost, it would release Kris's spirit to return to her body. We could then save the innocent and vanquish the ghost once and for all. I called Father Greg and had him look up the spell we'd need. The vanquishing spell would be a bit different from the one we use for demons, but it's easily learned. I think you are all quick studies." He smiled and looked at each of them around the table. "Of course, we'd have to get the ghost out of the young lady she is possessing, first."

Roman heard a cry from the nursery and after giving Rupert his coffee, went to check on Otter. He found the youngster kicking his feet and making gurgling noises.

"What are you up to, young sir?" Roman smiled at

him and put his hands down to pull the baby up into his arms. Otter's hands latched onto Roman's wrist and wouldn't let go. Roman brought him up and looked him in the eye. He heard a voice in his head.

I want to hear the plan, Dad.

Roman smiled and went back into the kitchen with Otter. Just as they arrived, the back door opened and Omar and Marcus walked in.

"Omar, what did the Oracle tell you?" Roman asked, and silenced all other conversation.

"The Oracle believes that Rochelle may have the ability to hold spirits. If this is the case, then while we were distracted with abolishing Pelonus, Rochelle pulled Kris out, but..." Omar frowned. "Ah, I don't know. Something isn't right."

Cassie moved into his arms. "What is it, Omar?"

He looked at Roman and shook his head. "I'm not sure. Have you ever just felt there was something wrong? The Oracle didn't act like herself. And it's bothered me for a while, the number of visits she's granted. I don't know, maybe it's just everything that's happening right now and I'm reading too much into it."

"I noticed it, too. Her light seemed to fade. It was strange," Marcus added.

"We can discuss this later, gentlemen. For now, is there any way of getting Kris back?" Roman asked.

Omar nodded. "Yes, the Oracle gave me some instructions. The hard part will be finding Rochelle. We'll have to get her attention somehow and then do the split spirit thing. Roman, since your connection to Kris is the strongest, we need for you to do it the way you did when Meshach stole her soul. There are going to be some differences since Rochelle is a ghost." Omar saw Father Rupert smile. "Which I believe Rupert already understands."

"I do, Omar." The priest continued to sip his coffee. "We should compare notes."

"Good. While Father Rupert performs the exorcism and keeps Rochelle busy, we empower the split and Roman goes in to bring Kris out." Omar looked at Roman again. "This is when things get tricky. We have to hold the circle because once Rochelle is out of Lorrie, we'll be vanquishing a ghost. It's best to burn the bones of the ghost, but who knows where Rochelle came from? Since she's been around so long, it would be difficult to find out who she really was. We could open a portal and send her to another realm, but what would stop her from coming back?" He looked at everyone around the table. "I don't know about you all, but I'd prefer not to continue facing off with her on a yearly basis."

"I agree," Roman said. Otter clapped his hands and gurgled. The rest also agreed.

"Okay, we have some work to do. One other thing of interest. The Oracle said that Rochelle has a major interest in Cedric. As did Pelonus," Omar added.

"When she came to me in temple and mentioned the young one, I thought she meant Otter. The interest apparently is Cedric," Marcus said and crossed his arms.

"If the Oracle knows why, she isn't sharing either," Omar said and put his hand on El's shoulder. "Could I speak with you outside for a moment?" he asked. This question surprised both Roman and Cassie.

El looked up at him suspiciously. "Why?"

Omar walked to the back door and opened it. He

held out his hand. "Please."

El pushed herself up. "Man, I don't remember a time when you guys used the word please so much." She walked past Omar to the back deck and he followed, closing the door.

Roman looked at Marcus. "What's going on?"

"He's telling her she can't participate. She has no powers and if, for some reason, we can't get Kris back, she mustn't be harmed," Marcus said. "Roman, I know the reality of this hasn't hit you, but we must take precautions."

"We're getting her back, Marcus, that is the only reality," Roman said angrily. He noticed a strange look on his brother's face and realized Marcus was staring at Otter. Looking at his son, he saw a stern, scrunched up face. He laughed. "My son agrees with me."

Out the kitchen window, they could see El continue to argue with Omar. She wasn't taking this well. Her face turned red and she said something to him, pointed a finger and poked his chest.

The back door flew open again with a bang and she stormed into the kitchen. "This is not fair. What am I supposed to do? Nothing except be a cow for my nephew!" she shouted and started to cry. "Kris is important to me, too, and I know I can help, but, no, I can't help. I can't have sex or experience any human feelings. What good am I? What's my real purpose?" She stared at Roman.

He motioned for Cassie to take Otter and stood up. He walked toward El, who backed up.

"Stay away from me Roman. I don't want to hurt you," she threatened and put up her fists, prepared to fight.

Roman grabbed her wrist and pulled her toward the bedroom. "Start preparations, we'll be back," he said over his shoulder.

The bedroom door slammed.

Chapter Twenty-Three

"I don't know, Lorrie. I like the days when I get up and do some work and watch Otter eat Cheerios. I go outside and help Roman do yardwork, or laugh at him when he fusses with something around the house. Those days are so peaceful. I hate having this crap hanging over us all the time. So far, they've only come after me, but what if they come after Otter? Then what do we do?" Kris asked and adjusted her position on the floor. She pulled her knees up, rested her arms across them and looked at Lorrie. "We never asked for any of this. If I hadn't drunk that stupid wine, this wouldn't have happened. Your house would still be standing and—"

"You wouldn't have Roman or Otter," Lorrie interrupted.

"Yeah, I know." She put her hand to her forehead. "I sometimes wish I'd done the binding spell before it all got out of hand. I'd like to think it is worth it and try not to think of what might have been." Kris gasped, and felt the air leave her lungs. She tried to catch her breath and wondered what happened. The dungeon began to spin. Her head started to feel light and everything around her went black.

When Kris woke up, she lay on her side in her own bed. Morning sunlight streamed through the windows and she could hear birds chirp outside. She felt a hand move up to her hip and leaned back into the warm arms. She closed her eyes, letting his fingers explore around her stomach and could feel his shaft grow with excitement.

"Good morning, sweetheart," he whispered in her ear.

Kris felt her brows crease as her eyes reopened. Something here wasn't right, but she couldn't tell what. She didn't remember this quite right. It wasn't the voice she expected to hear.

"Kris, is something wrong?" he asked. "You've gone all tense."

She rolled over and rubbed her eyes. Once they'd cleared, she smiled up at him. "I'm fine, just having a strange dream."

"You were moaning a little during the night." He moved his hand into her hair. "Do we have enough time for me to make you moan?" He smiled and his blue eyes looked down at her.

"I'm sorry, Jeff. I've got to get to the gallery early. The caterers will be showing up by noon and it will be a crazy day."

He flipped onto his back and sighed. "How late will this one be?"

"The gallery closes at 9:00 p.m. and since the showing goes throughout the month, there won't be a reason in the world for me to stay late," she said and leaned over to kiss his chest. She ran her tongue up his neck and nibbled his hairy chin. "You need to shave." She kissed his lips. "Tell you what." She propped up on her elbow. "Promise not to give me beard burn on my face and you can have a half hour."

He rolled her over and pushed her legs apart. "Deal. I may burn your boobs, though." He moved her pajama top up. "Ah, my favorite. Come to daddy," he whispered.

After they pulled apart, they both got cleaned up. While Jeff showered, Kris went out to the kitchen to get a pot of coffee started. As it gurgled, she looked out the back window. Lorrie squatted in her yard and pulled weeds, her lawn mower parked a few feet away. Kris felt surprised to see her and figured she'd taken the day off from her job.

Kris walked into the living room and sat down at her desk. Turning on the computer, she looked to the left at the hallway that led to the front door. She'd thought about putting in another room for an office, but hadn't gotten around to it. She couldn't figure out why everything seemed wrong. Maybe she'd developed some anxiety about the show tonight and denied it. Maybe it was PMS. No. That couldn't be the cause, it wasn't her time of the month.

She shook her head and checked her emails. Returning a couple with short, quick replies, she shut the computer down and finished getting dressed.

The shower shut off and she went into the bath while Jeff dried off. She watched him while brushing her teeth.

"You're staring at me." He smiled and arched his brow.

She turned to the sink and spit. "Sorry, Roman, I didn't mean to make you uncomfortable." She grabbed a hand towel to wipe her mouth. She saw him frown into the mirror. "What?"

"Who's Roman?" he asked.

"Who?"

"Roman? You just called me that." He stood next to her, and wrapped the towel around his waist.

"No I didn't." She thought to herself, *Why do I know that name?*

"Yes, you did. Kris, are you seeing someone else?" he asked.

"No, no way, babe. It's you and me, remember? And I didn't call you anything but Jeff." She kissed his chest.

He grumbled under his breath. "Babe? When did you start using that one? Are you heading out?" He picked up his shaving cream and shook the can.

"Yes, there's fresh coffee in the pot. I'll see you tonight." She kissed his lips before he'd smeared shaving cream on his face.

"Hey, how about I make dinner reservations for a late supper?" he asked and kissed her back.

"That sounds great," she said and left the bathroom.

"Love you," his voice said.

"Love you, too," she answered and left the house.

She thought about this morning as she walked toward her car in the driveway. She and Jeff were a couple for a while, but she realized she couldn't remember how long they'd been together and when they'd met. They talked about moving in together, but he wanted to buy over on the eastside and she wanted to stay at Haller Lake. He also wasn't ready to give up his condo, which meant he wasn't ready to give up his freedom and commit.

Her other neighbor, Sylvia, stood in her yard and dug a hole in the lawn. Kris waved to her and was informed that they were putting in a Japanese maple.

Kris smiled and walked to her car. A breeze picked up and she felt someone watch her. She looked around and tried to figure out where the eyes were, but couldn't see anyone. Out on the lawn, the ducks and geese wandered around. She thought she saw something else move around in the water, but didn't think it looked her way. Shaking her head, she got into the car. When she looked out the front windshield, she could have sworn she saw a head look at her from between two geese in the water. She closed her eyes and opened them again, but didn't see the head again.

"Okay, I've lost my marbles," she mumbled and turned the key in the ignition. "I must be stressed out."

Chapter Twenty-Four

The day went along smoothly. Tom MacAndrew, the owner of the MacAndrew's Gallery, got the paintings up and they were well lit. They looked wonderful. The caterers set up and it all went smooth as silk.

Around six-thirty in the evening, her artist walked in the door. Derrick Schmitt was in his late twenties, but his work showed a modern flare with an old world charm. Although his paintings were of twenty-first century buildings, cars, people, and some landscapes, his technique gave them the feel and look of a product hundreds of years old. Kris thought him very talented, but he appeared high-strung at times. This evening, he'd either taken a Valium, smoked pot or meditated, he appeared so mellow.

Kris sent out one-hundred-fifty invitations for the opening and online posted one-thousand other announcements, though the economy was sketchy and she couldn't predict how things would go. She spent the evening on her feet and did her best to sell her artist.

She walked about, shook hands, made small talk, and checked to be sure everyone had enough to eat and drink. She spoke with other gallery owners, writers from the local newspapers, and other artists. Some of the people she knew, some she did not.

One of her other clients, Cassandra Nelle, waved at her from a corner and Kris made her way over to her.

"Hey there," Kris said and gave Cassie a half hug. "What do you think?"

"You've got a really good turnout. Has anything sold?" she asked.

"That's not what I meant, but no, nothing's moved yet." Kris turned and looked around the room.

"I know, you meant how do I like the artist? Hmm, let me think. His technique is different and I may have to see if I can utilize it with my own works."

"Utilize? Horrors, you don't look to me like a copycat." Kris arched her brow and smiled.

"Copycat? Me?" Cassie opened her mouth with fake astonishment. "How could you ever think I'd do that?" Kris tilted her head and they both laughed. "Is Jeff coming tonight?" she asked. "I'm in need of a good attorney."

"He does estates, Cass, not traffic tickets." Kris hugged her arm.

"Ha, ha. I need to sue my agent for thinking I'd steal technique." She nudged Kris back.

"He'll be here around closing time." Kris looked around the crowded room again and hoped someone might need a little push.

"By the way, I've got a new series you haven't seen. Can you meet me here tomorrow to have a look at them?" Cassie asked. "I'd like to get your impression."

"Yeah, I'm free about eleven o'clock. I'll check with Tom to see if we can use the office upstairs. Should I be getting excited?" Kris opened her eyes wide.

"Wait and see, my darling agent. I'll have my fingers crossed all night. They are a bit different from my last works." Cassie sounded anxious.

"I'm sure they're wonderful, as always," Kris said and heard the bell above the door jingle. She turned toward the main entrance and saw a tall, dark-haired man come through. He wore jeans and a blazer. As he opened the buttons, Kris could see that he had on a rust-colored shirt.

"Damn," Cassie said. "Who the hell is that? He's hot."

Kris barely heard her friend. She looked at the man and felt that she knew him from somewhere, but couldn't say where. The palm of her hand began to itch and the strange tickle became a burning. It annoyed her as the man approached one of the paintings.

"I'd better get back to work," Kris said to Cassie.

She followed the tall, gorgeous man around the gallery, and tried to remember how she knew him. She'd stop and speak to other costumers, but it started to drive her nuts not being able to figure it out. Her hand felt on fire and it caused her to clamp her fist shut. She looked at it and there seemed to be a bright red spot forming. Shaking her hand out, she didn't think she'd touched anything hot.

Finally, Kris made her way up to the man and tapped his shoulder. He turned around and smiled down at her.

"Good evening, I'm Kris Bennett. I'm about to give myself a headache trying to figure out where I know you from." She smiled and held out her hand. When he took her hand in his, the itch and burning went away from her palm.

"I've seen you at the lake," he said. Looking at her with the lightest brown eyes she'd ever seen, he continued. "I live at the south end of Haller. My name is Roman."

When he said his name, Kris felt startled and continued to stare up at him. Comfort and warmth enveloped her and she could only think it came from him. "I apologize, I'm staring." She let his hand go and stepped back. "How do you like the paintings?"

"They're interesting." He took in a breath. "They aren't really anything I'd care to have in my home, but interesting," he said and looked up at the wall.

Kris suddenly felt a great loss and thought she might start to cry.

"Are you all right, Miss Bennett? You've gone a little pale." He offered her an arm and led her to a place to sit down. "Would you care for some water?"

"No, no, I'm fine." She put her hand up to her chest and stopped him. "Please, continue looking around." She excused herself and went into the ladies room. She put some water on a paper towel and held it to her neck and forehead. She'd grown very warm in the presence of that man.

When she returned to the gallery the tall, dark-haired man named Roman was gone. Jeff arrived and spoke to Cassie. Kris did her job, but by closing at nine o'clock not a single painting had sold. Derrick said it would be fine. There were still several weeks to go. He acted positive.

She found Jeff by the front counter talking to Tom and grabbed his hand. Tom excused himself to begin shutting down the gallery.

"Sweetie, I know we talked about going out for dinner, but can I get a rain check? I'm exhausted." Kris leaned into him.

"No problem. I'll cancel the reservations and see

you at home." He hugged her and turned to leave.

Kris finished up and said goodnight to Tom. Derrick walked her out to their cars and thanked her for a terrific opening. He said he felt a little anxious about not selling anything, but thought it would go better with time.

She sat in her car and thought about some of what happened that day. She couldn't figure out what made her feel so unsettled. She realized there were holes in her life that she'd ignored. Was Jeff really the one who could fill all the emptiness she experienced? Who was this Roman? She couldn't remember him from the lake. Maybe Sylvia or Lorrie would know him.

Kris got home in record time, the traffic being pretty light. Jeff waited for her in the kitchen. He'd poured a couple of glasses of wine and heated up some soup.

"Hey, sweetheart. Are you hungry?" He smiled from the stove.

"That's so nice." She walked up beside him and looked in the pot. "I'm done in. I'm going to hit the sheets. I'm sorry I'm being so boring tonight."

"No worries. You get some rest." He kissed her forehead.

She went into the bedroom, stripped off her clothes and put on a nightshirt. Washing her face and brushing her teeth seemed to wake her up a little. She looked at herself in the mirror. She thought she saw something move in the glass, but the longer she stared, the more the sleepiness returned. She turned off the lights and went to bed.

Jeff came in after a while. She felt his hands move

around her. As tired as she was, she found it difficult to settle down and go to sleep. Her brain wouldn't shut down. She closed her eyes and the next time she opened them, it was after two o'clock in the morning. Jeff breathed deep and snored. She pushed the sheets off and got up.

Going into the kitchen, she found the blinds still up and the moonlight shone through the window. She got a glass out of the cabinet and turned on the tap. She saw the bottle of wine on the counter. Drinking the water, she looked at the bottle and discovered it was one she'd never heard of, Brael Mist Peach Chardonnay. Kris's brows creased. Since when does Jeff like foofie wines? she asked herself. Setting her water glass down, she looked through the window at the dark outside. Something moved by the water and after she stared at it for a second, realized it was a duck.

Kris turned and leaned against the counter. Looking through the kitchen into the next room, she thought she saw a hallway leading to the right of the house. She knew that couldn't be possible. There was a solid outside wall along this part of the house. Her eyebrows folded in when she couldn't see her desk. She blinked and stepped forward, but discovered the dark and shadows played tricks on her.

She rinsed out her glass, but then refilled it and thought. For some reason this evening or morning, her life didn't satisfy her. She pictured Jeff in her head and, even though he seemed a good man, she didn't think he was what she wanted for the long haul. He had a good sense of humor and work ethic, but the relationship seemed one-sided. He pleased himself, but didn't think about pleasing her. He'd warmed up a pot of soup, but she realized this wasn't the type of pleasing she missed. She couldn't remember the last time she'd experienced an orgasm and found herself thinking about the tall, good-looking man Roman and wondered why just thinking about him made her warm.

She set her glass down and scratched her neck. *What is my problem*? she thought and felt that she had a good man and should count her blessings.

She glanced out the window, about ready to return to bed. This time, she saw something taller than a duck by the lake shore. She leaned over the sink and saw a woman who stood in the middle of the grass. The woman had her back to the house, but Kris could see she was tall and slender. She wore a long beige gown and didn't have any hair on her head. The moonlight made her skin look translucent.

Kris moved to the back door and undid the lock. When she walked out on the deck, watching the woman, Kris noticed she didn't turn around, but continued to look at the water.

Kris felt herself move forward, not because she wanted to do, but because she needed to. Her feet developed a mind of their own. The grass was wet and when she stepped down off of the deck, her feet became cold. She thought she should have put on some shoes.

She walked toward the woman and heard a strange crying. It sounded like a baby and then she felt a sharp stabbing pain in her hand. It almost caused her to double over, but she continued forward. When she stood about ten feet from the woman, she stopped.

"Excuse me, but why are you standing on my property at two o'clock in the morning?" Kris asked.

The woman turned around and Kris saw her eyes

flash. She sucked in her breath, and realized what her problem was all day. Kris knew this wasn't her realm.

Are you happy Kris? The woman asked without moving her lips.

Kris felt stunned and couldn't think of what to say.

You've whined so much about not asking for your abilities, I thought you might like to experience your world without them. Do you feel the difference since you didn't drink the tainted wine? Are you happy?

"So you're sort of the 'ghost of Christmas past'?" Kris asked aloud. The woman didn't answer her. The eyes flashed again and Kris felt all of her memories return to her. She looked around. The lake disappeared, as did the houses and the moon. "Oracle, I'm not sure I'm understanding any of this." Kris could feel anger build in her system. "What is the point you're trying to make?"

None of us have choices, Kris. Your destiny was set before you were even born. You denied your powers for many years, hiding them from yourself and now, although you are aware of your abilities, you choose to continue to ignore them. I'm giving you a one-time-only offer. Stay here in this realm without your magicks and live out your time. I'm tired of hearing you bitch and moan about your lack of choices.

The Oracle turned away from Kris and they were back at the lake, but it changed. The water looked brown and smelly, the trees were cut down and all the houses looked derelict.

This is what becomes of this world if you choose to stay. This will happen to the water-ways around the world and evil will prevail.

"What you're saying is, I have no choice?" Kris

asked.

You do have choices, Kris, she growled. *You can choose to be ignorant and without, or lead a productive life and protect your realm. Your husband and son will go on, but do you want to stand with them and devote yourself? Or will you continue to doubt your abilities and complain about this not being what you asked for?*

"Oracle, I'm presently stuck in a dungeon and chained to a wall. How is it possible you're showing me this?" Kris asked.

Your spirit is stuck in the cell, Kris. There are many possibilities out there if you'd only open yourself to them, she answered and smirked. Kris saw her eyes turn black. The Oracle turned to her and started to laugh. *So what, we have a job to do. What humans feel really, in the long run, means nothing.*

"Speak for yourself, sister. Feelings are everything." Kris crossed her arms. "If you ever do this again, I'm going to be pretty pissed off."

Pissed is better than whiny and needy, the Oracle said.

"Touché. Put me back into my own time. There's nothing here I want," Kris said. The scene around her flashed and all went black again.

She wasn't certain how long it took to get back, but when she opened her eyes, Kris was back in the dungeon. Lorrie watched her.

"We're getting out of here, my friend," Kris said and sat up.

Chapter Twenty-Five

Roman sat on the end of the bed, and let El rant and rave. She stomped back and forth in front of him. At some point, he'd stopped listening and just waited until she burned herself out. She finally sat down next to him and put her hands in her hair.

"I can't stand this, Roman. I feel like I'm going crazy," she said.

"I wonder if that's what Rochelle is trying to achieve. If she makes you lose it, would you turn over the body? If she has both you and Kris, she holds all the cards," he said.

El went silent and looked up at him. "I never thought of that."

"I could read you the riot act for acting like a spoiled brat, but I won't."

"Gee, thanks for the humanity," she answered sarcastically.

"You're welcome," Roman said with equal sarcasm.

"Kris is really lucky to have you, you know?"

"I'm very lucky to have her and we are getting her back. Now we have some work to do." He stood and looked down at her. "Because you won't be participating, doesn't mean we don't need you. In fact, I'll need your help with Otter. Would you watch him while we prepare?"

"Of course, yes. Kris would kill me if anything happened to him or you. I'll look after him."

Roman stopped and felt something wrong. He looked at the palm of his hand. He saw a red scratch mark down the center and it started to burn like crazy.

"Roman, what's wrong?" El asked, and stood next to him.

He looked at her and smiled. "Kris just got my attention." He held his palm up. Blood started to roll down his wrist.

"Oh, my Lord." El moved into the bathroom and grabbed a towel. "Does it hurt?" She put the towel over his hand.

"Hurts like stink, but she's there. I can sense her." He pulled the towel out of her hands. "Come on," he said and moved through the bedroom door into the other room.

Father Rupert taught the others the abolishing spell for ghosts. Cedric joined the group. Cassie sat on the couch with Otter and played peek-a-boo. She looked up, as did the baby, when they came out.

Roman's brow creased at Cassie. "Why aren't you learning the spell?"

"Remember, I don't know Latin? Rupert could be speaking French for all I know. Cedric is taking over for me," she said and clapped hands with Otter.

Roman walked into the kitchen.

"I've explained to Cedric what's going on," Omar said.

"I will be glad to help. Mrs. Lake treats me very kindly." Cedric looked up at Roman.

"You're sure you've explained everything, Omar?" Roman asked. Omar nodded.

"I can't begin to understand why this ghost would have any interest in me, sir. I only have standard powers. I'm nothing special," Cedric said.

"He's agreed to be used as bait, Roman. If Rochelle is after him, we can draw her out," Omar said.

Roman put his good hand on the young man's shoulder. "Thank you, Cedric." He looked at the rest, and held up his injured palm. "I believe we've made contact."

Omar's brows shot up. "What happened?"

"I'm not certain." Roman shook his head. "But I can feel Kris. Wherever she is, she's working very hard at getting us to pay attention."

"Can you hear her?" Marcus asked.

"No." Roman turned around as he heard Otter cry out from the couch. He saw his son on Cassie's lap with his arms straight out. Roman walked over to the baby and took him from Cassie. "Hey, little man, what's going on?"

Otter maneuvered his hand into Roman's and touched the tear in the palm. He felt a stabbing shoot up his arm into his temple. He heard Otter say *Dad, I want to help. I can help.*

Roman sighed, and looked down at his son. "Okay, but you're sticking close to me. I'm not going to lose you. Your mother would kill me." Roman looked at El and smiled.

Otter reached up and grabbed Roman's nose and laughed. He turned to the group. "Are you four ready with the spell?" They all nodded and Father Rupert turned in his seat, looking at Roman and the baby. "Okay, this is what we're going to do..." He walked up to the table and began to explain.

****

Kris rubbed the palm of her hand raw and it now bled, but she didn't care. She tried to remain positive and felt that she'd reached Roman. She continued to move her thumb over the spot, even though it stung like crazy.

Lorrie stared at her for a long time. Kris couldn't tell how long this went on, since she didn't understand how time worked there and she refused to believe she'd been gone eight years. It might be a day or two, but no way could eight years have passed.

She stopped rubbing her palm and focused on Lorrie. "Sweetie, we need to figure out how to get the door open," she said and stood to look at the wall.

Lorrie looked over her shoulder, then up at Kris. "What door?"

"The door Rochelle came through earlier." She looked and pointed to where she remembered the ghost came into the dungeon.

"Kris, there's no door. We're stuck here."

Kris felt her eyes squint. "You do remember that Rochelle came in a while ago?"

"Yeah, maybe a year or two ago. We haven't seen her for a long time," Lorrie said.

"No, no, she came in an hour ago. There's no way it happened that long ago." Kris focused on her palm to try to get the heat up.

"I've been here for over thirty years, Kris. I think I can understand the way time works," Lorrie sounded angry.

"I'm not going to argue time issues with you," Kris said.

"I remember Rochelle's last visit. She told you to

behave," the one called Sarah commented.

"Yeah, she did." Kris felt heat build in her hand.

"What are you doing?" Lorrie asked and got onto her knees.

Kris wrapped her hand around the chain. "Hush, this is going to take some work and I need to concentrate." She closed her eyes and focused her energy on her hand.

After a minute or so, she could feel the metal warm. She leaned back and started to pull on the chain. She kept the heat coming. After a few more pulls, and putting her foot up on the wall, one of the links opened. She unlatched it and slid the chain through the loop on the wall.

She heard the other women whisper, and saw her friend's mouth hang open. Kris smiled at her and winked. She moved to Lorrie's chain and began to work on it. After a while, she finally got all four of the women in the cell released. She sweated buckets and her hand shook and bled. She also felt a good headache stab her temple. The metal bracelets felt heavy on her arms.

The other ladies walked around the room and looked at the walls. Kris went to where the door appeared and looked around it. She couldn't see any way the barrier would open. Shifting a couple of rocks, Kris hoped there was some sort of lever, like in the movies when someone pulls a book off a shelf and it opens a secret passage. No such luck.

****

Roman asked Cedric to walk out to the back lawn alone. He and the other two Lakemen stripped the houses and surrounding area of all protection spells.

They knew it could open the door for all kinds of problems, but it needed to be done to draw Rochelle in. He hoped that she wouldn't figure out what they were up to, but she might not know about Father Rupert's involvement. They were going to try to save Lorrie along with Kris.

Roman handed Otter off to El, who watched Cedric out on the lawn. He tweaked his son's cheek, went through the door, swung himself over the deck railing, and moved to the front of the house. He cut across the driveway into Sylvia and Fred's yard, and crouched behind the bushes. Omar went into Cassie's yard and hid. Marcus swam out in the lake. Roman could see Father Rupert on the deck with a newspaper up to cover his face. Cassie and El stood in the kitchen window. The sun shone bright and the day turned warm.

Cedric started doing some exercises he'd learned in training school. Part martial arts and part yoga, his body and extremities became fluid as he moved. It looked to all watching as though he'd taken dance all his life, his movements were that smooth.

After waiting over an hour, Roman wondered if their plan would work, but suddenly he saw a brilliant flash of light. Peeking through the bushes, he saw Rochelle approach Cedric. The young man stood facing her with his muscles clenched and sweat running in rivulets down his back and chest.

Rochelle walked up to him, and grinned ear to ear with lust in her eyes. She circled around Cedric a couple of times and licked her lips.

"My, my, my, but aren't you delicious-looking. All that sweat," she said.

Cedric followed her movements, until she stopped

with her back to Roman. He could hear every word she said to Cedric. There were times Kris would speak to him that way and he'd be instantly hard and excited, but not now. Hearing the filth that came from Rochelle's mouth, sounded disgusting. Roman could see it effected Cedric, though.

Rochelle moved up to him and ran her fingers over his wet chest. "Lovely, just lovely. May I?" she asked, and looked down at his pelvis. She moved her hand down to his waist.

Roman knew what this would lead to and decided the time had come to make a move. He rose and leaped over the bushes. He walked up behind her without making a sound and put his merge hand up, grabbing her neck. Roman began reciting a freezing spell, and hoped he could keep her still until the others could get into place. Cedric fell into saying the spell along with him.

Father Rupert threw the paper aside and flew off the deck as Omar and Marcus came from opposite directions.

When the priest moved up, Cedric stepped to the side. The priest put his hand on Rochelle's forehead and looked over her shoulder at Roman. "Hurry," he said.

As Roman continued the spell he saw El and Cassie come out of the house. Cassie held Otter, who began to cry and point toward the group on the lawn. They said something to each other, El took Otter from Cassie's arms and then moved down the deck stairs to the lawn. She walked up to the men.

Rochelle made it difficult for Roman to get into her head. When El came close to him, Otter reached out both little hands and latched onto his father's arm.

Roman's eyes popped open and started to get angry, but stopped. He felt a zing of electric current run from his son's hands into his arm and straight down into his hand. He closed his eyes again and let himself be pulled with it.

When he opened them again, he stood in three feet of brown muck. He saw the adult Otter about ten feet away from him.

"Geez, Dad, what is this shit?" Otter asked and looked around him.

"I'm not sure, but since we're in an alternate realm possessed by a ghost, I imagine it has something to do with it. Otter, please don't let your mom hear those words come out of your mouth. She'll have kittens." Roman started to move toward his son.

Otter looked at him and frowned. "You mean the brown goo is something like *degenerating rotting corpse*?"

Roman laughed. "Yeah, like that."

"Gross." Otter continued to look at the muck he stood in. He moved forward a bit and started to come out of the sludge. "Hey Dad, do you see that blue light down there?"

Roman looked where his son pointed. "Yeah, I do," he said.

"Do you think it could be Mom's aura? She's usually blue."

"It could be her." Roman stood next to his son.

Otter arched an eyebrow. "Want to check it out?"

"Yes, I do. Let's go, we haven't much time." Roman patted Otter's back and they both started toward the blue light.

They wound up in what looked like a tunnel. The

brown sludge got shallower and only came to their ankles. Half way down the tunnel, they were stopped by a tall, red-haired woman. Her eyes blazed red and orange.

"What are you doing here?" she screamed and put her arms over her head. "Get out of my head, priest, or I swear I'll kill you all," she threatened.

"Hello, Rochelle. Having a bad day?" Roman motioned to Otter to keep moving while he diverted her.

"Lakeman, I swear..." And she screamed again.

****

Otter hurried forward, and saw the light get closer. The blue became more brilliant, but died out as he reached a dead-end. He looked at the block that came up in front of him. He could hear his father's voice behind him.

Dad, it's weird. I've reached a dead-end and the light is gone. Maybe it wasn't Mom, Otter thought.

I can still see the light, son. Keep looking. She's there somewhere.

Otter examined the wall. As he looked, he saw an area that seemed raised. He pressed his head against it and saw a door. It looked like the wall and was colored the same. He ran his fingers along where a joint seemed to be and felt an opening. He put his fingers in and started to pull.

"Mom, if you can hear me, I need you to start pushing," he shouted. He felt something touch his finger in the hole. "On three, Mom. One, two, three..."

The sound of a loud crack started and the wall split down the sides. Otter pulled harder and the block began to crumble into pieces. He backed up and watched it fall into a pile of dust. When it cleared, he saw his mom on the other side with five other women.

"Hi, Mom." He smiled.

Kris jumped out of the dungeon and grabbed Otter in a tight hug. "Baby boy, please tell me I haven't missed your first words or steps?"

"I don't think so, I'm still only three months old." He kissed her cheek. "Come on, Dad's waiting and we have to get out of here."

****

Kris turned back to the other women. Holding her hand out, she said, "Ladies, time to go." Lorrie moved forward, took her hand and the other four followed.

They all trailed behind Otter to the tunnel. Kris could see a golden glow toward the end with a black hole in the center.

"Otter, what's down there?" she whispered.

"Dad's trying to distract Rochelle." Otter laughed. "I think he's doing the annoying bug flying around your head thing."

"How do you know?" she asked.

"I can hear him, can't you?"

Kris creased her eyebrows and concentrated. "I hear..." She stopped. "What is Father Rupert doing?"

"An exorcism. Come on, Mom, keep moving." Otter pulled her arm.

"I swear, if you become as bossy as your dad..." Kris realized she could see Roman. She started to run the last part of the tunnel.

"Mom, slow down, there's..." he started to say, but stopped as Kris went face first into the brown muck.

She pushed herself up onto her knees, and wiped dirt off of her checks. "Oh Lord, Otter, you could have warned me." She looked back at him.

"I started to, Mom, but you were moving too fast," he said and helped the other ladies down into the goo.

Kris turned around and saw Roman trying to move around Rochelle.

"Hey, babe. We missed you at breakfast this morning," he said.

When she got near enough, they both reached out and locked fingers. Roman pulled her around Rochelle, whose hands pulled at her hair and she'd hunched over at the waist. Kris reached him and they put their arms around each other.

She looked up at him. "How long was I gone?"

"About twenty-four hours," Roman answered. She put her head against his chest and started to cry. "Hey, hey. Kris, what's...?"

She shook her head, and put her hand over his lips. "It's not important. Get us out of here."

The tunnel began to shake and the walls started to melt down into the sludge around their ankles. Rochelle screamed and her eyes turned black.

"Yes, ma'am. I think that's a very good idea." Roman got everyone together. They stood in a circle and clasped hands.

Kris closed her eyes and with Otter's strength, felt herself being pulled. A hot breeze blew through her hair and Roman's hand tightened around hers.

When she took in a deep breath, she peeked her eyes open, and found that they were back on the lawn outside of their house. She looked across the group and saw Roman. He smiled and made the "I love you" sign with his fingers.

Kris walked around the circle, and held Otter in her

arms. She started to walk away, but noticed the four other women from the dungeon stood on the lawn and watched the exorcism. Kris realized Lorrie wasn't there with them. She turned back to the circle around Rochelle and saw Lorrie's spirit standing behind Marcus.

She saw her friend's body twitch and writhe in the circle. Lorrie's arms flailed and she looked like she wanted to scream. Her mouth would open, but no sound came out. Her head tipped back and her mouth widened. Black wisps of smoke flew out of it and into the air. Some of it went up into the sky and disappeared and some went down into the ground.

Lorrie's spirit walked into the circle and reclaimed her body, which fell straight down onto the lawn and left a tall, red-haired woman with black eyes who screamed profanities.

The men began what sounded to Kris like the abolishing spell, but it seemed different. She watched and listened. Otter wrapped his little arms partway around her neck, and held on tight.

It occurred to her that Father Rupert said something different from the other men. It was Latin. Kris thought she'd have to remember to ask Roman about it. She watched as the five men wove their spell.

Kris realized she knew a lot of information. It would be impossible to eliminate Rochelle completely, but if what the men planned worked, her ghost would be sent to another realm. Her brain went into overdrive trying to figure out how she knew all of this. She thought it might be a vision, but no, she saw the current situation.

She stopped, and heard a voice in her head reciting

the Latin spell. It was Roman's voice and besides the spell, he was thinking - *other realm, my lady is back, what a relief.* How could she hear all this? She knew they could communicate mentally, but she could hear his every thought and the words that he spoke.

El went silent and Kris tried to get her attention, but she pulled way back into their mind. Kris wasn't certain, but thought she could hear El cry. Kris hugged Otter tighter in her arms and rocked him back and forth. He pushed his head under her chin and began to doze.

Looking back at the circle, she watched as a black cloud swirled above the men's heads, with flashes of light swirling in it.

Cedric began to recite something Kris didn't recognize. Out of place, a light began to shine behind him and move around in a clockwise direction. As she watched, Cedric backed away from the group, and created an opening in the circle. The black cloud growled at him. The four men continued to chant the spell louder and with more force.

Kris thought her head might explode. Roman's voice shouted outside and inside her head, and caused her ears to hurt.

Cedric put up a hand and pointed at the portal to the other realm. He said the strange words and the black smoke pulled into a straight line and slipped into the bright light. He said a few more words and the portal closed with a loud pop.

Roman moved to Kris and held her and Otter wrapped in a tight hug. All she heard in her brain was, *love, love, love, love,* which caused her to smile against his chest. She saw Marcus go down on his knees by Lorrie's side. His hand went to her neck, and felt for a pulse. Relaxing his face, she saw a smile curl on his lips. Lorrie was alive and hopefully would be all right.

Kris looked up at Roman. "Why don't you go talk to Beatrice?"

He looked over at the four spirits who waited near the shore of the lake. Looking back down at Kris, he smiled. "I love you. I'm so relieved we found you."

"I love you, too, and believe me, I'm glad I'm not where I was any longer." Roman leaned over and kissed her. "I'm going in to put Otter down. He's getting heavy," Kris said and adjusted the baby in her arms.

"I'll be right behind you."

****

Roman turned and went toward Beatrice and the other ghosts. She looked as beautiful as he remembered, even though it was a long time since he'd last seen her.

"Hi, Bea." He smiled.

She clasped her hands in front of her stomach. "Roman, it is very good to see you."

"I never... If I could have stopped Abednego.... I'm sorry it happened," he said.

"As am I, dear man, but happen it did. I'm as much to blame. I've had time to think of the things I could have done differently. I should have trusted you and not been fearful of the merge. Rochelle must have sensed that fear and used it to weaken me. I was not very wise," she said.

"Hindsight," Roman added.

"Yes, I suppose, but all is not lost now. You are happy, yes?" She seemed to be trying to comfort him.

"Yes, very happy."

"The woman you chose is very clever and strong. She was able to break the chains that held us for so long and set us free. I'd only been there for one-hundred plus years, but poor Françoise had been there much longer. Now we get to go home to the Lord and we couldn't be more pleased." Beatrice raised her eyebrows and turned to the other women. "I must go, Roman. Please thank your woman for us. She has given us a wonderful gift, one I never thought would be possible."

"I'll tell her. Hopefully, one day we'll cross paths, again."

"Perhaps. Stay well and keep your family safe." Beatrice smiled and turned away from him.

Roman watched as the four women took hands and began to fade. Beatrice turned and smiled back at him. He started to lift his hand to wave, but they were gone. He put his hand up to his face, circled around, and faced the others. Marcus sat on the ground with Lorrie in his arms. She'd woken up and had her face buried in his hair, crying softly. Cedric and Omar spoke with Father Rupert.

Roman thought he should join them, but turned to the house and bolted toward the steps. He blew past Cassie on the deck and made his way to the nursery. He found Kris leaning over the crib. Walking up behind her, he touched her back and she straightened.

"Hey," she whispered, and put her hands around his waist.

Roman pulled her into his arms and put his forehead against hers. "Hey, babe," he said. He felt tears roll down his cheeks and tried to stop them, but couldn't.

Kris moved her hands up to his shoulders and pulled him closer. His hands circled around her back and he rested his face on her shoulder.

They held each other until Roman gained control of his emotions. Kris kissed his cheeks. "Let's go into the living room and talk."

He nodded and turned to leave. He looked over his shoulder at their brilliant son and smiled. Following behind her, he closed the door and went to the couch where she sat next to him. They held on to one another for some time.

Chapter Twenty-Six

Roman never showed such emotion except during their wedding and the day Otter was born. Kris knew there were a multitude of subjects they needed to discuss and hoped they wouldn't argue. Roman seemed upset enough.

"Roman?"

"Yes, my love."

"Do you want to know something weird?" she asked and tried to lighten his mood.

"Of course I do. Today, the weirder the better."

She turned on the couch and sat lotus-style so she could look in his eyes. "I can hear you. Not like when we were at the church, it's more concentrated now and all the time." She looked into his eyes and his brows furrowed. "You just asked, *What on Earth is she talking about?*."

Roman sat up straight, and his eyes opened wide. "When did this start?" he asked.

"When I returned from Rochelleville, I think." Kris took his hand and held it tight. "At the church when we were training, I could hear you think about me, but not all the time. Now, I seem to be tuned in to you loud and strong." She put her fingers over his lips. "Yes, it is weird, and I don't know how to shut it off."

"We'll have to ask Father Rupert. He can probably help," Roman said. He put his hand up to her cheek, and ran his fingers through her hair. "Otherwise, are you all right?"

"We have a lot to talk about, babe. The Oracle took me from the dungeon, somehow and.... " It occurred to Kris that what she wanted to tell him might hurt very much. "But, we need to get your voice turned off. I love you dearly, but I can't concentrate," she said and put her hand over his and kissed the palm.

"I'll go get Rupert." He returned her kiss, stood up and headed to the back deck.

Kris felt sick at her stomach and raced to the bathroom to throw up. She'd been stabbed with a sword of guilt like nothing she'd ever felt before. Not only did she say she'd never asked for this life and there were no choices, which Roman would include himself as a part of, but she'd also been with another man. Even though the Oracle put her in another realm and at a different time, it could hurt Roman. During the dry heaves, Kris cursed the Oracle for mucking around with their lives and her head. Before their wedding day, she'd wondered how much the woman would intrude into their lives. Now she seemed to have the answer.

No matter what, she needed to be honest with Roman. She never wanted there to be any secrets between them.

She went from throwing up to crying her eyes out and curled up into a ball on the bathroom floor. Roman sat down and scooped her into his arms. She could feel the difference between his touch and that of the other man's and the guilt ripped her open again.

She remembered hearing Father Rupert's voice say a prayer or chant or spell. Slowly, Roman's voice quieted in her head. Then the door closed and they sat alone for some time. Burying her face in his chest, she'd created a large wet stain on his shirt.

Kris moved to get up and he helped her. Once standing, she turned the cold water on in the sink and rested her elbows on the edge of the basin. She rinsed off her face a couple of times and the cold water helped her to calm down. Roman handed her a towel and she dried off. She could feel her eyes tear up again and couldn't believe she still was hydrated enough to produce more tears.

"Roman, sit down." She looked up at him and saw he didn't want to leave her side. Another stab of guilt hit her heart. "Please, babe, sit for a minute," she whispered.

He lowered himself and sat on the edge of the tub. "Kris, what happened? What did you see that is upsetting you so?" he asked.

Kris took a deep breath, and wiped her eyes with the towel. "First of all, I want to apologize to you. I've been such a complete and utter idiot this last year, it's amazing I can walk upright at all." She pushed herself up onto the counter.

Roman cupped her heels and put her feet on his knees. "Your feet are frozen," he said, grabbed a dry towel and put it over her feet.

Kris felt a tear roll down her cheek. "Roman, for the last year I've done all I could to ignore my powers. I walked around like an ungrateful bitch and pushed them and you away."

"You didn't always push me away." He grinned up at her.

"Babe, serious up. I need to be hard on myself right now." She twisted the towel around her hand. "The

Oracle took me somehow to another realm. In her weird teaching way, she wanted me to see what my life would have been if I hadn't drank the wine. I experienced about a twenty hour period in that other realm and I had no memory of ever meeting you." Her bottom lip twitched. "You and Otter weren't in my life over there. I saw you and felt that I knew you from somewhere, but I wasn't with you." Roman frowned slightly. "I had no abilities, no vision, and for some reason I'll never understand, the Oracle had me living with someone else, a man I used to go out with, but didn't get seriously involved with in this life," she whispered.

She watched him and realized what she said registered in his head.

"What?" he asked, and looked hurt and angry at the same time.

Kris took her feet off his knees and they stared at one another. "Roman, I'd like to blame it on the Oracle—you know, point the finger at her—but I can't. It's my own stupidity that got me into it in the first place. I just don't understand why she felt I'd learn anything—"

"Stop." Roman interrupted.

She could see the hurt in his eyes as he stood up. He opened the bathroom door and walked out, but stopped and turned back to her. "Did you...did...did you fuck him?" he asked low, and stood in the doorway.

"Yes."

"When was this?"

"The day of Dwight Schmitt's opening at the MacAndrew's Gallery."

"You didn't know me then."

"You came to the gallery the night of the show, but

you didn't like Dwight's work. I introduced myself to you," she said and twisted the towel.

"Would you have left him for me?" Roman stopped and she saw him grimace. "Don't answer, how could you possible know that?"

"Roman, I did choose you over him. The Oracle gave me the option to stay in the other realm with no magick's, or come home. I picked you and our son, once she gave me my memories back." Kris started to cry, again. "Before she did that, I didn't remember a thing about our life, nothing."

Roman swallowed and backed up a step. "I've got to think," he said, and walked away.

Kris stayed alone in the bathroom for a time. She wasn't certain what to do. Should she panic or cry more? Should she get angry and have a temper tantrum? She felt empty until she heard Otter crying in the nursery and went to him, finding he'd pulled himself half way up the bars of the crib.

"Hey, sweet boy, come here to me." She lifted him out and got his diaper changed. They sat down in the rocker and she pulled her shirt open, bringing her breast out to him. As he started to nurse, she did cry. She felt frightened that she'd screwed up her marriage. Would Roman ever forgive her?

She looked down at Otter. His eyes met hers and he smiled. When he finished feeding, he burped and wanted to play. He started to gurgle and then went into "Ma, ma, ma, da, da, da, ma, da, ma, da." He put his hand on her chin.

Kris hugged him and sighed. "Otter, if those are your first words, I'm not telling your daddy. You'll have to do it for him."

"Ma, ma, ma," he said and then gave her a wet, open mouthed smooch on her cheek.

Kris tried to stop crying, and rocked the baby, humming a little. There was a knock on the door and it clicked open. Cassie put her head in.

"Hey."

"Hi." Kris tried to smile.

She came all the way into the room and sat on the edge of the twin bed. "Well, let's see, what have you missed? Father Rupert left, but said he'd see us all again soon. I gave the keys to Sylvia's house to Marcus and he and Lorrie have disappeared. Marcus said they'd be by in the morning. Roman pulled a part of the deck railing off and pulverized it to pieces. Omar says it shouldn't be a problem to fix. Roman went down to the shore and Omar is trying to talk to him. How are you doing?" She tilted her head and smiled.

"Great, my spirit was taken by Rochelle and I got chained to a wall in a dungeon for the equivalent of about eight years. The Oracle got tired of hearing me complain about my abilities and somehow managed to put me into another realm back a year ago on the day of Dwight Schmitt's opening at MacAndrew's Gallery. I cheated on Roman, although I hadn't met him yet and, silly me, I was honest and told Roman what happened. I, of course, feel guilty and not certain what to do to correct the whole fucking mess," Kris concluded.

Otter looked up at her and slapped his little hand over her mouth. "Ma, ma."

"Sorry, baby boy, I shouldn't say bad words." Kris looked up at Cassie.

"Wow, all this in less than twenty-four hours, go figure." She sighed. "Let me get this straight, the Oracle put you back to a year ago? If I remember right, you weren't seeing anyone, then."

"She put me into a realm where I was still involved with Jeff, who wasn't very memorable to begin with." Kris smirked.

"The Oracle is a bitch. I never did like Jeff. He didn't deserve you," she whispered.

"Cassie." Kris looked at Otter who fussed with her shirt buttons.

"I know, watch my language, but really it's nervy of her to do that to you." She shook her head. "Do you think Roman will talk to Omar and calm down?"

"I hope so. Omar will be able to fill you in." Kris hiccupped and started cry.

"Oh, sweetie, I'm sorry." Cassie started tearing up, too.

"I'm praying to God that I haven't screwed things up." The water works opened and she sobbed.

"Oh Kris." Cassie stood up and took Otter from her arms. She settled him in the crib while Kris blew her nose and tried to get back in control. Cassie turned to her and pulled her up into a hug. They cried and held each other for a long time.

Kris pulled back and looked at her. "What the hell are you crying about?"

Cassie wiped her eyes. "You know I can't stand letting anyone cry alone."

Kris checked Otter and then they linked arms and went out to the living room.

"I've been thinking. Let Roman calm down. Once he's thinking more clearly, he should realize the one to blame isn't you. He loves you so much, Kris. I'm sure his manhood is smarting some right now. He should be okay," Cassie said.

"Good advice. Thank you." Kris tried to smile again.

"Terrible grin, you look done in. Get some rest. Tomorrow is a new day and things will look better." Cassie hugged her again and squeezed her arm.

Kris watched her leave and stood for a few minutes at the kitchen window. Looking at the back deck, she saw part of the stair railing and the long top banister had been pulled off. It lay in the grass in pieces. Roman stood down at the shoreline with Omar, who kept nodding.

She tried to figure out what to do next. Going to the bedroom, she stripped off her clothes, took a shower and put on her fuzzy, flannel pajamas and crawled into bed. Grabbing Roman's pillow, she held it up to her face and smelled his scent. She lay on her side and held onto his pillow tight. She wasn't going to let it go for anything, unless Roman fell into her arms. It became hard not to think or worry and she couldn't sleep. Every move or creak of the house caused her heart to speed up and pound. She also listened for Otter on the baby monitor, but he was quiet.

The back door squeaked open and she heard Roman lock up and turn off the lights. He went into the nursery and spent some time in there with his son. Kris felt glad of that and hoped Otter did his "ma, ma, da, da" thing for Roman.

The nursery door closed and she heard Roman's footfalls come into their room. She recognized the sound of his pants unzipping and he sat on the end of the bed to take them off. The bed moved a little as he got up and finished undressing.

"I know you're awake," he said and walked into the bathroom.

Kris froze, and didn't move an inch. She put his pillow back in place and moved to her side of the bed. He came out of the bathroom and the bed depressed behind her. In the darkness, she could feel him looking at her.

They remained silent for a long time. Kris thought he'd gone to sleep and then heard him sigh. "Why are you wearing those pajamas?"

"Comfort. I'm more frightened than I've ever been in my life," she said. She felt his arm come around her and pull her to his chest.

"Kris, don't ever be afraid of me. I'll never hurt you. I swear it with all the honor I possess."

"I know," she said. She wanted to say, *I hurt you*, but went another direction. "I'm terrified that I've wrecked my life with you because I wanted to be honest and not keep any secrets." She put her hand over her eyes, and tried not to cry again. He tightened his hold and she could feel his warm breath on her neck.

"Shush, babe, I love you and always will. I appreciate your honesty and would expect nothing less from you." He rolled her over to her back, but she wouldn't look at him or take her hand away from her eyes. "Kris." His fingers moved her hand, wiped the tears away, and turned her face to him. "I know in my heart, there is nothing to blame you for. The Oracle made a decision and put you in an impossible situation. I'm sorry it happened, but you must have handled yourself very well and I'm proud of you. I only wish I'd been there to help." He kissed her nose. Of course, this caused her to sob one more time. Roman held her in his arms as she cried herself out.

Chapter Twenty-Seven

The minutes ticked by while Kris rested her head on Roman's chest and listened to his heart beat. She wasn't sure which direction she should take with the conversation and brought up the first thing to enter her mind.

"Roman." She sniffed. "I told you a year ago I felt nervous about the control the Oracle had over us."

"I remember," he said.

"If I were to get my fingers out of my ears and build my powers, would I be able to block her?" Kris asked.

"I would think so, yes," he answered. "Or at least, it will make you more aware when someone lurks around and tries to remove your spirit. What do you remember from before we abolished Pelonus?"

"I..."

"Wait, wait a minute." Roman sat up, and moved her off of his chest. He started undoing the buttons on her pajamas. "You're baking me with these things and they have to come off. Babe, I think I've developed a flannel allergy. Just keep that in mind the next time you decide to put them on, okay?"

"Okay," she said as he pulled her back under the sheets, skin on skin.

"Tell me. What do you remember?" he asked again.

Kris thought for a moment. "I was in the bushes

and our son, the twenty-year-old, came up beside me from out of nowhere. He shifted into a cat, and distracted Pelonus. I turned things over to El. You and the others began the chant and I don't remember anything after that, until I woke up in the dungeon. I never saw Rochelle coming."

"You don't remember El chanting the spell?" he asked.

"No, not really."

"Is she talking to you at all?" He propped up on an elbow and looked down at Kris.

"No, she pulled way back into my head. I thought I heard her crying." She ran her hand over his chest.

"She wasn't very happy with me," Roman said.

"Why?"

"I wouldn't make love with her."

"Great, I have another black guilt sword in my heart. She's been after me off and on to switch places, but I refused."

Roman's brows furrowed. "Why did you refuse?"

"I knew you'd be able to tell the difference. And besides, you're mine, not hers. You told me she wasn't your type and you've always known when she pushed forward. Once my powers get built up, maybe we'll merge once and for all. It does get rather old having her scream at me." Kris adjusted under the sheets. "Speaking of which, how did Father Rupert get the speaker switched off in my head?"

"It was a simple blocking spell. Once you're more in control of your powers, we can remove it. You won't be picking up as many of my random thoughts," he said and pushed her onto her back. He rested half of his body on hers and put a leg between her thighs. Looking down at her, he continued. "I will want it removed. I'm going to want to play hide and seek in the forest again, eventually."

He kissed her chest. His shaft pressed against her leg, hard and warm. Kris almost started to celebrate, but kept silent.

"I spoke with Omar about going and telling the Oracle that I wanted to speak with her," Roman whispered and licked her neck.

"Tell her? You didn't petition for an audience with her?"

Roman arched his eyebrow and smiled. "I don't work for her anymore. Omar said there's been a rumor flying around Parcel, that my life in this realm isn't working, and I'm returning to the Guards. The story's been told for a couple of weeks." He looked up into Kris's eyes. "Babe, it's not happening. It's a load of shit and I wanted to know, firstly, how it got started and secondly, I want to have her explain to me why she could pull you out of Rochelle, and put you in another realm, but didn't bring you home. What was the point of returning you to the dungeon?"

Kris's brain kicked into high gear. "She kept saying that I had choices and she said, 'What humans feel in the long run means nothing...'" Her voice faded as she stared at him. She pushed Roman off of her and sat up. "Son of a bitch." Kris got up off the bed, grabbed a pair of jeans out of the closet, and put them on. She snatched a sweatshirt out of a drawer.

Roman followed her and put his clothes back on. Kris walked with purpose to the back door and unlocked it. She stomped across the deck, stepped barefoot into the grass, and moved carefully around the pieces of wood. The Oracle stood by the shore, and then turned with a smirk on her face.

"You bitch!" Kris spat as she approached. Roman put his arm around her stomach and held her back. "You sent Pelonus here. You told him about Cedric's abilities to entice him. How could you do that to Cedric?" Before she could blink, Omar stood with them and Marcus wasn't far behind. Cedric swam up and walked out of the water. "And you set me up," she hissed at the woman.

"Now what are you talking about, Kris? It sounds like madness to me. I didn't say a thing to Pelonus. You have Garda to thank for his being here," the Oracle said.

Roman watched the strange woman with interest. Something didn't seem right with her. Her eyes were black and she acted different from the time he'd met with her a year ago.

"You'd like that wouldn't you? For me to be nuts, right?" Kris looked up at Roman.

"I could erase all of your memories," the Oracle said.

"No, I don't think so." Kris put her shield up, and covered herself and Roman. She looked at him again. "It never occurred to me when I was in the dungeon. I was the only one there who wasn't a vessel." Kris looked back at the Oracle. "There's no way Rochelle has the ability to move spirits around. She's a ghost for crap's sake." She heard Roman's breath catch. "Lorrie was there because her body Rochelle inhabited, as were the others whose bodies Rochelle stole over the years, but how did I get brought there? And then flipped to another realm? That wasn't done by Rochelle. So my

203

question is why did you do it?"

Kris saw the Oracle's black eyes squint. "You took one of our best Guards. We wanted him back. I wanted him back."

"Interesting. I never would have guessed Oracles could be corrupted." Kris shook her head.

"I am not corrupt," she hissed at Kris. "I also didn't send Pelonus. You'll have to accuse Garda of that one."

"I bet against you, Oracle. How else could Pelonus have known about Cedric's abilities? The Lake Guardians don't divulge that kind of information. Who else would have known? Hmm... let me think." Kris seethed with anger. "And another thing, if you didn't tell Pelonus, where is Garda? Why hasn't he put in an appearance?"

"The puppet master does not do appearances, young lady. You're lucky so far, but your days could be numbered. You should continue to watch your back," the Oracle said with a smirk on her face.

Kris felt Roman's arms tighten around her waist. "If it wasn't you, and it was Garda, why are you so different? Why are you here? What are you? Oracles have a code of ethics, and you broke the rules, why?" he asked.

"As I said, you were one of the Guards' best, Roman. We wanted you back," she whispered.

"My time of service ended long ago. Parcel was lucky I..." Roman frowned and let go of Kris's waist. He put his hand on her wrist, and pulled her hand down. The shield dissolved. "You set up Beatrice, didn't you?"

The Oracles eyes flashed at him. "There has never been one worthy of you, Roman. No one in this realm deserves you. You are too beautiful for this world."

"Why did you attend our wedding?" Kris asked. She was at a loss as to why an Oracle would take any position for or against a Guardian.

"Jealous Oracle," Marcus said under his breath.

"I watched because Roman wanted it. Then, to my surprise, I discover you're pregnant, increasing your power tenfold." She shook her head. "What a waste. You could have been a great seer and wizardess, but you sit and complain about what was given to you by the gods. I've never seen anything like your insolence."

Kris stared at her. "Oracle, this is where we part ways for good. If you ever come near me or my husband or children again, I'll find a way to vanquish you." Kris looked up at Roman. "If you wish to return to the Guards..."

He put his hand over her mouth and shook his head. "No way, never."

Omar and Marcus walked up on either side of them. "Oracle, we're going to file a report of your activities with our superiors, who, I'm certain, will file a grievance with the Oracle council. You have broken many codes and will have to answer for your actions. I'm sure they will want answers from you as to your involvement with Pelonus, Rochelle, and Abednego. You will answer for your actions," Omar said.

The Oracle looked at him and said angrily, "I've supported you Lakeman and for the last time, I didn't call Pelonus."

"I'll always be grateful for your support, but you've treated one of my family with a great amount of disrespect. I can't abide this behavior," Omar finished and turned away.

Roman took Kris's hand and pulled her toward their house. She hadn't realized both Cassie and Lorrie were on the lawn and listening.

They all walked into Kris's house and shut the door. The group stood around the kitchen and looked at each other.

Kris raced to the nursery to check on Otter and found him asleep. She breathed a sigh of relief and went back to the kitchen. She nodded at Roman to let him know the baby was fine. He held his arms open and she slipped into his hold. Love and warmth radiated from him.

"Guys, did that just really happen?" Kris asked and faced the group.

Roman put his arm around her waist and pulled her back to his chest. He put his forehead into her hair. "I think it did," he said.

"It makes no sense. The Oracle saves my life, and then she goes wacky and turns against me? Or was she always against me and Roman? I'm confused." She put her hands on Roman's arms and leaned her chin down to look at the floor.

"Is there any possibility that an evil has somehow leaked into Parcel? Did you see her eyes? I mean, come on, she wasn't radiating much warmth. And who's Garda?" Cassie asked as she sat down at the table.

Omar's cheeks puffed out. "Anything is possible. Evil can encroach anywhere there is an opening. As to Garda, I'm not sure who he is. Some research is going to be needed on the name."

"My mother dealt with a demon called Garda. The Oracle called him a puppet master. He likes to play with people. Is it possible he sent Pelonus?" She looked up at Roman who shrugged. She leaned against his chest. "We have to be sure Parcel is okay."

"There are safeguards in Parcel to keep the bad demons out of that realm," Marcus said.

"What?" Omar said sharply and caused everyone to jump. He looked at Cedric.

The young man adjusted his feet. "This may not have any bearing, but I got sort of bored one an evening a couple of months ago. You know, I played around with my magick's and opened a portal. It was very small, but..."

"Where?" Omar and Marcus asked at the same time.

"In my room at headquarters," Cedric answered and looked uncomfortable.

"We'll discuss this," Omar said. He turned and looked down at Cassie. "Lover, I've got to head back. Love you." He leaned over and kissed her.

Marcus kissed Lorrie and opened the back door. Omar pointed at Cedric and the three left.

"Ladies, I know we need to talk, but can we do it tomorrow? My wife and I need some sleep," Roman said.

Cassie got up and she and Lorrie started to leave. Kris left Roman's hold and grabbed Lorrie's hand.

"Girlfriend, I insist you come back home to the lake. We have to learn how to protect ourselves," Kris said.

Lorrie smiled. "We'll talk tomorrow. Goodnight."

Kris shut the door and locked it. She turned and looked across the kitchen at Roman. "Are we good, babe?"

He crossed his arms and leaned against the counter,

then pushed himself forward a step. "Meet me half way." He took another step. Kris took two steps and when he took another, she did, too. They meet in the middle of the kitchen floor. Roman brought his hands up and cupped them under her breasts. "Kris, just for the record and so we're clear, these are mine."

She felt her nipples harden as his fingers moved over them. "Yep, all yours," she sighed.

His hands continued down to her hips and one moved to her crotch. "Mine," he whispered and wrapped his other arm around her to pinch her bottom. "Mine, all mine."

She felt his fingers press into her pelvis through her pants. "Only you, no one, but you, my love," she whispered and moved her hands up to his chest. "I love you more than anything." Her hand trailed down to the front of his slacks. He still felt hard from earlier. "Would you like for me to show you just how much I love you?" She started to move the zipper down and gazed up into his eyes.

"I love you, too, babe and yes, please show me." He leaned down and touched his lips to hers.

She stretched up onto her toes and flicked his lips with her tongue. "Come with me, Mr. Lake." She moved toward the bedroom and Roman followed. He hit the light switch in passing and pulled his shirt off.

"Kris," he said, which caused her to stop and turn. "There is one other thing we need to be clear on. We're never going to mention what happened in the other realm again. It's done and over, no blame."

"Thank you," she said and took off her sweatshirt while she stared at him. "Roman, would you sit on the bed, please?"

He sat down on the end of the bed while she took off her jeans. She stood in front of him and looked down, running her hands over his eyes and cheeks. She put her hands on his shoulders and pushed him back. When he lay flat, she undid the button on his pants and finished bringing the zipper down. After he pulled them off, she straddled his hips and rubbed her opening over his shaft. He sighed and she kissed his chest and bit his nipples which made them harder. His fingers moved through her hair and along her neck.

Kris put her fingers around his shaft and placed the head to her opening, and pushed down impaling herself all the way. She sat up, arched her back and wanted to feel every inch of him inside her. Roman moved up, took a nipple between his lips, and flicked the hard peak with his tongue. He held onto her hips, and wouldn't let her move. She tightened around his penis.

"Mine," he whispered and licked her neck and chin.

Kris looked down and placed her lips on his open mouth. Their tongues swirled and flowed together. Moving up and down, she felt his length slide in and out and the friction and heat in her core grew with each motion. One of his hands came down and pressed on her spot. She sucked in her breath and continued to move up and down. His thumb moved in circles and caused her breath to come in quicker puffs.

"Roman...my love...oh yes." She moved faster and faster. His thumb kept the pressure coming and she climaxed very long and rode him hard.

Without leaving her, Roman moved Kris to the bed and lay on top of her. He began to thrust into her with intensity. He grabbed her merge hand and connected their souls. The heat and electricity from the connection caused them both to breathe harder and sweat started to roll from their bodies. She could hear the current snap and crackle as their motion continued. Roman moaned and pumped harder which caused the bed to creak. Kris panted in his ear and wrapped her legs around his waist. He kept the motion going long and steady. Kris felt the warmth from their hands flood her body down into her pelvis.

"Kris...oh my Lord...I can't...are you ready?" he stuttered.

"Bring it home, babe," she said between breaths.

He gave her several more hard pumps and then sucked his breath in. She orgasmed at the same time, and tightened her legs around him.

Chapter Twenty-eight

"Hello, Father."

Garda straightened up from the seeing pool and looked around the room. "I can hear you. Why are you hiding in the shadows?" he asked and looked back down into the swirling mass.

"Sebastian says Pelonus got himself abolished. Is it true?" the voice said from several different corners of the room.

"Yes, it is true." Garda placed a blackened fingertip on his temple and rubbed a new headache. "He was caught off Guard by a shifter, of all the stupid..." He stopped and bit his cheek. "He was very focused, but managed to get surrounded in the end. It's such a shame."

"You don't sound pleased, Father. It could be why I'm staying on the outside."

"Guillermo, have you finished wasting your time in Asia?" Garda sat up again, folded his hands on his lap and heard his son laugh.

"Yes, it has grown dull. The women don't scream as I like," the seventh son said and appeared behind a chair in front of the fire place.

Garda sighed at the sight of his youngest. "I take it, then, that you didn't find your perfect mate?"

The tall demon with black hair that hung down to his waist, wore a smirk on his face. "No, not yet. She isn't in Asia, that's for sure." He walked around the chair and flopped his long body down. "Sebastian says you've called for me. Sorry, I didn't hear you. He says you found the woman."

"Yes, but she is tough. I've tried to figure out a way to turn her, but other than stealing her squalling spawn, I'm at a loss," Garda answered and continued to look into his pool.

"Tell me about her, Father."

"She came into her powers as a child, but because of parental influences, she turned them off and ignored them for many years. Last year, with Abednego's help, her abilities were reawakened, but she's reluctant to use them. She is married to one of the Lake Guards and has a child. She still doesn't realize what she holds within herself."

"Why don't you kill the husband?" Guillermo said and adjusted his long legs.

"I thought about it, but it would only make her need for revenge grow. In the end, it wouldn't turn her." Garda stood and stretched. "Come have a look at her." He held out a hand toward his son. "I'm interested to see what you can come up with." He saw his son freeze in the chair. "I'm truly interested, son."

Guillermo stood and walked to the seeing pool. He stood on the other side from his Father and put his hands on the outer rim. "What am I seeing?"

Garda moved his hand over the boiling mass and the liquid contents cleared. They could see Kris and Roman making love in their bedroom.

"She rides him well," Guillermo commented. "Strong legs on this one. I suppose they could be put to use."

As they watched, the couple connected their merge

spots and the room lit up. He saw his son watch as an electric current shot about them.

"You didn't say they'd merged."

"It wasn't noteworthy, son. The merge would mean nothing if she were turned." Garda sat back in his chair.

"Have your visions told of an outcome, if I were to get involved?" Guillermo straightened his back and looked down at his father.

"Unfortunately no, it would be a bit of a crap shoot, but I believe you could handle the situation. Have you any thoughts?"

"I'm thinking. Is Bartolome still paying off his debt?"

"You're not thinking of turning her over to Bartolome?" Garda hissed and felt surprised.

"Not her, old man, the husband. Wouldn't it be fun to see him bleed?" Guillermo said.

Garda sensed his son's growing eagerness to get involved. The demon's pride began to take over his black heart and the headache began to fade.

****

Kris woke up with Roman's arms and legs wrapped around her. They hadn't enjoyed a marathon night or morning in a long time. She felt relaxed and warm. Opening her eyes, she saw the sun's rays shine through the bedroom window. The clock said nine-thirty-five and she realized she'd slept through one of Otter's feedings and felt another guilt pang in her heart.

She could hear Otter squeak in the nursery and then he said, "Ma, ma, da, da." She smiled and shook Roman's arm.

"Babe, wake up," she said and pushed herself up.

"What's wrong?" he asked and his eyes popped

open.

"Nothing...Listen," she said.

Roman's brow creased and his head lifted off his pillow. "What? Is that....Otter?" He got up and headed straight for the nursery.

Kris swung her legs off the bed, grabbed her robe and followed. When she walked into the nursery, Roman held Otter in his arms. The baby pinched his dad's cheeks in his tiny hands and said "Da, da, da." When he saw Kris walk in, Otter said, "Ma, ma, ma," and squealed, grinning ear to ear.

Roman looked at her with wonder. "I didn't think he would speak until he was one or two years old."

"I think it's around nine months that they begin to speak with real words, but our son is brilliant, so it doesn't surprise me he's speaking now." She walked up to them and kissed her son's cheek.

"He's also soaked," Roman said and made a face. He put Otter onto the changing table and began to get the wet diaper off.

"I see he leaked, too," Kris mumbled. She took the wet sheet off of the mattress and cleaned it before putting a clean fitted sheet down.

Once finished, she went up alongside Roman. He'd finished the diaper change and fastened the snaps on the baby's pajamas. Otter played and laughed. He kicked his feet against his dad's muscular stomach. Roman grabbed one of his little feet and pretended to munch on it. This caused peals of laughter from the youngster.

Roman picked him up and Otter seemed to focus on his dad's hand and placed his in the palm. "Da, da," Otter said, and turned to look at Kris. "Ma, ma?" he asked, and nodded.

Kris put her merge hand up with theirs and Otter pulled them into the other realm. He stood tall between his parents. They were by the lake again. He hugged them both and held Kris in his arms.

"I hope you two have learned some lessons," he said. Roman tilted his head with a questioning look.

Kris nodded. "I have," she said. "Trust my abilities and don't be so negative about them."

"What about you, Dad?"

Roman's eyebrows popped up and down. "Don't trust the Oracle."

Otter stared at him and then laughed. "You know it's a miracle you two have reached the age you are." He shook his head. "You're both so stubborn, it's almost ridiculous and you've got to trust one another one-hundred percent. Learn from each other and stop feeling dumb if you don't know something."

"Otter, I do trust your dad." Kris crossed her arms.

"Okay, so maybe trust is the wrong word. You're both control freaks and you need to learn to give in, or meet half way. Hey, I know, when you get me the Legos set for Christmas, why don't you two work on building something together," he said and laughed harder. "Never mind, yes, I've had a vision of the future. You two are so funny sometimes. Just keep loving each other..."

"Otter, I can't promise you that Dad and I aren't going to argue sometimes," Kris said.

"Mom, don't worry. I understand it better now. I know you two aren't breaking up, just expressing your opinions, which you both have in abundance."

"That's not a bad thing, Son," Roman said.

"I agree, Dad. Now, I'm starving and want

breakfast." He grinned and pulled them back into the nursery. Otter held out his arms and leaned toward Kris.

Roman handed him off. "Our son is developing an odd sense of humor," he said.

"I noticed that, too. He certainly didn't get it from my side of the family," she said, sat in the rocker and got Otter settled.

"Ha, ha, maybe it was from El. I'm going to get the coffee started," he said and stopped in the doorway with a blank look on his face.

"I heard that about El," she said and saw the strange look on his face. "Roman?"

"Omar will be here in a bit. I better make a full pot." He smiled and left for the kitchen.

Kris looked down at Otter and thought this might be a good day to get his swing set up. It seemed like he would be awake longer between feeding times.

After Otter finished feeding, Kris got out his playpen, set it up in the living room and put him in it. She got dressed, washed her face, and combed her hair. She started to think about the anniversary gift she'd gotten for Roman. It burned a hole in her nightstand drawer and she felt very focused on it. She decided to get the pendant out and give it to him today. She didn't want to wait until the actual day of their anniversary.

She smelled bacon cooking and it made her stomach rumble. She put on her half of the merge pendant, the side with RGE on it, tucked his box in the waist of her pants and went out to the kitchen.

"Babe, that smells heavenly," Kris said, poured herself some coffee and then set the table.

"Hungry?" he asked over his shoulder.

"Starving." She put four slices of bread in the toaster, got the butter and marmalade out of the fridge, and waited for the toast to pop.

Roman tossed a couple of eggs into the bacon fat and fried them. Within a couple of minutes, breakfast was on the table and they sat down to enjoy a scrumptious meal.

They talked, drank too much coffee and made plans for a mini-vacation. Roman wanted to take Otter up to Whistler, in Canada, when the snows came so he could play and build a snowman. Kris wanted to know why they couldn't just go up to Mount Rainier or Baker. Roman explained that he'd never been to Canada. He'd been close, but had never gone over the border.

Roman's brow furrowed and then he reached over to her and put his fingers under the neck of her sweatshirt. "What are you wearing there?" he asked pulling the chain up and out. Looking at the pendant his eyebrow arched. "RGE?"

"See, next week is our anniversary. However, now that I'm really pissed off at the Oracle for all her shenanigans, I think our anniversary should be the day we merged, which would be in March. I'm a little late with your gift, so please, forgive me." She pulled the box out and handed it to him.

He opened the box and found his half. The chain she picked out was thicker and a little longer. He looked at it and smiled. She leaned toward him and he fit the halves together.

"I gave you the ME half. Since I'm yours anyway and you laid claim to all my parts last night, I wanted you to have ME," she said.

"I'll take it." He leaned over and kissed her. "Wait here." He set the chain down and went into the bedroom. Coming back out to the kitchen, he held two small boxes. He bowed and handed them to her. "Open this one first," he said and sat down. He put the chain around his neck, and watched her open the box.

She found a framed picture of Roman and Otter. "Oh, my two men are looking so handsome," she whispered with tears in her eyes.

"Do you like it? Omar thought I was crazy," Roman said.

"Omar's the crazy one. I love it, babe. Now what's in this one?" She opened the second box and a key fell onto the table. She looked at Roman. Checking the box once more, she saw a set of folded papers. She took them out and found the title and bill of sales record for a building down on Fifteenth Street. "What the..."

"I thought this would be a good time for you to open your own gallery." He smiled.

Kris's eyes opened wide and she became tongue-tied.

"I bought you a building. It's about ten minutes from here, just north of the university. Cassie helped me start to get it set up. That's the reason for the picture. You'll need it for your desk in your new office." He sat back in his chair and smiled proudly.

"I'll have my own space to meet clients?" She gasped.

"Yep."

"I won't have to bug Tom anymore." She crossed her eyes. "I'll be Tom's competition. He's going to be mad."

"He's in Everett. You'll be in Seattle and can

share," Roman said. "Do you like it?"

"Yes, I'm stunned, but, oh my goodness this is incredible. I could even have employees. I could offer Lorrie a job. She's an accountant," Kris said, breathless.

"Yeah, you could do that." He put his elbow on the table, and cupped his chin in his hand.

"Thank you, this is incredible." She stood up and moved to his lap. "How did I ever get so lucky?" She kissed his lips and ran her hand through his hair.

"Now you're feeling lucky?" He hugged her tight.

"Yeah, I am. And thankful." She kissed him again. "The power of positive thinking, you know?"

Roman chuckled and held her for a couple of minutes. "Kris, I haven't thanked you for telling me to talk to Beatrice yesterday. Thank you for that," he said.

Kris felt her throat tighten. She took in a breath. "She cared for you very much and wanted to make sure you were happy. She thought very highly of you."

"She's with God now, in a better place," Roman said. "You and Otter are my life, but thank you."

"You're welcome."

Roman picked up her half of the pendant and smiled. "Hmm...RGE, what could we have the letters mean?"

She looked down and grinned. "I did a little thinking about that. How about Roman Gets Erection," she said with a mischievous smile.

Roman whooped and started to laugh. "Perfect, I love it."

They both were laughing when there was a knock on the back door. Kris said "Come in," and the door opened with Omar looking in. "It's okay, we're dressed," she said, and stood up to start clearing the table.

Omar walked in with Marcus behind him. They both looked at Roman, who still laughed so hard he'd started to cough.

Roman waved his hand at the chairs and said, "Private joke, please forgive me."

"Would you like some coffee?" Kris asked.

They both were up all night and said yes, then sat with Roman at the table. Kris poured two cups, handed them to the Lakemen, and went back to the dishes.

"Brother, we have more than one problem this morning," Omar said. "The temple has gone dark and cold. The Oracle did not return to Parcel and her whereabouts are unknown. Headquarters will send out trackers before long. They've requested a replacement for the temple from the council, but it could be several days before the new Oracle arrives."

Kris turned from the sink, and dried her hands. She looked at Roman, who gave her a nod and she waited. Sitting next to Roman, she looked at the playpen. Otter lay on his back. He watched them and seemed to be listening to the conversation.

"We found Cedric's portal, which was left slightly open. It has been sealed, but we have no idea what might have come through. Trackers are already investigating in Parcel, but nothing has been found. Cedric was demoted by the leaders, but before his abilities could be stripped, he disappeared, too. I'm being penalized for Cedric's behavior, but also because I didn't think his abilities should be censored. His power is too great and good to just throw away. I've been suspended for six months and Marcus is now the lead."

"Temporarily," Marcus added.

"Until my suspension is over, Roman," Omar looked across the table at his friend, "we need a third. Is there any possibility you'd consider returning, just to fill in?"

Roman shook his head before Omar finished. "No, I'm sorry Omar, but no. I have a family now. I'm staying on this side." Kris put her hand around Roman's arm and squeezed it. "I served my time, but I will help on this side if I can."

"That would be appreciated, brother," Omar concluded and frowned.

"Is it possible Cedric was turned?" Kris asked. The silence at the table gave her their answer. "Unknown, I see." She looked at the top of the table. "Is it likely he joined up with the Oracle?" The others continued to say nothing and stare at her. "Again, unknown."

A thought came into her brain. She stood up, walked to the back door and went out to the deck. She didn't know where the idea came from and hadn't ever done it, but wanted to try.

The men followed her. Cassie walked over from her house and met Lorrie in the middle of the lawn. They both stopped to watch Kris. Cassie put her hands up to her mouth and pointed at her.

Kris felt her aura change, put her hands out and closed her eyes. She began to chant under her breath in a language she'd never studied.

****

Roman started toward her, but stopped when he saw her aura turn to a metallic gold, shiny and bright. It looked so brilliant that it made his eyes water.

When Kris opened her eyes and continued the

chant, he saw her eyes were white. Light began to radiate from her hands. It shot out over the lake. For a moment, the water and air glittered a sparkling gold. It floated over the area, and touched the animals, fish, frogs, and birds.

Roman realized she'd just incanted a protection spell over the area. How she knew the chant, was a mystery to him, but he felt so proud of her for using her ability with such strength.

Kris suddenly sucked in her breath and stopped speaking the words. Her brows creased and a deep frown formed on her lips. She started to speak and stopped several times, then calmly said, "Cedric's soul is not lost, but he's close to being taken by an evil from another realm. He was marked soon after the portal opened. His..." She stopped. "He is walking this realm, frightened and feeling a great amount of shame for his actions. The seer has sent a familiar from his vessel and will take another..." Kris flew backwards and landed hard on her bottom on the wooden flooring.

Roman crouched by her side and held her. She brought up her head and smiled at him. Her eyes were their normal blue color. Her hands were very warm on his arms. "Hey, babe," she whispered.

"Where on Earth did that come from?" he asked.

She looked around at her friends gathered near her. "El says it's Middle Ages Mediterranean." She stood up with Roman's help, then grabbed his arm and he caught her as she passed out.

Chapter Twenty-Nine

Roman felt thrown as he watched Kris's eyes roll up and held her in his arms in a split second. "Cassie, would you straighten the sheets on the bed?" he asked.

She bolted through the door and by the time he carried Kris into the bedroom, things were back together. He laid her down and grabbed her merge hand in his. Closing his eyes, he began a spell to reach her. The merge spot was blocked and he couldn't get to her.

Roman opened his eyes and looked down at her. "Omar, there's elixir in the cabinet above the stove," he said.

"I'll get it mixed," Omar answered and left the room.

They all watched Kris. Her aura changed colors rapidly, going through everything in the rainbow. Roman watched her aura go mostly golden, to white, to blue.

"Cassie would you get Otter, please, and bring him to me?" He sat on the edge of the bed, and held his wife's hand tight.

Cassie came in with Otter. She lowered him into Roman's arms and they all stood and watched as Kris continued to change colors.

Otter looked at his mom and leaned over. He slid his hand over hers. "Da, da," he said and looked up at him.

Roman put his hand over theirs and felt the pull.

He closed his eyes and concentrated.

****

Kris knew she blacked out, but when she opened her eyes, she wasn't on the deck, but stood by the lake. The day felt warm and she became aware of someone standing next to her.

When she turned her head, she saw El. She wore her black spaghetti strap dress, the three-inch heels and her hair in an updo.

"El, what's going on?" Kris asked.

"I've decided it's time to turn everything over to you. You'll have the knowledge I've been withholding from you. I didn't think you'd ever be ready, but"—El turned to her—"you are. You handled yourself so well against the bitch Oracle. I'm proud of you, sister."

Kris felt stunned and turned to face El. Looking down, she found that she wore a white spaghetti strap dress. "El, I don't want you to go."

"I can't deal anymore. Sure I'm useful, but he won't touch me and he won't let me go somewhere to experience being touched. I can't stand it. I feel, I don't know, unloved?" She took Kris's hand and an electrical charge radiated between them. "I couldn't do this until you'd wrapped your head around it. The protection spell told me you were ready."

"El, I need you with me always. You're my strength and I do love you." Kris choked, and her eyes teared up.

"Sister, you have the power, you always have. Just trust it and don't let anyone push you around or take you anymore. You can do it and you're going to kick ass. I've seen it." She smiled and gave Kris another blast of electricity.

There was a flash of light and when Kris looked over her shoulder, she saw Roman and her adult son appear. She tried to smile.

"Kris." Roman took a step forward.

"It's okay, babe."

"You passed out," he said and took another step.

Otter took hold of Roman's arm and held him back. "Wait, Dad," he whispered.

Kris looked at El. "Okay, sister, but you need to do one thing first."

El looked at her and raised her eyebrows. "You think?" She looked at Roman. "He won't like it."

"I know." Kris squeezed her hand.

"Well...okay." El looked at her and pulled her into a hug. "I love you, sister. Keep making me proud."

"I'll do my best."

They let each other go and El headed straight up to Roman. She put her hand up to his cheek. "This was not my idea. You're so damn hot, Roman, and I know you belong to Kris. Protect her or I'll come back and kick your butt." She stood on her tiptoes and moved her hands around his neck. Putting her lips on his, she gave him a long thought out kiss.

Kris almost started to laugh and put her hand over her mouth to maintain herself. She felt a little jealousy work its way into her head and she shut it off. Roman's hands shot to El's arms and began to pull her away. Otter started laughing and made kissing noises. Roman took a step back and disconnected himself with shock on his face.

El turned back to Kris and shook her head. "Terrible kisser, he's all yours, Kris."

"Thanks, sister. I'll keep him. I love his kisses."

Kris winked.

"Time for me to split. I'll see you again in the between or the next life, whichever comes first." El smiled. A very bright light enveloped her, and carried her up into the sky.

Kris walked into Roman's arms, and hugged him very tight. His hands ran down her back.

"Did you just set me up?" he asked.

Otter still laughed and made the kissing sounds. They both looked at him. Roman put his hand around his son's neck and pulled him into the hug.

"Wow, Mom, you feel charged," Otter said.

"That's from your Aunt El." Kris ran her hand up Roman's spine.

He shivered a little and smiled. "Me like."

"Let's get back, guys. I believe Dad and I have some things to discuss." She closed her eyes and felt them move back to their own realm. It felt nice to do it herself for a change.

Kris opened her eyes and saw two sets of beautiful brown eyes. "Hello, handsome boys." Otter gurgled, smiled down at her and drooled on his dad's arm.

"Hey beautiful lady, what just happened?" Roman wore a questioning look on his face.

Kris sat up, and took Otter out of his arms. Her little one put his hands around her and leaned his head in the crook of her neck.

Omar came in the room carrying a cup. "What have I missed?" He handed the cup to Roman who set it on the nightstand. Omar and Cassie wrapped their arms around each other and Lorrie sat down on the end of the bed with Marcus standing behind her.

"Okay, so El pulled me into an alternate realm and

I guess downloaded the information she's held for me. We are now merged and she's gone somewhere else." Kris looked at Roman, who nodded.

"Was that why your aura kept jumping colors?" Cassie asked.

"I suppose so," Kris said, and tried to unlatch Otter from her neck, but he wouldn't let go. She patted his bottom. "It's more than likely. When El passed the knowledge, it felt like an electrical surge. It caused my circuits to overload a bit," she continued.

"Now you have her knowledge?" Omar asked.

"Yeah." Kris's eyebrows creased. "I'm going to need some help sifting through it, because I'm already feeling all kinds of new things flying around. I'm almost afraid to lift my arms." She kissed the side of Otter's head and whispered in his ear. "Baby boy, I need to talk to your daddy. Would you go out to the living room with your Aunt Cassie?"

Otter leaned back, put his hands on either side of her face and made a popping noise. Then he reached up for Cassie to lift him.

"Guys, I need to talk to Roman for a minute, we'll be right out." She smiled and watched as her friends filed out, closing the door behind them.

Roman put his fingers through her hair. "What's wrong, babe?"

"It's not really wrong, I'm just wondering something. El was a part of me, I mean a split part, and she said she knew where the knowledge came from, but how come I didn't know any of this stuff before? Where does it originate from? I mean, why don't I know where it originates from now that she's left? Am I making any sense?" She looked at him with more questions than there were answers.

"Yes, you're making sense. We know from what El told us, that you'd buried the magicks and they weren't active for you for some time. It was the poisons and spells in Abednego's wine that activated the power for you. Where it came from originally, is hard to say. We may never get that one answered. We could do a little checking around, though. I'm sure Cassie and her group could help us out. Father Rupert might know something," he said. "We have all of those files your mom put together and could use them, too. I doubt very much we'll ever discover the why of it."

"It's just strange to find out what is zipping through my brain right now. Even when I was a kid, I don't think I knew how much power I would develop."

"Kris, how could you have known? You were just a kid and your mom held you back, remember?" Roman put some lose hairs behind her ear.

"I've never had a clue." She looked up at him. "The Oracle called me a wizardess. I suppose I'll have to buy a pointy hat."

"Swear to me you'll never grow a beard," Roman said.

"Ah babe, you don't want me to look like Gandalf?" she teased him.

He pulled her into a hug, and kissed her neck. "Not Gandalf, please. How about the Lady of the Lake?"

"She had an evil sister, but she did have Excalibur. I could deal with a sword." She kissed his cheek and leaned back.

"Queen Mab was only on TV. She didn't really exist back then. Do you know how to use a sword?" Roman asked.

Kris looked into his eyes. "Roman, love of my life, you've never really fessed up to me how old you are. How exactly do you know Queen Mab didn't exist back then?"

"Wife, who I adore more than anything else on the planet, I'm not that old. I'm very well read, remember? I've read many myths and legends over the years. Besides, it says I'm thirty-two years old on my driver's license." He smiled and slipped his hand up the back of her shirt. "That electric charge is really nice. You know, we have a rain check floating around from a couple of nights ago."

"Hey, that's right. Are you wanting to collect on it?" she asked, as his hand came around to her breast and he kissed her lips. "I guess that's a yes. How about we say goodbye to our neighbors, I'll get Otter fed and then we'll meet, say, in the shower?"

His fingers pressed on her nipple. "I wonder if you'll electrocute me in the shower." He saw her frown. "Just kidding, babe. I can't wait," he whispered.

"If we continue in this vein, we won't be leaving this spot for the rest of the afternoon," Kris said.

His hand slid out of her shirt and she whimpered and whined under her breath about ungrateful neighbors, which caused Roman to chuckle.

They walked into the other room and found Omar holding Otter and playing "zoom around the room." Otter laughed hysterically and kicked his feet out behind him.

Kris walked over to Lorrie and hooked her arm. "Girlfriend, I have an offer for you." Lorrie looked up at her with an open mouth. "My darling husband bought me a gallery...well, a building where I can start a gallery. I'm going to need someone that has computer savvy to help me start a website, plus accounts and contracts and whatnot. I guess it would be sort of an assistant-type position, but it would be more of a managerial post because you'd be second boss when I'm unavailable. Please tell me if this makes any sense at all. This day has become something of a jumble."

Lorrie smiled and laughed. "Kris, are you offering me a job?"

"I am, indeed."

"Yes, yes, and yes. I've never done art before, but it shouldn't be too difficult. Thank you so much," Lorrie said and leaned against her.

"The only thing up in the air is a place for you to live," Kris said.

"No rush there. When I spoke with Sylvia the other night, she said they found a place down in Arizona and are about ninety percent sure they're going to stay. This means that when they come back up to Haller Lake in the spring, their house will go on the market. Now that I have a job, I could make them an offer and be back at the place that's really home," Lorrie said, and looked up at Marcus.

Kris saw he wore happy look on his face and he hadn't been happy for months.

"Good. I mean, I'm sorry to be losing Sylvia and Fred, but hey, this works out really well," Kris said and smiled at Roman.

"I do need to go over to Moses Lake and see what I can find of my stuff. Hopefully, someone put my furniture and clothes into storage," Lorrie finished and frowned.

"What do you think about starting in a month? I've

got to do some figuring, particularly since I haven't even seen the building yet. Speaking of..." Kris walked over to Roman.

He smiled down at her. "If you think you're leaving this house today, I'll fight you tooth and nail."

"Oh that's right, we have a date," Kris whispered and moved her hand to his tight behind and pinched it. "So, we'll talk more this week. We'll need to decide on a salary and all the trimmings too," she said and looked back at Lorrie. "If you need any help with moving things, just give us a shout, okay?"

"Got it, thank you." Lorrie smiled. She latched onto Marcus's arm and pointed to the back door. "We should get out of the way." They moved toward the exit and left the house.

Omar still flew Otter around, but brought him over to Kris, and put the boy into her arms. "I get the message." He smiled. Turning to Cassie, he held out his hand. "Come on lover, these two are having a hormonal moment." He winked at Roman.

"Are we that transparent, Omar?" Kris asked. Cassie wore a huge grin on her face. "What?"

"Kris, between your nipples and the size of the bulge in Roman's pants, it's more than a little obvious what your minds are on," Cassie said. "And fortunately, it's rubbing off on me, too. Omar, darling, let's go home. Time to eat," she finished and licked her lips.

"Got to go," Omar said and both turned to the back door. "We'll talk tomorrow, Roman. We need a plan for Parcel," he added over his shoulder as he closed the back door.

"Roman, my love, would you lock the door, please? I know it's early in the day, but close the blinds, too. I want no interruptions the rest of the day."

"You got it," Roman smiled.

Chapter Thirty

The next month seemed to fly by and between making plans for the new gallery and how all of that would work, Kris trained on her extra powers and conjuring. She found herself exhausted and the days went by so fast, she wasn't certain if she was coming or going.

Roman helped out in Parcel and tried to wrangle in the demons that slipped through Cedric's open portal. He told Omar that he would only help out on their side of the lake and didn't want to be far away from home. Finding it possible to be gone for a few hours during the day, he would swim through the portal, which the administration reopened for him, and be back home in time for dinner. He assisted with tracking - a talent Roman knew well.

They were not only trying to find the demons, but also Cedric, and the missing Oracle. The religious order that trains Oracles sent another seer to Parcel. Because of the disturbances caused by the evil in their realm, the new Oracle found it difficult to get settled.

Cedric was another matter entirely with his talent for opening portals. The leaders weren't certain how many demons got through, but the ones that caused some mental turmoil among the trackers were being caught. Cedric vanished and some thought that he'd slipped through a portal of his own. The Guard leaders hoped the new Oracle would get evened out soon, and be able to help them. Trackers were on both sides of the portal trying to find the young Guard.

Kris experienced a vision that he'd been taken by one of the black demons, but hoped the vision was wrong. If Cedric fell into the grip of some evil, she wanted him found so it could be expelled from him and they could find out what he might know about the demons that ran amok in Parcel.

Roman came home every night exhausted. He'd eat dinner, play with Otter a little, and then crash land into bed, dead to the world. One night, he didn't come in until after midnight. He slid under the sheets and comforter, and snuggled close behind Kris.

"There you are," she said and rolled over to face him. "I was worried. Roman, your feet are freezing."

He gave her a kiss. "Sorry, babe. We searched pretty far today." He moved his feet away from her warm side of the bed.

"How far?"

"We were over on the Russian peninsula around Vladivostok. We checked several water- ways and a couple of lakes. It's frustrating. Wherever Cedric's hiding, he's doing a good job at covering his tracks." Roman brought his fingers up to her lips. "Tell me what my beautiful wife and son did today?"

"We finished painting the walls at the gallery. I think Otter would like to have participated more, but he had fun running around in his walker buggy."

"I wish I could have helped." His fingers made their way down her cheek.

"You're working hard enough, babe."

Roman took in a deep breath. "Speaking of, I've told the leadership that this is my last week in Parcel.

I'll Guard this side of the lake until Omar and Marcus find a third, but then that's it. It's messing with my family life too much and I don't want to miss Otter's first steps or first anything."

"Roman, have I mentioned that I love you more than anything else?" she asked.

"You may have, but I've been so tired I think I missed it. See? I'm not going to miss anymore," he whispered.

Roman finished out the week, slept in until eleven o'clock on Saturday morning and got up to announce that daddy day care was now open for business. While Kris sat at her computer and pounded out prospectives and advertisements for the gallery opening early next year, Roman kept Otter occupied. The boys played inside and outside.

One afternoon, after she'd responded to a multitude of emails, she realized there were no sounds coming from the living room. She looked out the door of her office and saw father and son crashed out on the couch. Otter lay on his dad's chest and they both looked as though they were having good dreams. Kris turned around and tiptoed back to the computer to do some more work.

In the last few weeks, she'd spent evenings working with Cassie on spells and conjuring. It amazed Kris how much information El passed on when she'd departed. There were a few things Kris needed to sort out, but she got ingredients and their uses down pat.

Lorrie stayed over in Sylvia and Fred's house for the winter. They decided to purchase the place down in Arizona and would be back in the spring to pack up the house. In the meantime, Lorrie made them an offer to buy it. All that needed to be done was sign on the dotted lines and it would be taken care of when Sylvia and Fred came back to Haller. Lorrie went to Moses Lake and found that her personal items from the apartment she'd rented before being taken by Rochelle, were put into storage. With Marcus's help, they got the back rent on the storage locker paid, loaded everything into a truck, and brought it over to their side of the mountains. Lorrie spent a day sifting through it to see what she what might be missing. She'd lost some furniture, books, kitchenware and her computer. She also found some clothes she didn't remember buying and a lamp she never would have bought. She'd have to start from scratch.

Cassie ragged on endlessly to Kris that she went too easy on Lorrie. The two never saw eye to eye, but tolerated each other as best they could. Cassie and Kris were painting the walls of the gallery when the topic came up again.

"You know, Kris, you're too nice. Your employee, and you know who I mean, is going to walk all over you," Cassie said from a ladder.

"Cass, my sweet friend, when you've been taken and possessed by a ghost in the same year, I'll be just as nice to you," Kris said and tried not to knock herself out with the wall primer.

"Ah, how nice." Cassie batted her eyelashes. "You'll have to start kissing butt soon. Hey, did I mention I started a new series?"

Kris shook her head. It shouldn't surprise her how fast Cassie could change subjects, but it always did. "That's great. I wondered when you were going to get off your butt and start working again." She smiled at

Cassie.

"Great, you're going to heap the abuse on me, just great," Cassie said with fake disgust.

"What's the focus?" Kris asked.

"Stuff from around the lake. In fact," she said and stepped down the ladder. "I was wondering if you and Roman would pose for me?"

Kris's mouth dropped open. "You want us as subjects? What's the catch?"

"Yes, you and Roman and maybe one of you and Otter, but there's no catch." Cassie smiled.

"Let me see what Roman says," Kris said. She wondered what Cassie had in mind.

"What Roman says? I thought you wore the pants in the family," she teased.

"Cassie, I've told you before, its panties, I wear the panties. Unlike your house, where I'm sure you're the boss," Kris teased back.

When Cassie explained to Roman and Kris what she wanted to paint and the word nude entered the conversation, Kris said no way. Roman mentioned that they'd talk about it and get back to Cassie with a decision. Kris expressed herself in the negative and if he thought they were posing naked in front of Cassie with him wrapped around her and not getting turned on...she asked him what pill he'd taken that day. Roman liked the idea of the painting, but wanted to buy it for himself and put it up in Kris's office in the house. She explained the difference between commissioning a painting and just buying it. Cassie would charge big bucks for a private sitting. Roman thought Cass would do it with taste and liked the idea of one of Kris and Otter.

For the time, Cassie worked on another piece and Roman and Kris continued to discuss it. If Kris got her way, though, the only one she'd sit naked for was Roman.

Chapter Thirty-One

As Kris started to go cross-eyed looking at her computer screen, she felt warm strong hands massage her shoulders.

She leaned her head back and looked up at her gorgeous husband. "Hey, babe."

He leaned over and upside down, kissed her lips. "Hello there, wife."

"The last time I looked, you and the wee one were sawing logs on the couch," she said and shut off the computer.

"Otter's still out." He leaned over her farther, and ran his hands around her breasts. "I had the most erotic dream."

Kris reached up, found his neck and patted him. "Tell me about it."

"I'd rather show you." He started to pull her sweater up.

"Does it take place in here or the bedroom or...." Kris could feel pressure and warmth start to awaken in her pelvis.

"No, in the bathroom." His hand moved under her shirt, and then he pulled her up and kicked the chair out of the way. "We don't have to go in there." His arms wound around her. She could feel him press his wonderful erection against her backside. "Trust me?" he asked and shimmied his hips from side to side.

"One hundred percent," Kris whispered and felt his

hand cup her crotch.

He slid her sweater over her head, and dropped it on the floor. Carefully unhooking her bra, he took it off and threw it on top of the sweater. His hand covered her breast, massaging it firmly, the way he knew she liked. She pressed her bottom against him. Kris tried to turn and heard him say, "No", and growled. He picked her up from behind and they moved to a wall by the door. He pushed her face first into the wallpaper and pressed against her.

This position seemed unusual and they'd never tried it, Kris thought. Roman usually preferred face to face.

"Take your pants off and do not turn around," he whispered and backed up to let her lower her slacks and panties.

She heard him unzip his own pants and he took them off. He pressed her against the wall, grabbed her wrists and moved them up over her head. She could feel his erection, hard as a stick, moving around her bottom.

Suddenly, she realized she moved up the wall and her breath caught. Something wasn't right.

"Roman?" Kris opened her eyes and tried to see his face over her shoulder. She heard deep laughter as something bit into her shoulder.

"Shut up, woman. I'm going to fuck you and you'll scream for mercy, of which, I can guarantee you, I have none. Now spread your legs," a voice ordered.

Kris could feel her legs move apart and something hot and searing started to burn its way into her.

She shot out of her chair so fast that she knocked the computer keyboard off the desk, caught her foot on the chair, and crashed to her knees on the floor. She lay on her stomach, breathing hard, and knew she'd just experienced a nightmare, but couldn't grasp anything. She felt a hand on her shoulder and started to scream. She rolled over and kicked and punched as hard as possible.

Roman somehow got her wrists in his grasp and pulled them behind her back. "Babe, what's happening? Come back to me," he said into her ear.

Kris leaned her head on his chest, and gasped for air. He let go of her wrists and pulled her to him. She buried her face in his shirt, smelled his scent and let out a breath.

"Holy shit, that was weird," she mumbled.

"Babe, what happened?"

She heard Roman's voice, but leaned back to look at him. She let out a sigh, and put her fingers on his lip, which bled. "I just had the weirdest dream." She moved out of his arms, leaned up to the desk and pulled down a tissue box. "Let's get your lip to stop bleeding," she said.

He took a tissue, pressed it to his mouth and looked at her.

"I guess I fell asleep at the desk. I dreamt you came in and said you'd had an erotic dream and you wanted to show me what it was about. At some point, I realized it wasn't you..." Her voice faded and she put her head down in her hands. "It seemed so real," she added and shook. She looked back up at Roman. "Where's Otter?"

"He's in his crib, still sleeping. I wore him out today." Roman looked at the tissue. His lip stopped bleeding.

"Please don't have me arrested for spousal abuse," she continued.

"You've only ever hit me twice and I'm well aware you weren't in your right mind when it happened. No abuse, babe." He pulled her back to his chest.

"Roman, when you were crashed out on the couch, did you have any kind of a dream?" she asked and looked at him again.

"Not that I can remember. What exactly did this person do?" He ran his hand through her hair.

"I was at the desk. He leaned over me and sounded just like you. He even looked like you." She sucked in her breath and looked at the desk. "I am such an idiot. I should have known something was wrong when he carefully took off my bra without wrecking it. You do that once-in-a-while, but only when I want to save the bra." She looked at him and saw a frown on his lips. His eyes were focused on her shoulder. "What is the possibility that it was real?"

Roman's eyes came up to hers and he sat up straight. "I suppose it's possible you were pulled into an alternate realm." He put his hand on her shoulder and touched the mark. "Kris, how far did this go?"

Turning her head to try and see her shoulder, she said, "He took off my bra, pushed my face to the wall and that's when I started to fight." She'd never withhold information from Roman, but felt she didn't tell the whole story and didn't want him to think she'd turned into a slut. She knew by the mark on her shoulder that it hadn't been a dream. There were red marks that looked like teeth on her skin and her sweater sat in a pile next to her.

"This alternate reality crap is getting old, Roman. If that is what happened and it was more than a nightmare, I've got to learn how to block myself so it doesn't keep happening. It's starting to drive me bats," she said.

"Me, too. Let me call Father Rupert and see if he can give us some help." Roman stood up, and held out his hands to help her. He leaned over to retrieve her bra and sweater and handed them to her. She wobbled a little when she put on the sweater, which caused him to put his arm around her and help her stand steady.

"Roman," she said and bit her lip. "I can't lie to you, whoever it was said he would fuck me and I'd scream for mercy." Her lip quivered as she started to choke up. "I thought it was you... I..."

He pulled her tighter into his arms. "Babe, what's upsetting you?"

"I don't want you to think I'm asking for this stuff to happen. I only want you, period, end of subject. You know that, right?"

"I know, my love. I'll never think you're asking for this, know that." He put his hand on her cheek. "You've given me two of the greatest gifts I could ever hope for and you're mine."

"What two gifts?" Kris grabbed a tissue from the desk to dry her eyes.

"Your love." He wiped a tear with his thumb. "And my beautiful son."

"I do love you." She kissed his thumb. "I hope I can give you more gifts down the road."

He pressed his lips together and looked at the ceiling. "Let me think, anything in the shower is a gift." He scrunched his nose. "We've only made love outside, in a forest once. We should do that again." He smiled down at her and arched his brow.

"I'm going to have to work on that one since

winter's coming on," she said and wrapped her arms around him. "I'm going to check on Otter. You call Father Rupert." She started to move away and stopped. "Babe, can we freshen up the protection spell?" She tilted her head and looked toward the living room. "Something's lurking around out there. I can sense it."

****

That evening, when Omar and Marcus came in from the lake, they joined Kris and Roman to reinforce the protection spells around the three houses. Once they'd finished, Kris spread another spell over the lake.

Roman beamed, he felt so proud of Kris. Her pronunciation of the Latin spells was spot on and he could feel the electric current radiate from her soul. He watched her aura and it amazed him how far she'd come with the magick's.

They stood around the lake and talked with the others for a short time, then went back into the house to relieve Lorrie who'd watched Otter.

Lorrie made it clear to Kris that she wanted nothing or little to do with magicks. She would work at the gallery and watch Otter, but didn't want to participate in anything else. Her relations with Marcus were good, but she felt scared and didn't trust herself not to be turned again. Lorrie said that she thought the Guard leadership and the new Oracle would say *third strike, you're out* if she got taken once more and tell Marcus he couldn't see her anymore. When potions were mixed or spells were being cast, she excused herself and looked the other way.

****

That night, Guillermo, the "something" Kris had sensed, lurked around the lake. He watched the spell casting with interest. Earlier in the day, he found his way into Kris's reality and enjoyed tormenting her a bit. She smelled and tasted very good and he could still feel her breasts in his claw-like hands.

He wanted to slip back into the house, but they'd beaten him with the spell and he smirked to himself. It was fine. He could wait and watch for an opportune time.

The new one, Cedric, whose capability of opening portals, still mastered his abilities, but managed to somehow stay out of this demon's reach. Guillermo felt shocked when he arrived at the precious Haller Lake. Even from the other side of the lake, he'd been drawn to this woman's power. The magick's glowed within her and he developed a huge desire to possess it. He would find a way to take her to his realm and she would be his, body and soul and he might keep her for a time.

Guillermo was the seventh son of a long line of tormenting demons. Some of his brethren would only tease, but he worked with no such methods. He desired nothing less than screaming and terror or pain. He watched the woman walk into the house with the Lakeman. He almost got her today, but she'd alerted herself to his presence, which almost never occurred. There would be another day. The anticipation made him hard and he could feel the seed within him burn for release.

Guillermo could sense another being lurking around in the darkness. He'd seen the bright red eyes that could see in any light or dark.

****

The other sat hunched in the bushes and watched Guillermo. He, too, smirked, and thought the idiot demon believed himself so sneaky that no one would notice him. What an idiot this demon was. They'd had several run-in's over the years and it never turned out pleasant. So far, they were tied two to two. This being was of the Vitterfolk who'd battled demons for a million years or more. It seemed the fights took more out of him as the time went by. He watched the demon lurk around, and waited. If he beat the demon this time, he would return to Sweden and rest for a very long time.

Chapter Thirty-Two

The next morning, getting up felt very nice. Otter slept in late, and gave Roman and Kris time to explore one another's bodies, have a nice hot shower, and breakfast with the best coffee. All of this meant that Kris wasn't running out the door to go to the gallery or they weren't getting ready to fight some evil weird thing. They sat at the kitchen table and stared sappily at one another. She with her feet in his lap, and he massaging said feet with his strong, warm hands.

Roman turned a little in his chair and maneuvered her foot under his bathrobe onto his penis.

"Oh, Mr. Lake, what big teeth you have," she said and batted her eyelashes.

He grinned and turned her chair to face him. Then he pulled her foot out of his robe, put it onto the floor and parted her knees. Sliding himself down between them, he ran his hands up her thighs to her hips.

"All the better to eat you with, my darling Mrs. Lake," he said deep in his chest and opened her robe. He kissed her breasts, stomach, and thighs, nipping and licking the soft skin and he heard Kris sigh.

And then he heard a squeal come from the nursery. Otter was awake and they needed to stop their play time.

Roman looked up at her and raised his eyebrows. "I'll get the bottle ready, Mrs. Lake."

Leaning over to kiss him, Kris hugged his neck.

"Thank you, Mr. Lake."

He helped her stand and she made her way to their son.

Just as she was finishing the diaper change, Roman walked in with the bottle. Otter had advanced to the stage of holding himself up in a sitting position and held the bottle himself, a step he shouldn't have reached yet, at five months old. He'd grown very well and seemed to be ahead of the normal curve. When the doctor shared how amazed she was by his progress, Kris only smiled. She knew her son was brilliant.

Roman picked him up and gave him the bottle. The baby sat with his back to Roman's chest, and his feet hanging over his dad's arms. This seemed to be Otter's favorite position. He liked being able to watch things going on around the house. His coordination with the bottle wasn't great, but it would come together.

Kris looked at the clock and he realized she'd lost some time.

"Oh, my darlings, I've got to get moving." She wrapped her arms around them.

Roman kissed her over Otter's head and she snuggled Otter, snorted in his ear, and saw him grin around the bottle.

****

When she arrived at the gallery, Lorrie had opened all the doors and windows and tried to air the place out. Rug cleaners and floor polishers worked the last two days and the place smelled of cleaning fluids.

Kris found Lorrie in the room they called her office. She looked through the computer at accounting forms wearing her coat. She held a cup of coffee in her hands. Kris waved and said good morning as she went to the room they'd designated as her office. She closed the window half way and felt glad she'd worn a wool sweater.

"Kris, Kris, Kris," Lorrie said coming down the hall. "I think I have good news. Ready?"

"Yep, hit me with it." She sat behind her desk.

"Okay, the floors, painting, window washing, etcetera has finished, finally. We can start moving furniture around, getting the stands up and all that. The company that does coffee carts called with a lower offer," she said and flipped through her notes.

"I'd still rather rent out the space on the west corner and let someone else schlep the coffee. If we have a stand and happen to get no customers in, well, you do get my point? Plus I'd rather not have to deal with the licensing and health standards." Kris leaned forward.

"Gotcha. I'll tell them that the final answer is no." She raised her blonde eyebrows, moved her hair behind an ear and smiled. "Drum roll please. Now I have the really good news. Howard Salt." She tilted her head to the side.

"Yes, the artist from San Francisco—"

"—Has agreed to some of his works being shown here for the opening in January," Lorrie finished cheerfully.

"Hey, that is good news." Kris clapped for Lorrie as she bowed.

"Thank you, thank you. He's going to send an email with some photos. You choose what you want to show and he'll ship them up. If we sell any... are you ready for this?" Lorrie looked at her. "Thirty-five percent goes to the gallery."

Kris's mouth dropped. "Wow, I mean wow, that's really...don't let Cassie know that. She'll have a fit and think I'm going to demand the same rate from her. I've got a couple of prospects coming in this week. The list grows, this is good," she said.

They went down the stairs to the main floor and checked the wood and carpets, which looked excellent.

"Roman's coming down tomorrow to start putting up shelving and the wall units for hanging," Kris said and examined the floor. She turned to head back upstairs, but noticed someone stood by the open front door. He looked to be one of the chubbiest kids she'd ever seen. She moved toward him.

"Can I help you?" she asked.

She heard a sigh and a deep male voice said, "You should be very careful who you let in your doors, Mrs. Lake." He looked up at the ceiling with red eyes.

Kris realized it wasn't a child at all, but a very small adult, maybe only three foot five. His head seemed too large for his body and he had a huge nose. His blondish-gray hair stuck out in disarray.

Kris followed his line of vision to the ceiling and saw a wisp of black smoke dance up on the plaster. She pushed Lorrie behind her and brought up the protective shield to cover them both.

The small man came into the gallery and watched the smoke above him. "It's a lesser demon, Mrs. Lake. No need to worry. They are annoying, like mosquitoes." He took something out of his pocket and flashed it up. It held the smoke in place. After coaxing a little, the smoke moved to the object in his hand, which turned out to be a mirror, less than three by five, and went right into it. The little man put the mirror back into his pocket. "You should have your man put a spell here. There is too much evil out beyond the doors." He seemed to smile.

Kris brought the shield down. "What is your name, sir?"

When she called him sir, he seemed to stand taller. "I am called Gaspar Vitterfolk, Mrs. Lake."

"Do you know my husband? Have you met Roman?" she continued.

"Yes, yes... husband, that is the word. Yes, we met. Many years ago we fought an evil together. The demon Abednego, who was a lesser, but managed to cause much, much trouble," the small man said.

"Mr. Vitterfolk, thank you for your help. Have you been to Haller Lake recently?"

"Yes, I have been watching. There is another evil watching, too. He is called Guillermo. He is old, very old and very mean. Warn your man. Tell him the little man held his hands together and looked at me with hope."

"Mr. Vitterfolk, who is the little man you are talking about?"

"No, no, you must call me Gaspar, please," he interrupted.

"Gaspar, I will tell my husband, but who is the little man?" Kris asked again.

"Your husband will know what I'm saying."

"Well." Kris felt a little stumped. "He might want to speak with you and ask some questions. Does he know how to find you?"

Gaspar got a blank look on his face, then said, "Oh yes, I understand questions. I will find him." He nodded and turned toward the door. "Remember, Mrs. Lake, need spells here to protect you. Be sure to remember." He waved his stubby fingers and went out the door.

Kris and Lorrie watched as he disappeared from the sidewalk outside.

"Oh, my God," Lorrie whispered.

Kris pulled her cell phone out of a pocket and hit the speed dial. "Hey, babe, we just had a very interesting visitor. He was a really short dwarf, named Gaspar Vitterfolk. Do you remember him?"

Roman went silent for a moment. "You have got to be kidding me. Yeah, I remember him. He's a troll though, not a dwarf. Oh wow, I didn't know he still lived. Is he still there?"

"No, he removed a lesser demon and left. He said he'd find you." She looked at Lorrie, and said "Troll," and rolled her eyes.

"He's one of the good guys, babe," Roman said.

Lorrie's mouth hung open and Kris heard her mumble "They're real?" under her breath.

"Gaspar says we need a protection spell here. Apparently, there's a lot of bad out on the street," Kris said into her phone.

"What?"

"He did some strange thing with a mirror. The demon went in and didn't return. How can we do the spell?" she asked. "He also said to tell you, 'the little man held his hands together and looked at me with hope.' Do you understand what he's talking about?"

"I'll get everyone together and we'll head your way," he answered. "And, yes, I understand his meaning. I'll explain it to you later."

"Babe, isn't he small for a troll? I thought they

were supposed to be giants?" Kris asked and tried to remember the folklore she'd read.

She heard Roman chuckle. "Gaspar used to joke that he was the runt of the litter. I believe they come in all sizes, babe."

They wrapped up the phone call. She and Lorrie closed windows around the building to keep the black demons out as best they could. They looked around and didn't sense any others. Kris dug a cleansing spell out of the multitude of files stored in her brain that were passed down by her alter-ego, El. Lorrie ran out to a convenience store to buy votive candles and together they did the cleansing spell. Lorrie grumped that she shouldn't be participating, but helped out anyway.

At one point, another wisp of black whizzed past them up through the ceiling. Kris could see a crack up there that would have to be patched.

By the time they finished, the others arrived. Roman walked in with Otter in a backpack-style carrier. Omar and Marcus were in a big hurry, as they needed to get back to the lake. They did the protection spell. Cassie drove the boys back home and Lorrie got into her car to follow them. Roman stayed with Kris in the gallery.

He'd brought some cast iron pots and baggies of sage and lavender. They arranged those around the building and let them burn. The scent covered the acrid smell of carpet cleaner.

Roman also went up onto the roof, found the crack and filled it with tar. When he came back down, he said he hadn't realized the roof needed some work. He would call a roofer and get them there pronto.

Otter was in heaven in the backpack and got to

accompany Roman all over the place. He watched over his father's shoulder and it amazed Kris how he concentrated on the things going on around him.

By the time they'd finished, the sun started to go down. Kris accomplished half of what she'd planned for the day, but it would work out all right. They went around the building and checked the pots. It would be really bad karma to burn the building down.

They met back in the middle of the main floor. Kris held her bag and coat. Roman carried the diaper bag. Otter conked out in the pack and his head rested on his father's neck.

Roman pulled her into a hug. "Hello, beautiful lady. We've been way too serious today, don't you agree?" He kissed her cheek.

She looked up at him. "Yes, I do agree. In fact, I'm a little upset with you. You haven't patted my behind once this afternoon." She reached around to his rear end and held his cheeks firmly.

"See, I knew there was something I'd forgotten to do. I think I had one of those momentary blank spots. It's caused by the sun, you know. Please forgive me." He leaned over and kissed her. His tongue tasting of his usual cinnamon, caused her to warm up.

"Babe, let's head home, have a good dinner, get Otter to bed, and then screw each other's lights out. We haven't done an all-nighter for awhile," she said.

"Is my wife horny?" He smiled and brushed her lips with his finger.

"Let's put it this way, if horny is hot and steamy, a volcano has nothing on me. I'm burning up south of the equator." She smiled up at him.

Roman laughed. "We'd better get you home, then."

Chapter Thirty-Three

On the drive home, rain poured down. Roman drove carefully and watched out for other vehicles splashing and going too fast. They talked about the day's events. He slowed the car for a red light.

"Your friend Gaspar said we were being watched by a baddie named Guillermo. Who's he?" Kris asked.

Roman glanced at her and his brows came together. "He said Guillermo? Really?"

"Where would I come up with that name? What are we up against? Is he very bad?" She watched him.

"I know you're not making up the name. He's very bad. We may need to head back up to Father Rupert's for an extended stay," he said. Roman looked at the intersection as the light turned green and a car sped through the opposing red light. He put his foot on the gas and started the car forward.

"Extended stay? No, no, babe. I'm not going to run. I also have work to get done for the opening. Time moves too quick." She looked at him again.

Roman smiled. "Let's discuss this later, Kris. We need to get home, I'm starving." He maneuvered the car into the center lane.

Kris looked out the side window at the dark night. She watched as rain streaked off the front window, slid around and streamed across the side windows. As they moved, the lights glistened in the drops, and changed colors and textures. Kris stared, and realized she was being pulled mentally. Something tugged at her brain. She'd either have to fight it or accept it and let it in. Before she could decide, she was pulled into the vision.

She stood by the lake or what used to be the lake. The water level looked low and fish and ducks lay in the mud, dead and rotting. The smell of decay wafted around her. The trees were flattened and the homes looked old and decrepit. She turned her vision towards what used to be her house and saw someone standing on the deck.

As she pulled herself closer, she saw Roman frown at the lake. His face showed deep wrinkle lines around his eyes and gray peppered his beautiful brown hair. It hung down past his shoulders and he held a glass in his hand. If Kris didn't know better, she'd say he was drinking.

As if on cue, a brown-haired young man came out the back door. He walked up to Roman.

"Dad, isn't it a bit early to be into the bourbon?" the boy asked.

The look on Roman's face shocked Kris. He'd become instantly angry and snarled at the boy, who was Otter. Roman turned from the boy, and told him to shut up.

He stomped into the house and Otter followed. "Dad, you've been wallowing for too long. Get over it already. We need your help," her son pleaded.

Closing her eyes, she felt herself move and found that she stood in her kitchen. The cabinet doors were falling off or pulled away. The floor, her wonderful linoleum, looked black and trash lay all over it.

Roman went to the sink, and refilled his glass from a large bottle. Otter walked up behind him.

"Dad, Mom left us both, we need to move on," Otter said and sounded like the father.

Roman swung around and hit their son in the face. Otter's lip started to bleed. Kris felt as if she'd been the one hit and brought her hands up to her face.

"Shut up, Elliott. Your mother turned out to be a bitch. One we never should have trusted. It was my own stupidity that allowed me to be sucked into her game and I'll be paying for it and reliving it for the rest of my life," Roman growled and pointed a finger at his son's chest. "Don't ever mention her to me again." He stormed out of the kitchen.

Kris felt herself choke up. What happened? Why were her boys fighting each other? What did she do?

Again, as if on cue, the scene shifted. She found herself in a very dark, plush bedroom. Someone sat at a round table.

A woman with long, white hair, wearing a black silk robe, sat with her back to Kris. She couldn't see who the woman was and shifted a little to the left of the woman and looked into a mirror to catch the woman's reflection. It was her, Kris, sitting at the table. Her eyes were black and her hair whiter than salt.

She looked at a set of tarot cards. Her nails were long and painted ruby red to match the red on her lips. She concentrated very hard on the cards.

Kris felt shocked again and looked around the room. A huge bed sat against one wall, with a brilliant red comforter and black silk sheets. Pillows were scattered about the mattress and floor. She saw something flash on the headboard and realized she saw handcuffs.

The carpeting looked black and seemed to move.

This is not good, she thought and tried to remove herself from the scene.

She heard a door open and looked to her right. A man, about six foot four with long black hair and black eyes, came into the room. He wore black silk leisure slacks and carried a glass of something red.

He walked to the back of the woman's chair, and leaned over to watch her turn the cards. Kris watched them in the mirror, and her horror grew.

The man's black hair fell over the woman's shoulder. The Kris at the table put her hand into it. The strands wrapped around her fingers and wrist of its own volition, but she never took her eyes off the cards.

"What do you see?" the man asked, leaned into her neck and licked her shoulder.

"Our strength continues to grow. It's only a matter of time. The other realm will be ours soon, lover..., very soon." Kris heard her own voice coming from the woman.

"The brat who was your child is continuing to cause trouble," the man said.

Kris saw the woman's eyes flash and she yanked the man's hair. "Nothing must be allowed to stand in our way, Gee. Kill him." The woman looked at the man through the mirror.

The man reached down, cupped the woman's breast and pinched her nipple. "As you wish, my harlot. Come back to bed, I'm growing hard for you." He pulled the robe open and massaged the woman's breast.

She smiled at him. "I can feel it pressing against my neck." She moved her head against the man's crotch. "I think I'd rather swallow you whole this evening, Gee." The woman stood up and let her robe slip off her shoulders. She got on her knees in front of the man and looked up at him with a sinister smile.

Kris thought she knew what would happen and closed her eyes. She tried to will herself back to her own realm. She tried a chant, but knew it wasn't working. Her eyes opened and what she saw caused bile to flame in her stomach. She felt it crawl up the back of her throat.

Suddenly, she'd returned to the car and looked out the window. Roman shouted at her with his hand on her arm. She realized the top of her sweater was soaked and tears ran down her cheeks like the rain on the car windows.

She looked at Roman. "Stop the car," she whispered.

"What? Babe, I can't hear you," he said.

"Stop the car!" she shouted and pulled at the seatbelt, wanting it off.

A gas station sat lit up ahead and Roman pulled the car into the driveway and stopped. Kris's door flew open and she jumped out. Running to a garbage cylinder that sat on the island with the gas pumps, she started to throw up and spent several minutes with the dry heaves. The kid who worked the station came out the door and wanted to know if they needed any help. Roman waved him off, and said she might have food poisoning.

Kris held onto both sides of the metal canister. She felt Roman's hand on her back. He helped her straighten and handed her a couple of paper towels.

Wiping her mouth, she looked up at him. Tears continued running from her eyes and she thought, *Sweet Jesus, please let this one be wrong.*

Roman put his arms around her and she leaned onto his chest. She tried to control the sobs.

"Babe, what happened?" he asked.

"Vision...really bad," she sobbed and held onto him tight.

"Come on, let's get home and warm. We'll talk about it then," Roman said and turned her to the car.

Kris looked across the street over the roof of the car. Standing in a circle of light from a streetlamp, was a man. It wasn't easy to see his face because the rain came down so hard, but she knew who it was. His hair looked black hair and he grinned at her. His hand moved down over his crotch as though he waited for her.

Chapter Thirty-Four

Kris and Roman moved Otter's crib into their room for the night. They didn't want him out of their sight. Roman knew they would move Otter to sleep between them later.

Kris didn't eat much dinner and stared at her food. Putting her fork down, she excused herself and went into the bedroom. He heard her throw up again.

Roman got the kitchen cleaned up and put the dishes into the washer. When he finished, he saw that Otter had fallen asleep in his highchair. Roman got him up into his arms and went into the nursery to ready the youngster for bed.

He worried like crazy about Kris. The vision she'd experienced knocked the wind out of her completely. From past experience, he knew she'd tell him what happened when she could wrap her head around it. He knew better than to push.

Roman brought Otter into the bedroom, and put him into the crib. He saw Kris lying on her side. He put a blanket over Otter and tucked it around him. He then turned out the lights and stripped off his clothes.

Crawling under the sheets, he moved to her back and put his arm around her. She moved back and pressed against his chest. She shook.

"I love you, Roman. Nothing will ever change the way I feel for you," she said, her voice trembling.

"Babe, I love you too, heart and soul." He tightened his grip around her.

"What time is it?" she asked.

"Just after nine o'clock. Are you ready to tell me about the vision?"

She pulled out of his arms and got out of bed. Starting to redress, she slipped on jeans and a sweatshirt. Roman sat up and watched her.

"Kris, what's going on?"

"I have to go talk to Cassie. I'll be back in a few minutes." She put on a pair of loafers and headed out of the house.

Roman heard the back door close and fell back onto the bed.

****

Kris ran across the lawn, jumped a hedge, and took the stairs up to Cassie's deck two at a time. She pounded on the back door several times before a light came on. Omar opened the door buck naked and yawning.

"Kris, hey," he said, as she pushed her way in. "What's wrong?"

"Omar, where's Cassie?"

"Asleep."

"I've got to talk to her." Kris started to move toward the bedroom.

Omar grabbed her arm. "Wait a minute, she's asleep," he said.

"Dude, bite me. I need to talk to her," she hissed back and tried to release his tight fist.

"Hey, love of my life, let her go. It's okay," Cassie said, walked out of the bedroom and slipped on a robe. She walked up to Omar and patted his arm. "Why don't you go see if Marcus needs any help with the watch?"

Omar's brows creased as he let go of Kris. "Fine,

but I won't be long." He kissed Cassie and stomped out the back door.

Cassie smiled. "Men, go figure. Want something to drink?"

"No, let's sit. I need help."

Kris told Cassie about the vision, started to cry again and reminded her about the Oracle sending her to another realm to experience what her life would have turned into if she hadn't drank the wine. In the other place she'd slept with another man. Kris told her about the weird dream and how after the vision she'd seen the man called Guillermo standing by the road.

"Let me make sure I have this right," Cassie said. "You were turned, Roman went bitter, and you were with the demon Guillermo? And you saw him along the road on your way home from the gallery?" Kris nodded. "You said Otter was a teenager, right?"

"Right."

"Okay, so it's way ahead in the future and subject to change. We know the visions are subjective, right?" Kris nodded again. "You said this Guillermo showed up in the dream sequence where you thought he was Roman?"

"Yeah, it was really creepy, too, and I bloodied Roman's lip coming out of it." Kris pulled a napkin out of the holder on the table, and blew her nose.

"You know, I'm wondering," Cassie said half to herself. "You haven't told Roman any of the vision stuff, right? The dream was before the protection spells were put up."

"Roman knows about the dream. The vision was between here and the gallery, and there's no protection spells on the car. Is it possible Guillermo...." Kris's voice faded. She looked at Cassie. "Damn it, I'm such an idiot."

"What are you thinking?" Cassie asked.

"He's playing with me, teasing. I should have realized." Kris stood up.

"Shoulda, woulda, coulda. You can't know everything, particularly what demons are going to do." Cassie rose from her chair. "What's the next step?"

Kris started to answer, but the back door opened. Omar and Roman walked in, both looked anxious and pissed at the same time.

"Good timing, guys." She walked up to Roman who hadn't dressed and put her arm around his waist. "Who's watching Otter?"

"Lorrie." He looked down at her. "Kris—"

Putting her fingers over his lips, Kris shushed him. "I knew talking to Cassie would help." She saw Roman frown. "I needed a woman's point of view, babe." She looked at Cassie and Omar. "Guillermo is trying to puppet master me. He did it with the dream and again with the vision. He's trying to make us not trust one another and it almost worked."

"You didn't trust me?" Roman sounded hurt.

"No, no, Roman, no. Don't ever think that I don't trust you. I just needed Cassie because of her female levelheadedness. You know how I like to panic sometimes," she said and looked into his eyes. "I trust you one-hundred percent, babe."

"Did it work?" he asked, and looked at Cassie across the room. She stood with Omar behind her. His arm wound around her stomach and she patted it with a grin.

"Yeah it did," Kris smiled at Cass. "Girl power

rocks my boat. Why don't we sit down and I'll explain."

Roman sat at the table and pulled Kris onto his lap. Cassie sat across from them with Omar next to her. Kris explained the vision to the men. She did edit some of it, and didn't tell Roman he'd hit Otter and nothing about the sex. She wanted to abolish Guillermo for that alone. She felt afraid that if Roman knew, he'd begin to hunt the demon. Kris did choke up again and tried to hold it back. She felt so tired of crying.

"It seems the protection spells are holding for now. It's when I'm outside the zone, that he can get at me. Although now I'm very aware of what he's up to, I don't think it will be so easy for him to fool me. One thing I don't understand is, why it makes me so sick at my stomach. I mean I know he's a demon, but why?"

"The disruption of realms could cause it. You know, it messes with your balance," Omar said. "Did you smell sulfur or anything rotting?"

"The rotting animals and fish by the lake, but nothing else that I can remember," Kris answered.

"Kris, is there any possibility you might be pregnant?" Cassie asked.

She thought about the calendar a little and tried to remember her last cycle. She looked at Roman who watched her. "I'm not certain, Cass. I can't remember," she said and didn't take her eyes off him.

"Cassie, I think you should pack a bag. We'll need to get you, Kris, and Lorrie to holy ground to be sure you're protected," Roman said.

"I'll let Marcus know to prepare Lorrie," Omar said.

"Thank you." Roman began to stand up while

holding Kris. "Cass, don't leave the house anytime during the night. We'll head to Father Rupert's in the morning." He walked to the back door with Kris in his arms. "Hold tight, babe. I'm going to run us home."

Kris put her head down, and closed her eyes as Roman moved back to their house. He'd taken her clothes off and got her back in bed before she could blink. Roman lay next to her with his hand on her stomach. He kissed her belly several times.

"Roman, if you'd let me get up and check the calendar, we'd know for sure." She ran her hand through his hair.

He looked up at her and smiled. "I'm sure."

"Dr. Roman Lake, OB-GYN?" She raised her eyebrows.

"Roman Lake, who is a knower of all things wifely. Do you want a boy or a girl?" He put his lips against her skin and rasberried her stomach, which caused her to laugh.

They needed to quiet down with Otter in the room and managed not to wake him.

"Kris?" he said, and propped up on his elbow.

"Yes, Roman."

"We never really have talked about how many children we want. Have you given it much thought?"

"I haven't really thought about the number much. Otter keeps us busy, but I would like a little girl maybe." She smiled and touched his lips.

"How about a baby who is as beautiful as her mother with reddish-blonde hair and blue eyes?" Roman kissed her chest, and moved up to her lips.

"With her father's brown eyes, thank you very much." She kissed and nibbled his lips.

"What would you want to name her?" he whispered.

"Would you mind Elzabeth?" she asked.

"Elzabeth Lake? I think I like it. We could make her middle name Krista or Kristiana." His lips found her ear.

"Or just Kris," she said and could feel the warmth of his body pressed into her side. He grew hard and firm. "Roman." She sighed.

"I know we agreed never to make love with Otter in the room," he whispered and licked her chin.

Kris rolled on her side, and put a leg over him. She found his erection and gently laced her fingers around it. "There's no negotiating around that one either. What do you propose?"

As her fingers moved, Roman caught his breath. "Damn, you have incredible hands." He caught his breath again. "What if you were to straddle my hips and lay on top of me? If we hold the position and move very little, then use the merge spot to other realm us, we'd climax here, but...." He opened his eyes as she moved to straddle him. "I take this to mean you like the idea?"

"Very much. I told you earlier today, my furnace is on high." She impaled herself on his erection, and pushed it all the way in. She leaned over him and held up her merge hand.

Roman slid his into hers and their souls connected. They were out on the back lawn in each other's arms.

Kris lifted her head and found Roman's eyes smiled at her. She sat up, lifted her hips and eased back down. It caused Roman to move his hand to her other hip and hold on while he began to pump.

"Hey, look, my love. We're making love out in

nature again." He smiled.

This was the first time they'd ever done anything like this. They hoped it would keep them from scarring their son for life.

The merge spot shined and, as many times before, increased the intensity. When Kris leaned back, and felt her orgasm approach, she saw colors and lights float around her and Roman. It seemed to last longer than ever and they lay together like that the rest of the night, refusing to let each other go.

Chapter Thirty-Five

Roman woke up first in the morning. He heard something or someone pound on the back door. Kris said she heard it, too, and they both got up. She grabbed her robe, and put it on as they walked out to the kitchen. He motioned for her to stay in the bedroom with Otter. She stood in the doorway and watched as Roman went to the door. When he looked out of the blinds, he swore under his breath.

He opened the door and could see Marcus standing on the deck. Roman moved forward and Marcus bent at the waist and bled from his nose and lip.

"Roman, Guillermo cornered me," Marcus said, out of breath.

"Come in, Marcus. Let's get you patched up." Roman held out his hand.

"No, brother, we must go and face him." Marcus straightened a little. He pointed toward the master bedroom side of the house. "There, he is there. We must go."

"Roman, don't walk out that door. This isn't Marcus," Kris said and came up behind him.

He could see that the being, who stood on their deck, didn't have an aura, which meant it wasn't alive. A deep growl and hiss came from the demon. It looked like Marcus, but it wasn't him. The eyes were black.

"Kris, what are you saying? Of course, it's me," it said and smirked at her.

"If it were really Marcus, he'd come in. He can't get past the protection spell," Kris said, as Roman moved back and stood half in front of her.

The demon changed and shifted into its true form. He was tall, slightly taller than Roman, with long black hair and black eyes. He wore black leather pants and a bright red silk shirt.

"You're very good, Mrs. Lake. Can't get anything by you, can I?" When she didn't reply, he smirked again. "Cat got your tongue?"

"You haven't said anything that I feel is necessary to reply to, demon." Kris smirked back.

"This measly protection spell won't hold forever. You'll have to face me very soon."

"It's holding fine, demon. What do you want?" Roman snarled and crossed his arms over his chest.

"Lakeman, why don't you stand aside and let me gaze at the beautiful woman behind you. She will soon be mine." He grinned.

"Roman, shut the door. It's not worth it." Kris touched his arm.

"Yes, Roman, close the door. Then ask the little harlot why she hasn't told you the whole story. Ask her why she's withholding information," Guillermo said with laughter in his voice.

****

Kris felt her stomach twist. She thought to herself, *What goes around comes around* and knew she should have told Roman everything from the vision.

Roman closed the door and stared at the knob. "What is he talking about?"

"He's a demon, he'll say anything to come between us," she said and turned toward the bedroom. "He's playing with us, just like last night. He wants us not to trust one another." She went in and looked at the crib. Otter still slept. Kris took off her robe and began to dress.

Roman stood in the doorway and watched her put on her clothes. "Kris, you know I hate it when your aura goes dark pink," he said.

Once dressed, Kris pushed past Roman and returned to the kitchen. She loaded the coffee maker with grounds and water. She snapped the lid onto the canister and held it. "Roman, you're staring at me and it's making me nervous." She put the coffee back into the refrigerator.

Roman cornered her between the cooler and the closet door. "What was the demon talking about?" he asked.

Kris felt herself squirm. She closed her eyes, held her breath and didn't want to tell him everything from the vision. They'd had a moment like this a year ago when she hadn't told him all the details of a vision she'd witnessed. They'd gotten into their first argument and she'd called him names and accused him of trying to intimidate her. She'd almost sent him back to Parcel and didn't want to fight with him about this.

When she opened her eyes, he watched her and still blocked her way. She couldn't stand being cornered. It tended to make her very angry. "Roman, it's not important. The visions are subjective, remember?" She put her hand on his chest.

"Did you tell Cassie?"

"No." She felt her lip tremble.

Roman's brown eyes burned a hole into her skull and he wasn't giving an inch. "You know how I feel about lies, Kris."

"Fine, fine. Yes, I told Cassie." She felt her brows crease together. "You were drinking and very bitter. Otter was a teenager. You hit him and caused his lip to bleed. Yes, I'd left you for some reason unknown and I was with Guillermo." Her voice began to rise. "Do you want the gross details about my sucking his cock? Will that give you peace and closure knowing all of it? Do you want to know why I threw up? Because it made me so sick seeing what could become of us. I'm not pregnant, Roman, and I'm not certain it's such a good idea at this particular moment."

She pushed away from him. Roman caught her wrist and she swung around. "You know, Roman, there have been several times in the last year I've wished I'd never drank the stupid wine. I've not wanted visions or powers, but I've accepted them." She pulled her wrist out of his hand and pointed at him. "The one thing I've never wished, was to be away from you and Otter. So either I do something which will screw it up, or you do." She raised her eyebrows. "We'd both better pay attention to our actions and not say the wrong things, right?" She stormed through the living room to the door of her office and slammed it behind her.

****

Roman watched Kris walk into her office sanctuary. He heard something crash against the door. Moving quickly, he went the same direction. He opened the door and found Kris on the floor. She held her head and cried. A vase lay in a million pieces on the floor by a wall. He squatted next to her and put his hand on her neck. "I'm sorry, Kris. I shouldn't let anger overtake me so fast. I let the demon make me doubt you and could dropkick myself into the lake. Please forgive me," he said.

She lifted her head and looked at him. "Forgive me for withholding information. I should have told you everything. It could have been important. I didn't want to hurt you again after what the Oracle pulled last month."

Roman put his hands out. She put hers in and he stood up, pulling her with him. She put her hands around his waist and rested her head on his bare chest. He felt guilt in his heart and thought he could have handled the situation better.

"Roman, if Guillermo can get onto the deck, how do we get past him to the car? We have to get out of here." She looked up at him.

"I think this would be a good time to call in some distraction. Why don't you get a bag packed and I'll bring you some coffee. Then, we'll get Otter up, by which time Lorrie and Cass should be ready." He put his hand on her cheek and wiped a tear away. "Kris, I am truly sorry for being such an idiot and treating you the way I just did. I love you and get crazy jealous some-times. I learned a lesson, though and swear never to do it again."

"I won't hold back information anymore. Roman, do you really want more children?"

"With you, yes. I'd like a few more to support us when we're old and still chasing each other around the bed. Someone will have to keep us from breaking our hips." He leaned over and kissed her lips. They hugged and moved together back to the bedroom.

Otter woke up and pulled himself up on the side rail. He'd never done this before and they both smiled.

Otter grinned back, and tried to bounce, but fell over onto his back.

Roman went to the crib and picked him up. "Good morning, wee one. Look at you all standing up and playing."

Kris came up to them and kissed her son's head. Otter gurgled and laughed. Roman kissed her, patted her behind and said, "I'll get him changed and then get some cereal in him. You want coffee, yes?"

****

"Yes, I want coffee, and thank you for understanding. I'll start getting things packed." She watched Roman change the baby's diaper as she got a small duffle bag out of the closet. She also pulled out a larger travel diaper bag. Roman and Otter left the bedroom and she heard noises in the kitchen. She could hear Roman getting Otter into his high chair and then pouring Cheerios into a bowl. It sounded so sweet to her ears.

She went into the bathroom and pulled a plastic bag out of a drawer. It held old make-up brushes, which she emptied back into the drawer. Pulling several sage leaves out of a pot by the bathroom window, she put them into the palm of her hand, and opened a poison spell in the file cabinet of her brain. She recited the incantation, and watched the soft, green leaves turn brown and shrivel. Once the spell was finished, she put the remains of the leaves into the baggie and folded it up and jammed into her jeans pocket.

Kris packed the diaper bag for Otter first, and got changes of clothes and pajamas to put in. She stood up and listened for sounds from the other room. It seemed too quiet out there. She went to the bedroom door and looked right to the kitchen. Otter sat in his highchair and looked straight ahead. When she moved in closer, she saw that the back door lay flat on the floor. She wondered briefly why she hadn't heard it happen and walked toward it to look out to the back of the house. She couldn't see Roman anywhere.

Chapter Thirty-Six

Roman felt sideswiped. All he'd seen was black and then something wrenched deep in his chest. He thought he might be having a heart attack, but then the back door blew in and he got pulled out. He watched as a dimensional doorway opened. It swallowed him as though a hand reached out and pulled him into the swirling clouds.

When he came to and his senses returned, he found himself chained between two thick oak trees in a dark and vile forest. The smell of sulfur was strong and there was another hideous aroma in the air. It smelled of death. He could see eyes looking at him. Something ran past his thigh and he felt a stabbing pain in his calf. He tried to see what lingered in the darkness, but the shadows enveloped the small thing.

Roman worried about Kris and Otter and what they could be going through. He prayed to God that she'd gotten into the car and driven out to Father Rupert's church. He begged for God to watch over and protect them. If he knew anything, though, Kris would be stubborn and try to find him, which doubled his worry.

Out of the corner of his eye, he saw a light move toward him. He looked over his shoulder and watched it come closer and closer. He heard a squeaking noise that reminded him of a bad shopping cart wheel at the market.

Through the shadows and darkness, came a

disfigured man. He'd broken and re-broken parts of his body many times and limped, hunched over a cart. He wheeled it up to Roman, who could see torture devices and whips of many varieties on the cart.

Roman looked at the man and thought because of his build and looks, he might be an ogre, but realized the man was as mortal as any of the Lakemen.

"Master Roman," the broken man said. "I've been assigned to you. It will be my job to beat you for a time. Lord Guillermo is unsure if he wants you dead or not. It depends on the decision of another." The man picked up a whip with three tails, with metal bolts attached to the tips. He made his way around behind Roman.

"Sir," Roman said over his shoulder. "What is your name?" He could hear the man's congested breathing.

"My name is Bartolome."

"Where is this place?"

"You have been brought to the under realm, Master Roman. You must pay for your sins."

"Sins? What sins?" Roman wanted to know why he needed to be punished. He didn't think he'd sinned much. Guillermo just wanted to sway Kris to his dark side.

"Lord Guillermo did not share that with me. I only do my job." Bartolome walked around Roman and flicked the whip to the side, making it crack. He then brought it around and snapped it on Roman's back.

Sucking in his breath, Roman kept himself from screaming. The pain seared, but he refused to give in and wrapped his hands around the chains that held him to the tree.

****

Kris stood in the kitchen, and tried to make sense

277

of what she saw. "Roman? Babe?" She looked from the kitchen to the living room. "Where are you, Roman?"

Otter pounded the tray on his highchair, which caused Kris to jump. "Ma, ma, ma," he said, over and over. He held out his hand to her and moved his little fingers, beckoning her to come to him.

Kris pulled him out of the chair and held him in her arms. "Otter, where did Daddy go?"

He turned to the door and pointed. When Kris turned her attention to where he looked, she saw Guillermo just outside. He stepped through the doorway, and looked smug, but stopped just inside.

"I told you the spell wouldn't hold, Mrs. Lake. I have your man. Come with me and I'll release him unharmed," the demon said. "We can continue from where your vision left off."

"Why won't you just leave us alone?" she hissed.

Guillermo laughed. "Oh, Kris—may I call you Kris?—you are worth more to me and my family than all the gold in the world. Your powers are so very enticing. With you as my woman, I'll have the realms in my hands. It will be so delicious." He licked his lips. "I can taste it even now. I've looked for a mate for so long and here you are. Think of all the fun we can have."

Kris felt stuck and didn't know what to do. She knew she carried enough power to blow this demon into oblivion, but he'd taken Roman.

"Put the brat down and come with me. I'll give you all you've ever desired. There are worlds you've never seen and I'd love to show them to you. Together we can take them one by one." Guillermo held out his hand. "Come with me," he whispered.

Kris took in a breath to say something, but another voice came from behind the demon. "Guillermo, leave the lady alone," it snarled.

The dark eyes closed and he hissed, "Troll, why is it you stalk me?"

"I have nothing better to do than to follow you around God's creation. Get away from her, you spawn of Lucifer." Gaspar stood on the back deck between Omar and Marcus. Cedric emerged next to Omar.

When Kris saw them, her jaw dropped. She thought of the Knights of the Round Table, but threw that thought away and focused on the situation.

Gaspar flung a powdery substance at Guillermo and said, "Shoo, shoo, evil creature, be gone. Go back to your slimy rock."

As Kris watched, Guillermo sneered and faded from view. She blinked and he'd disappeared. The troll and the three men walked into her kitchen.

Gaspar approached Kris and smiled up at Otter. "Hello there, little one. My, my, aren't you glowing," he whispered and held up his hand.

Otter gurgled, leaned over and held onto Gaspar's hand while they concentrated on each other. Kris felt a sizzle of electricity run up her arm.

Gaspar nodded. "Yes, yes, I see. Not good, not good at all." He let go of Otter's hand and turned to the Lakemen. "Gentlemen, it would seem Guillermo's thugs caught Roman unawares and have taken him. We will need to begin a search immediately." He looked back at Kris and she felt tears well in her eyes. "Ah, dear lady, do not fret. Your man is very strong. We will find him. Of this I am certain." He patted her hand. "Omar, please, put a protection spell around the womenfolk and get them up to Father Rupert."

"No," Kris said. "No, I'm not leaving. We have to find Roman. With the merge spots, he and I are connected, so I can help." She saw Omar gear up for an argument.

"Mrs. Lake, if your husband is where I believe he is, the merge will be of no use," Gaspar said softly.

"Where do you think he's been taken?" she asked.

"More than likely, Roman is in the under realms." Gaspar's red eyes seemed to brighten. "But have no fear. I believe we can save him. Yes, I do believe this with all my heart." He turned once more to Omar. "This Lakeman will see you to safety and then return to help with the search."

Kris suddenly registered Cedric's presence. The last she'd heard of him, he'd possibly turned evil and assisted the old Oracle. "What is he doing here?"

Cedric looked surprised. "I returned to face my punishment. My brother, Omar, spoke in my defense. I've been suspended for a while, but our leaders aren't going to strip me of my powers. I'll be re-evaluated in ten years. Until then, I will intern with Omar and Marcus. They are good teachers," he said..

"I had a vision you were turned and gone," Kris whispered.

Omar smiled. "I know I don't need to remind you, Kris, that your visions are subjective. Cedric is back where he belongs and is definitely not turned."

She glared at him and growled in her throat. "I remember, and you don't need to tell me again, Omar."

"Mrs. Lake, I swear I'll help out as much as I can. We'll find Mr. Lake," Cedric said.

"Please, please, big reunion at a later time. We

must get the ladies to safety, please," Gaspar said and shuffled out the door to the deck.

Kris walked up to Omar. She looked in his eyes. "Are you sure there's no other way? I really want to help."

"I know you do," Omar said and patted her arm. "I can't worry about Cassie, you, and Lorrie while we try to find Roman. Father Rupert will take good care and keep you all safe." He squeezed her arm.

She pressed her lips together. "I don't like it."

"I know, you just want to fight with me." He grinned. "Kris, we'll find him, I promise."

"I'm holding you to it. You better pray you don't have to face off with me. I will hurt you." She poked him in the chest.

Chapter Thirty-Seven

The old man, Bartolome, sat on a downed tree. He'd started a fire and boiled something in a pot, which smelled vaguely familiar, but Roman couldn't place it.

After he shredded Roman's back with the various whips, Bartolome unchained him, and tied his wrists behind him. Roman lay on his side, in a pile of wet mold and nettles.

"Lakeman, you shouldn't have sinned against the lord. His wrath is vicious," Bartolome said and chewed his food.

"I didn't sin against him," Roman answered and opened his eyes.

"That's what they all say. Lies, lies, and lies."

"He wants my wife. He's using me to weaken her."

There was silence for a moment and Roman thought he'd lost the conversation thread with his torturer, but he heard a cough.

"I had a wife, many years ago. She was such a sweet little thing. Miri was her front name. She made wonderful blood pie," the old man remembered. "One of those damned highland scum's stole her from me. Told her I'd died at Trafalgar, which was a load of horseshit. I was nowhere near that battle and never would have lowered myself to be a ship swabby, ever. Stupid woman should have known," he finished.

"Did she give you children?" Roman asked.

"Yeah, several, but they never amounted to much.

You?"

"Yes, a son. We were only married a little over a year ago." Roman could see Kris and Otter's faces in his head.

"She was with child before the marriage?"

"Yes, we weren't aware of it until after the wedding. She's a very strong wizardess and that's why Guillermo wants her."

"Shame," Bartolome said.

"Bartolome, how is it you came to be here? Why are you doing this job?" Roman asked. He wanted to keep the old man talking.

"The master did something for me, once. I owed him a debt, which I've spent some time paying off. I still have a few hundred years left before the contract is through."

Roman heard what sounded like an old man standing, lots of popping and creaking. Bartolome walked up to him, and pulled him up onto his knees. Roman saw the black jack in the man's hand as he grabbed a handful of hair. He jerked Roman's head back and looked him in the eye. "You seem like a right proper man."

"Thank you, Bartolome," Roman swallowed.

"But I have a job to do. Will you accept my apology?"

"Of course, I understand you have to carry on."

Bartolome nodded, and brought his hand back.

****

It took an hour to get to Sedro Woolley. Omar drove Cassie's car and the silence lay heavy between them all.

Kris felt torn about leaving. She wanted to help

them abolish Guillermo and all those involved with him. If one hair on Roman's head looked damaged, she might turn evil just to kill demons.

Cassie didn't think she needed to leave her home, but Omar insisted and didn't want her anywhere near what might be coming. If Guillermo got his hands on her and Kris, it would be ugly.

Lorrie mumbled about how she'd moved to Moses Lake to get away from the magicks and couldn't understand why being at a church would make any difference. Marcus explained to her about the church being on holy ground, protected by God, and that no demon... not even Lucifer... would dare try to materialize there.

Kris sat in the back with Otter in his car seat and Lorrie on the other side. With her mind spinning, she convinced herself she wasn't running, but protecting her son.

When they arrived at the church, Fathers Rupert and Greg came out to help them unload their bags. Kris and Cassie remembered the way to the rooms where they'd stayed before. Father Greg showed Lorrie to another room.

Kris walked into the main hall of the church and held her sleeping baby in her arms. She lowered Otter onto a pew and sat down. Looking at the cut glass windows and the cross above the altar, tears started to roll down her cheeks. She hated herself for crying and for leaving the lake. She wished she'd dry up and quit bawling like a baby.

After a while, she blew her nose. Her eyes were closed as she rocked Otter back and forth. She found herself praying for God to watch over and protect

Roman. When she opened her eyes, she found Father Rupert next to her. She adjusted Otter to lie in the pew beside her and blew her nose again. "Hello, Father."

"Hello, Kris. Omar tells me things have been very difficult since last we met," he said.

"Up and down, yesterday and today. I don't know." She shook her head and rested it in her hand.

"Would it give you any comfort to know that God hears you and will do his best to protect Roman?" he asked.

"Father Rupert, the only way I'll ever be comfortable again is when Roman has his arms around me and I've sent every demon that's loose on the planet back to Hell," she said and marveled at the strength in her voice.

Rupert nodded. "Remind me never to get on your bad side. Roman is a very strong man."

"I don't mean to interrupt, but if I hear one more time how strong Roman is, I may go insane. I'm married to him. I know he's strong."

"Forgive me, Kris. Of course, you're right."

She held up her hand. "There's nothing to forgive, Father. I do need some advice, though. I don't want to spend the rest of my life having to pack up a bag whenever a vision happens or some demon decides to come annoy us. How do I get them to leave me and mine alone?"

"I'm sure you are aware of the binding spell?"

"Not an option."

"It would seem, Kris, that you need to make a stand. If there was a way for you to abolish Guillermo on your own, it would be a loud statement to the evil that roams the earth, about your strength and power,"

Father Rupert said. "It would keep some, not all, but some from wanting to cross your path. I would say, though, perhaps we should wait for the men and Gaspar to return before you plan any action."

Kris looked at the priest and tried to smile. "Of course, Father."

"Kris? I sense that you have already decided on a course of action?"

"No, not really, but something is nagging me. I'm just not sure what. I'm tired and think I need to get a good night's sleep before two and two will equal four again."

"Why don't we get you some dinner and then you can rest?"

"Good, thank you. I'll go and get the others." She picked Otter up from the pew and went back to the guest quarters.

She knocked on both doors and they all walked to the kitchen for an early dinner. Kris got a bottle ready for Otter and he fed while she ate. The silence at the table felt as heavy as on the drive up to the church.

"Ladies, if you don't stop giving me the silent treatment, I swear I'm going to lose my mind," she said and looked at them both.

"It just doesn't seem fair. We have our men, but Roman ..." Lorrie started.

"...Was taken," Kris finished the sentence.

"Right, and Guillermo isn't after us. It's you he wants." Lorrie sat back and looked at her plate. "I'm sorry, I know I'm whining."

"Guys, number one, Roman will be back, Hell or high water, cliché, cliché. You two are important to me, and Guillermo must know this. He would be too

286

tempted to use you against me, too, and I don't want you in that danger. Neither do Omar and Marcus," Kris said.

"You sound certain it will be worked out and Roman will be returned." Cassie looked at Kris across the table.

"I am certain. Now, please, I want to be clear on one thing. No matter what happens, you two must stick together. I know it's been a difficult friendship for a while, but get over it, okay?"

Cassie and Lorrie looked at each other and nodded like schoolgirls.

"But Kris, it is we three staying together, right?" Cassie pointed at all three of them.

"Of course," Kris said and heard voices come from the hall.

Fathers Rupert and Greg came into the kitchen looking angry. "There is a problem," Father Rupert said. "Guillermo has sent his spawn to surround the church. They're around the outside fence and blocking the main entrance. They've also cut off our phone service. Miss Cassandra, can you communicate with Omar?"

Cassie sat up straight and took in a breath. She ran her thumb over her merge spot and closed her eyes. She hummed and then opened her eyes. "The number I tried to reach is unavailable. It's blocked, I can't get through." She put her hands up.

Kris hadn't thought of trying to reach Roman. She felt stupid and pulled Otter onto her lap. He'd been playing with his bottle. "Baby boy, I need your help," she said.

Otter looked up at her and squeaked. He put his

hand over her merge spot and concentrated on it.

Kris felt herself pulled and kept repeating *find Daddy* in her head. When she opened her eyes, she stood in a deep, dark forest. Adult Otter was next to her and held her hand. He put a finger up to his lips. They heard a snapping noise through the trees.

Moving together, Kris and Otter tiptoed around a tree. What they saw took seconds to register. Kris started to move forward, but Otter grabbed her around her waist, put his hand over her mouth and dragged her behind a tree. They both breathed hard.

Otter pulled them out and when they opened their eyes back in the kitchen, he started to cry. Kris brought him up to her chest, and wrapped her arms around him. She looked at the eyes around the table that watched her. Finding Father Rupert, she addressed him. "We found Roman. It's really bad. There isn't much time."

Chapter Thirty-Eight

"What did you see?" Cassie asked.

Kris looked at her. "It was a dark forest full of mold and slime. Someone tortured... beat Roman. He was covered with blood and...." She closed her eyes again and tightened her hold on Otter.

"It sounds as though they have him somewhere in the under realms as Gaspar thought. This could be difficult." Father Greg frowned.

Kris looked at him. "Why difficult?"

"Kris, there are certain realms we are not allowed to enter unless invited. Gaspar may be able to delve there, but us, no. The under realm is not a place I would want to visit, it is pure evil and nothing survives," Father Rupert said. "We need to figure a way to rid ourselves of the lesser demons surrounding us."

Kris stood up and nodded. Otter stopped crying and put his hand on her chin. She looked at her son's brown eyes, so like his daddy's.

Otter sucked in a breath. "Ma, ma, no....," he said.

She took his little hand and held it to her lips. "Baby, I've got to try. It may not work, but I have to try."

"No." Otter's eyes filled with tears and he put his forehead against her chin. "No, no, ma."

"I love you, wee one. Your daddy and I will be back before you know it," she whispered in his ear. She wanted it to be true. Looking at Cassie, Kris tried to smile. "I hope you won't mind watching him for a bit?"

Cassie twitched and put her hands up to her face. "Kris, are you sure?"

Kris nodded and passed Otter into Cassie's arms. He fought her for all his worth and grabbed onto her shirt, but finally gave up. Tears rolled down his cheeks as she pulled away.

"Kris, I wish you would reconsider this. You're putting yourself in grave danger," Father Rupert said.

She started to leave, but stopped and looked back. "Hey, don't look so grim you guys." She smiled and flashed the *I love you* hand signal she usually reserved for Roman.

She went to the room in the guest quarters and picked up her coat. With the sun going down, it would be chilly outside. She pulled the plastic baggie out of her pocket and looked at what was left of the sage leaves. It turned into a fine white powder. She hoped the white dagger poison spell worked. She would need it.

White dagger poison was similar to nano-technology in theory. The white daggers, once ingested, begin to multiply as they hacked away at the person being poisoned from the inside out. She hoped she would have the opportunity to introduce it to Guillermo.

Walking out the back door of the quarters, she followed the driveway down to the wrought iron gates. Her shoes crunched on the gravel as she strode forward. She felt no fear or cowardice, but her heart broke for Roman and the situation she'd seen him in. Providence would lead her in the right direction.

The sun fell behind the mountains and it would

soon be very dark. She walked around a curve that led to the gates. Outside the bars, she could see a variety of demons stood Guard. There were black wisps of smoke floating outside the perimeter and tall and short people all with black eyes, watched her as she approached. Men and women in various types of clothing—some completely naked—looked at her with menacing glee. If she'd been asked to give a number, she would have thrown up her hands. She almost started to laugh, it reminded her so much of the movie *Night of the Living Dead*.

"Is anyone here in charge?" she asked. No answer came. "I'm coming out. Take me to Guillermo." She reached up with her hand and blew the lock on the gate with a bolt from her palm.

The minions mumbled and moved back. Kris made a small space in the gate and slipped through.

"Your leader, take me already," she hissed.

A little blonde-haired girl walked up to Kris and took her hand. Besides the black eyes, the child grinned, exposing a mouth full of razor sharp teeth. Kris's heart tugged and felt terrible for the child, but then realized it was a demon in costume.

As Kris watched, everything went sideways and took on a negative color. It all seemed backwards. She squinted as a wind kicked up and blew straight into her face. As the blonde imp moved them, Kris felt the temperature climb and knew she didn't need her coat. Whatever hit her face, felt like hot needles. She closed her eyes to keep them from burning and brought an arm up to cover her face.

Before long, she they'd stopped and her hand was empty. The little blonde child disappeared. She opened her eyes and found that she stood in a room. The room looked familiar and she knew it from her vision of her evil self and Guillermo. There was the king-sized bed with the crimson red comforter, the black carpeting, and the table where she'd looked at tarot cards. The mirror seemed bigger than she remembered, but hey, can't get everything just right.

After going through the blast furnace, she felt warm enough to take off her coat. She looked at herself in the mirror, pleased she didn't have a bunch of red, burn spots on her face. Thinking she stood alone in the room, something on the back of her neck said no. She went to where a drape hung from the ceiling to the floor and pulled it back. There was a window and outside the glass were flames. She could see humans being burned, blazing by the hundreds. Some were still alive and she could see hands reach anything, to grab, but there was nothing for them to grab onto. It looked like the fires of Hell.

"Believe me, Kris, you don't want to go out there," a voice said behind her.

She looked over her shoulder and saw Guillermo. He leaned his back against the door and wore tight, black jeans and a black shirt, buttoned half way up. Five o'clock stubble shadowed his face and his chest looked hairy. She remembered Roman's smooth, muscular chest and already missed it. Kris turned back to the window and looked out at nothing.

She felt him come up behind her. His finger traced her neck and it caused her to move away from him. "Gee, no touching until I'm certain you uphold your part of the bargain. I want my husband back with my son, unharmed, now!"

"You have a long memory, Kris," he said.

"It was just this morning, why wouldn't I remember? Release him, Gee," she said and turned to face him.

Guillermo's eyes flashed and he moved his hand. "Done, now ..."

"Prove it to me." Kris squinted.

He shook his head, rolled his eyes and pointed to the mirror. Kris moved to it and saw the lawn at the church. It looked dark, but she could see Roman being helped up by the Fathers. Cassie brought Otter out of the guest quarters. He seemed to connect with Roman and let him know what Kris tried to do. Her darling man looked at the others angrily. They all spoke at once. The mirror cleared and she saw her reflection.

"Gee, one other thing. I hate facial hair. You're going to have to shave." She watched in the mirror as he moved his hand up to his face to feel the growth. The stubble vanished from his cheeks and chin.

He put his hands on her hips and looked back at her. "Better?"

Kris nodded. "Thank you, much better. You don't look as old."

"May I take your coat?" he asked, reached around her and rubbed an elbow and forearm against her breast.

Kris held it up and willed it back home. She felt pleased when it went poof and disappeared.

His hand moved to her stomach and he pressed his pelvis against the small of her back. "Very impressive, Mrs. Lake."

Kris looked up at him over her shoulder. "If that's so impressive, will you have a heart attack if I do something big?"

He laughed. "Touché."

His hair hung over her shoulder and some of it moved around her neck. A section tried to work its way into the front of her shirt.

Kris pulled away from both Guillermo's hands and his hair. "Gee, I'm not comfortable with jumping right in there. I've never trusted your world and it's going to take some work. I can tell just by the look on your face, that you're only lusting for my body. You don't trust me, either, and aren't really certain you're going to keep me," she said and watched his brows crease. "How close am I, soon-to-be-lover?"

His black eyes flashed and the eyebrow fold went away. "You hit it right on the nose, my dear, right on the nose. Until I'm sure you won't kill me and will equally crave my body, I will have to reserve a decision on keeping you." He moved his hand again and a bar appeared. "Would you care for a drink?"

"Yes, I would, thank you." She walked over and sat on a stool.

"Courtesy isn't a necessity here, Kris."

"Old habits die really hard, Gee." She smiled.

"What would you like?" He moved to the other side.

"I'm not much of a drinker. Whatever you're having will be fine." She looked at him and watched as he opened a bottle of Brael Mist Merlot. It somehow seemed fitting that he'd serve Abednego Brael's wine. He was the bastard who started all of this. "Gee, is this wine similar to the peach chardonnay?"

He grinned. "Not as sweet as the chardonnay. Have you tasted the peach?"

"Yes, once over a year ago. It was too sweet, as

you said." Kris continued to watch him.

"The merlot is very full-bodied with a little kick, but not like the chardonnay kick. You won't have any lower level demons swimming around in you, only a larger level demon in you," he said and arched his brow.

"I guess that is some good news. I nearly coughed up my lungs after trying to burn up the peach and accidentally inhaled the smoke."

He poured a small amount into a glass, walked around the bar, and stood next to her. Taking a sip of the wine, his head shot down and his lips pressed onto hers. His hand moved to the back of her neck and held it tight. His tongue parted her lips and tore into her mouth. This demon didn't have any finesse as a kisser. Some of the wine leaked onto Kris's tongue, sliding down the back of her throat.

"God, woman, you are pulsing with energy, it's incredible," he said and licked her lips.

"Are you going to pour me a glass, too?" Kris asked.

Guillermo straightened up, looked down at her and put his hand in her hair. "You really want to drink?"

"We have plenty of time, Gee. Perhaps we should savor our first time together." She tilted her head and tried to appear coy.

Putting his glass down, he reached across her and poured wine into another glass. Handing it to her, he watched Kris take a sip. "Woman, my penis is as hard as a stick in these tight pants and I can't wait to set it free and feel your energy surround me. I think I may have to keep you." He licked her neck. His hand moved up her thigh into the V between her legs and then he started to lift her shirt and slipped the hem out of her pants.

"Gee, wait, wait." She grabbed his hair and pulled his head back. "Listen to me, listen." She looked into his eyes. "I had a vision of us. I wore a red negligee and you had on black silk leisure slacks." Kris felt a lie come to her, but didn't care. "I remember the feeling in that vision. Putting my hand down those leisure slacks and holding your cock in my hand." She brought her hand down onto the front of his pants and applied pressure. She tried to sound breathless. "I want it to be like that, but I need to get myself ready."

"You can do it now, magically." He started to move in again.

"Please, Guillermo, give me a couple of minutes. I'm going to have to put my old life behind me now. I want to be as presentable for you as possible." She tried to look as innocent as possible.

He let out a breath and looked down at her hand. "I'm going to want your hand right back on my cock as soon as I return. One more kiss." He looked into her eyes.

Kris stood and kept her hand on his crotch. She stood on tiptoes and put her lips on his. Their mouths parted at the same time. All she wanted needed to do was not heave into his mouth and convince him to get out of the room. She caught his lip between her teeth and pulled it.

He sighed and opened his eyes. "I'll be back shortly. Prepare yourself," he said, touched her lips and moved his hand down to her breast and pinched the nipple.

She watched him move to the door and leave the

room. When the door shut, Kris shook her head. "Boys and testosterone, what an idiot," she said to herself.

Kris pulled the plastic baggie out of her pocket and poured the contents into the bottle of wine. She saw the white powder start to swirl inside the bottle and turn the liquid clear. She almost fainted, but finally the wine went back to its normal dark color.

She put the bag back into her pocket, ran her hand up her body and changed into a red mini negligee. She looked down and realized she'd left on her bra and panties. "Kris, you dork, that won't blind him," she mumbled. She ran her hand again this time changing to a long spaghetti strap nightgown. A split ran down her leg and she grabbed the fabric to check underneath.

"Better, but we need more mind blowing," she whispered. One more time and she conjured the same gown, but much more sheer. Nipples and crotch could be seen. She looked at her reflection in the mirror. *Roman would love ripping this off. I'll have to remember it*, she thought to herself.

Kris looked at her nails. Clenching her fists she lacquered them with red polish to match the nightgown. "Rochelle would be happy to finally see me in red." She shook her head.

Going back to the stool, she sat and bared her legs. She discovered that she hadn't shaved her legs in a week. Moving her hands over them, she made her legs smooth and soft. Then she popped on a pair of red spiked heels. She organized the gown again, and slid one of the straps down her shoulder.

The door creaked open and Guillermo peeked in. When he came all the way in, he wore only the black leisure slacks and it seemed obvious that he felt excited.

"What took you so long, Gee?" she asked.

"I was so hard for you. It was difficult getting my jeans off without cumming. I wanted to save that for you." He walked over to her and put his hand on her thigh.

"Why didn't you just magic them off?" she said.

"I wanted you to have enough time to prepare yourself." He looked down at her and seemed to admire her breasts. "You look so stunning, Kris."

"My harlot," she said.

"What?"

"That's what you called me in the vision, my harlot."

"Ah, yes, how could I forget your vision?" He rubbed himself against her leg and chuckled low in his chest.

"Yes." She picked up her glass and took another sip. The wine tasted vile.

He grabbed the bottle and poured more into his glass and then moved toward hers. He poured more and she wanted to throw the glass across the room.

He picked up his glass and clicked it on hers. "Ladies first, my harlot." He grinned at her.

Kris put the rim up to her lips and let the fluid into her mouth. He continued to watch until she had swallowed, and then took a long drink of his.

Well, she thought. *That's it. I'm dead, but at least he is, too.* Kris felt something stab at her chest, but didn't think it was the poison. She'd never be able to tell Roman and Otter how much she loved them and never smell their scents again or feel their warmth.

Guillermo took the glass from her hand and set it on the bar. He finished his own and put it next to hers.

Turning to her, he uncrossed her legs and pushed them apart to move his body between them.

"Are you ready to be fucked like never before?" he whispered and hooked his finger under the shoulder strap to pull it down.

"You're such a romantic, Gee." She tried to think of a way to stall him.

His hand slid the strap lower and exposed her breast. He pushed her back against the frame of the stool and lowered his head to take her nipple between his lips.

"You are tasty, my harlot." His hand worked under the fabric of her gown and his fingers moved along her soft folds. She felt them slide into her and was ready to wretch.

"My cock is waiting to feel your hand upon...." His breath caught in his throat. He stood straight and looked at her. "What?"

Chapter Thirty-Nine

Roman rolled over onto his back and realized he saw stars in the night sky. The grass felt cool against his back and it didn't crawl like before.

Did he make it back? What happened? He heard voices say his name. Something touched his neck and shook his shoulders. He opened his eyes and saw Father Greg lean over him.

Otter screamed, "Da, da!" Roman could see Cassie try to hold the baby who fought her.

Roman tried to sit up, but his back and arms killed him. He could only imagine what he looked like. If Bartolome did his job properly, he felt sure it was what caused Otter to scream.

He watched as Cassie set the boy down beside him. Otter quieted, put his hand in Roman's and squeezed tight. He felt his senses being pulled again and let himself float free.

When he opened his eyes, he stood by Haller Lake on a sunny day. Adult Otter paced back and forth in front of him and stopped to look at him.

"Are you in there yet, Dad?" Otter asked. His eyes were red from crying.

"Yeah, I'm here." Roman tried to nod but something stabbed his neck. "I'm here, Son."

"Mom turned herself over to Guillermo. The church is surrounded by lesser demons and his minion," Otter said and started to pace again.

"How long ago was it?"

"About an hour. I could sense she planned something, but wouldn't give us any information. She's being her usual stubborn self."

"That's your mom." Roman put his hand on his neck and rubbed it. "Are we at the church?"

"Yeah, Aunts Cassie and Lorrie are here. Uncle Omar went back to the lake. Cedric's back. He turned himself in and is on suspension. He still has his abilities"

"Otter, could you please stand still for a moment. My head wants to catch up with the rest of my body. Your pacing is making me dizzy." Roman lowered himself to the grass.

"Sorry, Dad." He knelt by his father's side.

"Tell me what your mom said when she left," Roman asked and held his head in his hands.

"She said she needed to try. Meaning she planned something to get you back." Otter stopped and put his hand on his dad's arm. "She wasn't scared at all. No putting on a front to comfort those around her, she looked angry and it worries me, Dad," Otter finished.

"Me, too, Son. We have to get back." He looked into the young man's eyes. "There's work to be done."

"I prayed for her. God will protect her, won't he?"

Roman squeezed his son's hand. "God will protect Mom. We'll get her back."

"Father Rupert told her that if she could vanquish Guillermo on her own, it might make the demons think twice about coming after her anymore."

Roman sat up. "Get us back, Son." He closed his eyes and felt the pull. When he opened them, he found Father Greg still by his side. Otter's little hand still held tight. He looked around and found Father Rupert, Cassie, and Lorrie.

He tried to speak, but needed to clear his throat several times. "Okay, I'm caught up. What's the present situation?" With Father Greg's help, he sat up and shook his head. His back and neck would be stiff and sore for some time.

"I wish Omar hadn't gone back to the lake. We could use his help," Cassie said and picked Otter up off the grass. "Roman you look like shit. What happened?"

"No time for that now, Cass. What's the situation?" he asked more forcefully and looked up at Father Rupert.

"There's a group of lesser demons outside the church's gates. Guillermo's minions have left, but for some reason, the demons aren't leaving," Father Rupert said. "It's as if they're waiting for something to happen, perhaps the end of the story." He folded his hands.

"Does anyone have any idea what Kris planned? Otter said when she left she wouldn't tell her plan and was being stubborn." He looked around at the others. The silence in the group became thick. "Rupert, have you put salt down around the boundary?" Roman asked.

"Yes, many times. They're not getting in."

"Good." Roman looked around and felt watched. "Let's go inside, there are eyes watching us." He turned toward the church and the group followed.

Before they reached the building, the air became very thick and humid. Roman turned back to scan the grass and tree line. The hairs on the back of his neck began to prickle. The trees swayed as a breeze picked up. The breeze quickly turned into a hard wind. Dead needles flew from the taller firs and spun in swirls around the lawn. The sky lit up and there was a loud crash of thunder.

Father Rupert walked up next to Roman and looked at the sky. "I believe God is making a statement," he said.

"I don't think that's God, Rupert. Those clouds are too angry," Roman said. The clouds turned black and rolled, forming what looked like a funnel.

"Is that a tornado?" Lorrie asked.

"We don't generally get them in the Northwest," Roman commented and continued to watch the clouds. Another flash of lightning flamed through the air and hit a tree, splitting it in half. He moved in front of Cassie who held Otter. Part of the tree fell onto the lawn and threw bark and limbs into the air.

They continued to follow the storm above them. The funnel moved up and pulled in on itself. It began to look as though a portal opened.

Roman started away from the group. The wind whipped around and debris hit his face. A light formed in the center of the portal and he saw another bolt of lightning come down. "This is a big one," he shouted at the others.

The light from it became so bright that they all closed their eyes. Otter screamed and Roman saw his son become frantic. The bolt hit the ground with a loud crash and Roman would swear later that he'd felt the ground move up under his feet. It threw him off balance.

He raced over to Cassie and took Otter from her He held his son, whispered into his ear, and tried to calm him. He felt a hand on his arm and saw Cassie point at something.

When he turned, he found the storm over. The clouds were gone and the winds died down. Roman saw a body lay where the last bolt struck on the grass. It wore a white spaghetti strap dress.

"Oh sweet Jesus," he hissed and handed Otter back to Cassie. He ran to the burned grass and saw the body was facedown. He fell on his knees and moved to turn it over. He didn't realize he sobbed as he turned Kris onto her back. "Kris, Kris." He brushed dirt off her face. "Kris, speak to me, babe." He picked her up and her head fell over his arm. "Please, God, no. Don't let her leave us. Please dear God, bring her back to us, to me, please." Roman rocked back and forth as he held Kris to his chest. He screamed.

Chapter Forty

"You bitch. What have you done?" Guillermo swung his fist, and knocked Kris off the stool onto the floor. He kicked her in the ribs and knocked the breath out of her lungs. She thought she heard something snap.

Kris forced herself to stand, tasted blood in her mouth and gasped for air. "Sorry Gee. Well, not really sorry." She limped back from him as he moved toward her and watched as he tried to grasp what happened inside his human form. She happily noticed his erection went flat. "It's so demented. You didn't think I'd fight back? Maybe demons are just stupid, cranky souls who are too trusting in the end."

"You bitch." He started toward her again, but stopped and grabbed his chest. "What is it?"

Kris moved back. "White dagger poison."

He looked at her. "You conjured white dagger?" Kris nodded. "Ah woman, we could have been so good together. Not many can conjure the dagger. Too bad you drank it, too. My father is going to be so pissed at you," he said as the skin on his hand started to turn gray. He could still move fast and dug his fingers into her shoulders. "See what you have to look forward to?"

"If it sends you back to hell, Gee, I'd swallow the whole potion. It's too bad it doesn't work slower so you could suffer more. I saw what you did to my husband, you bastard. I hope you suffer for eternity." Anger and hatred boiled in her veins. She didn't like this side of herself. "The faster you go, Gee, the better, and then I can get on with dying and be done with it." Pain stabbed into her legs which caused her to fold onto the black carpeting. She slipped from his hands and gasped from the way the poison seared the inside of her limbs.

As she watched Guillermo, the skin on his hand, arm, and chest began to crack and crumble into dust. His body shattered, fell into a white wisp and disappeared into the black carpet.

Kris put her head back. She knew it would be only minutes and she'd be the second pile of ash. She could feel the daggers do their job and shred her insides.

She looked up at the ceiling and tried not to feel sad. She would miss her family more than anything. All those mornings Roman beat her to the kitchen to start the coffee and get breakfast going. She would miss Otter in her arms with his little head resting against her chest.

She marveled, for a moment, at the fact that here, in an evil realm and just taking out a demon, she looked up at a white ceiling. Who on earth would think the ceiling would be white and not black?

Kris felt something stab her neck and her breath caught. She saw a white light up on the ceiling and it seemed to get bigger and brighter. A hole opened. She tried to push herself up to focus better on the opening, but couldn't move her arms. She saw a familiar face appear and look down at her. Slowly, she raised her arm and reached for the hole. A muscular arm extended out and grabbed her wrist. She hoped she didn't disintegrate before she got out of this room.

The arm pulled her through the portal in the ceiling. She opened her eyes and felt strong arms hold her. The familiar face smiled and she remembered Roman told her the man was a troll. She smiled. "Mr. Vitterfolk, how nice to see you," she croaked.

He smiled at her. "Keep smiling, Mrs. Lake. We still have to get you out of the woods." He felt her forehead. "I saw you put the powder into the wine. What was it?"

"White dagger," she whispered.

He looked very concerned. "We must get you back. I haven't the necessary ingredients here to cure this and we need a good witch. Take my wrist, Mrs. Lake. We must be hurrying now." He put out his arm.

She took it and felt her body being pulled in fifteen different directions. She'd been thrown into a maelstrom and spun like a top.

****

Roman had a desperate hold on Kris. He prayed to God and continued to rock her back and forth. He cried out and called her name. When a hand touched his shoulder, he pulled away.

"Enough, Roman, that is enough. We have much work to do," a voice growled at him.

Roman turned his head and looked over his shoulder. He saw a familiar face. "Gaspar?"

"Yes, boy, but reunion later. We must fix Mrs. Lake now," Gaspar said and looked at Cassie. "Are you the witch?"

Cassie wiped her eyes, and nodded.

"Good. Mrs. Lake conjured the white dagger poison to kill Guillermo and drank some herself. It is very bad." Gaspar looked sad.

"Shit, shit, shit," Cassie said and put Otter into Lorrie's arms. "We haven't much time. Father Rupert."

She turned to the priest. "Do you have a spell casting compendium?"

"Kanter?" he asked.

"No, Wilhelm?" She started to move toward the church.

"Yes, we have it." Father Rupert hurried past her. "And I believe our cabinets have all the ingredients you'll need."

"Good, let's go." They moved together into the church.

Roman picked up Kris and carried her to the guest quarters. Gaspar followed behind them.

"I have Mrs. Lake in a stasis-type slowdown. It will keep the daggers from doing further damage. It will take your witch about thirty minutes to mix the cure, but it will be dicey for the next twenty-four hours. We must get all of the daggers out of her."

Roman heard him start to pray.

Lorrie walked in and after Roman put Kris on the bed and covered her, she brought Otter and sat him next to his mom. Otter tried to merge with Kris, but pulled his hand back. "Ow!" he shouted.

Roman began to recite the same prayer Gaspar said. He held Kris' hand against his lips. He could feel the same stabbing that Otter felt, but wouldn't let go. He tried to shift what little strength he could into her, but the poison blocked him. When he looked down, he saw one of her eyes was black. Guillermo must have hit her. He got up and went to the bathroom to get a warm washcloth to get her cleaned up. She always looked so clean and beautiful, except when she acted mischievous in the garden. On those days, mud and grass stains only added to her beauty.

Roman didn't realize that tears still rolled down his cheeks and when he'd cleaned her face as best he could, he leaned over her with his lips to her ear.

"Babe, you listen to me and only me. Otter and I are waiting here for you. You get your ass back to us, pronto. There's too much work to do. I heard Lorrie say she thought she'd paint the walls at the gallery in pastels. I know you hate that idea, but it's what she wants to do. You'd better come back and tell her *no* right away. Remember our wedding night, babe? I think often of seeing you come out the back door. You looked so gorgeous; it took my breath away. That was the most incredible night. When I think about tasting and kissing you, I always find myself getting excited. I had to stop remembering it at the grocery, though. It would be a bit embarrassing trying to make love to you in the fruit or vegetable sections," Roman continued to whisper. He told her what he planned to do to her when her strength came back and set up a scene for them in the shower. Telling her she would have to hurry up and get well because his patience grew thin.

Roman glanced up and saw Otter stare at him. "Kris, your baby boy is here, and he's concentrating very hard. Otter needs his mom. See... he's nodding and he wants you back too. See?"

Cassie came in and carried a steaming coffee cup. Father Rupert trailed behind her with two large pots in his hands.

Cassie set the cup down and picked up Otter. "Sweetie, I know you want to help, but we need you out of here right now. Lorrie," Cassie said as she went through the door.

Roman watched as Cassie handed the baby off to

Lorrie and walk back into the room. She slammed the door behind her.

"Okay, we've got some work to do. Roman, we're going to need Kris sitting up, first to drink the antidote. Second, she's going to throw up."

"We don't want her to choke," Father Rupert said and helped to adjust Kris.

Roman sat behind her. Rupert set the pans next to him.

"I've started a fire out back and salted a circle. Father Greg is waiting. The poison she throws up will have to be burned. Let's not have the pots get too full. No drops should be spilled on the way to Father Greg. Gaspar and I will take the pans out."

Cassie came out of the bathroom with towels and set them next to the pans. Walking around to the other side of the bed, she sat on the edge, patted Roman's arm, and smiled. "Here goes." She picked up the cup, and looked back at Gaspar. "You can release her now."

Gaspar bowed his head, said a few words and waved his hand. Kris sucked in a breath and arched her back. Roman held onto her as tight as he could.

Cassie put her hand on Kris's forehead. "Hey, sister, we're going to get those daggers cleansed out of your body. To do it, I need for you to drink every last drop of this potion." Kris tried to turn her head away. "Hold her, Roman." Cassie moved the cup towards her lips. Kris sneered and they could hear growling come from her chest.

Roman could see her eyes were open and black wisps floated in the whites. She stared as Cassie started to tip the cup and poured the mixture into her mouth. He saw her swallow and knew that, even though she had a vile poison in her system, Kris understood on some deeper level what she needed to do.

"Bring us back the one we love," Cassie began reciting the spell.

The three men began to chant a prayer.

"Bring her back from high above. Tortured soul is all we see, give her peace and set her free." Cassie began to say the chant along with the men.

Kris finished the potion and within seconds screamed at the top of her lungs. Although Roman held onto her body, Kris's hand found a way to her neck and tried to scratch something terrible. Her legs kicked, hit Cassie's hand and sent the cup flying across the room. Cassie tried to hold her legs down and chant at the same time.

Father Rupert continued the chant and sat next to Kris with one of the pans in his hands.

"Oh God!" Kris screamed, closed her eyes and tried to break out of Roman's arms. Her breath came in short pants. She let out a shriek and grabbed the pot from Father Rupert and started to throw up.

It went on for over two hours. Roman lost count of how many pots of bile Gaspar and Father Rupert carried out to be burned. The one time he glanced at the contents in the pot, he almost threw up himself. It looked like a combination of blood and some tarry substance. He didn't look again.

****

Kris felt exhausted and thought her throat was ripped to shreds. She couldn't speak, but saw Cassie in front of her. She felt Roman's arms around her. He whispered in her ear and prayed over her the whole time. He said her self-healing mechanism must be out of order since she still had a black eye. She tried to drink water, but it hurt going down.

At some point, Roman told everyone to go and get some rest. He thanked them for their assistance. As they started to leave, Roman asked Cassie to wait. She walked back to the bed.

Roman grabbed her hand and squeezed. "Kris couldn't have a truer friend. Thank you, witch," he said and kissed the back of her hand.

"Such a suck up." She leaned over and kissed his forehead. She turned before she left the room. "Call if you need any help."

Kris watched him get her out of the white dress, which looked covered with dirt, and got her comfortable under the covers. He slid under next to her, rested on his arm and placed his other hand on her stomach. They stared into each other's eyes.

"Roman," she whispered.

He put his fingers over her lips. "Shush, babe, rest your throat. We'll talk tomorrow."

She looked frustrated, and then brought her hand up doing the sign language for *I love you*.

Roman looked at her hand. "I love you, too, wife." His strength crumbled and he put his hand around hers, bringing it to his lips and started to weep. Trying to talk at the same time, he let it all come out. "Babe, I was so scared. When I first saw you on the grass, I thought you were dead. I can't live if you're not with me. With you, I have everything. You and Otter are the only life I can imagine."

"Shush, Roman." Kris put her hand on his face. He sniffled and tried to smile. "Babe," she whispered. "When I thought I was going to die and never be able to tell you and Otter how much I love you...I've never felt so desolate in my life and I never want it again." Her voice quit working. She pulled into his arms and they held each other throughout the night.

Chapter Forty-One

Sebastian heard a very loud rumble come from his master's divining room and his innards clinched. It couldn't be good.

He scrambled down the hallway and hurried to assist Garda. He stopped at the entryway and peered around the corner. The master's seeing pool lay sideways on the floor and water and goo pooled all around it. Other pieces of furniture were broken and cast about the room. The draperies were in shreds. Garda sat in a straight back chair with his hands in his hair. Sebastian thought he could hear his master moan.

He made his way to the chair. "Master, what can I—"

"The bitch killed my son," Garda's voice came from a mass of gray hair that covered his face.

"Guillermo is gone?" the small troll asked.

"Yes," Garda snarled and sat up. He smoothed his hair back.

Sebastian saw that his master's eyes were black and sweat streamed down his temples. The troll knew that only silence from him would keep him from being killed.

"She tricked the stupid boy and his essence is gone."

"His essence? Master, do you mean he isn't even in the under realm?"

"No, you imbecile. She conjured white dagger

poison and he no longer exists." Garda put his hands up to his temples and rubbed them.

"White dagger? My lord, isn't it illegal?" Sebastian felt shocked at the woman's guile.

"Yes, it is and she's going to pay. I'm going to take care of her and her stupid band of protectors. She has no idea what she has started." Garda stood and faded from the room.

****

The morning sun came up, birds sang around the windows of the church and Kris could feel the warm sun radiate through the window. It warmed her shoulder. Father Rupert came in during the night to let Roman know that the lesser demons were no longer surrounding the church. Kris heard the brief conversation and went back to sleep. She didn't know how long she'd slept and she'd had no dreams. Her throat hurt and she'd woken up coughing a couple of times. Drinking water was next to impossible, but she tried.

She opened her eyes and found Roman already awake. He smiled down at her.

"Witches, demons, and trolls, oh my," she whispered.

"Welcome back from Oz, Dorothy." Roman grinned and kissed her cheek.

"Where is our little one?"

"I think he's still asleep. Lorrie kept him last night. I haven't heard him yet. You know, he's being very well-behaved," Roman said.

"We have such a cool son." She rolled on her side and put her head against his ribs.

Roman reached down and pulled her up.

His hand hit her ribs right about where Guillermo kicked her and it caused her to jerk.

"Kris, what's wrong?"

She lifted the sheet and showed him the massive bruise on her side. "Guillermo kicked me in the ribs and I think one is broken."

"Oh babe." He sat up and moved the sheet lightly kissing her ribs. He looked at her. "Batteries still low?"

She nodded. "Babe, I'd like to look out the window and see the sunlight," she whispered. "I'm afraid my legs won't hold me up. I can hear the birds singing."

"Say no more, my love, your wishes and commands and all that." He got up, grabbed the shirt he'd worn yesterday, and smelled it. "Yuck, this won't do." He scowled and started to throw it aside.

Kris latched onto the sleeve and pulled it toward her. "It smells heavenly."

He helped her put it on and then put on his slacks. Wrapping her legs in a blanket, he picked her up and carried her out the back of the guest quarters. The sun shone through the trees and Roman found a spot where they could sit and feel the warmth.

"I only wanted to go to the window, babe," she whispered.

He held her on his lap. She rested her head on his shoulder. "This is better than the window, don't you think?"

"The fresh air smells good," she croaked.

"Yeah, it does." Roman closed his eyes and felt her weight and the sunlight, and thanked God for saving them.

"Roman?" She brought her head up.

"Yes, my love." He opened his eyes.

"Your back." She looked at his shoulder and her brows creased. "Somehow Otter got us to where you were being beaten. That demon was so cruel, but your back looks fine."

"When I came back, the skin healed up, but my neck and back are still a bit stiff."

She looked up at him and frowned. "Should I be sitting on your lap?"

"You weigh next to nothing and would have known if my back felt upset about lifting you."

"I'm walking back in then. No more lifting for you." She put her head back on his shoulder.

"Uh-oh, do I detect an argument coming on?" Roman asked.

"Not if you listen to your wife." She smiled up at him. "Seriously, babe, that beast...there was so much blood."

"Bartolome isn't a beast or a demon. He's a man," Roman said. "He's just a man who chose the wrong path. He owed Guillermo a debt, but I never found out what it was for. I forgave him for what he was doing."

"Roman, you have such a good heart," she whispered.

"What goes around comes around. We may meet up with him again and he'll remember the kindness. There's a saying about honey and vinegar, right?"

"Yeah, I guess it makes sense." She looked up at the trees and sky. "Roman, can we stay here for a while?"

"I'm not getting up."

"No, I mean here, at the church for a while. Can we stay for a few days at least? No demons can reach us and I need a little break," she said.

317

"I'll talk to Father Rupert. I'm sure it won't be a problem."

"Good...I..." She heard something gurgle and looked up to see Lorrie come out the door with Otter in her arms.

Otter shifted into his black cat form and jumped out of Lorrie's hands. "What the..." Lorrie's mouth dropped open.

Otter ran across the lawn, jumped onto Kris's lap and head-butted her. He then shifted back to his human form, put his head against her chest and grabbed at the fabric on the shirt she wore.

Roman looked up at Lorrie. "Did we forget to mention that Otter's a shape shifter?" Lorrie didn't answer and shook her head. "I guess we did forget." He leaned over and kissed Otter's head.

"Ma, ma, ma." Otter held on tight.

Kris hugged him. She looked at Lorrie. "Maybe you want to sit down. You've gone a little pale in the face."

Lorrie looked around and found a lawn chair next to the building. She brought it out and sat rubbing her temple.

"How did he do that?" she asked and still stared at the baby.

"We're not sure where it comes from. It's in the gene pool somewhere," Roman replied.

"That is amazing."

The back door flew open and Cassie walked out. Racing up to Kris, she put her hands around Kris's shoulders and hugged her.

"I heard voices and hoped," she whispered. She stood back up. "How are you feeling?"

"Pretty skanky. I can't heal myself just yet," Kris said. "My throat's sore. I owe you guys big time. I don't know how I'll ever repay you for your support."

"Kris, shut up. Give Lorrie a raise and me a lifetime showing in the new gallery and ..." Cassie grinned and raised an eyebrow.

"Oh crap, I'm in trouble," Kris whispered and leaned against Roman.

"You three pose for me." She paused.

"Wait for it. Here it comes." Kris smiled.

"Nude," Cassie finished.

Kris looked up at Roman. "Did I mention Cassie wants to paint us in the buff?"

Roman laughed. "Kris, we've talked about this already and you know I can deal with nudity." He arched his brow. "It's all about placement and I think Cassie would do it with class."

Kris huffed. "When did you develop such a good eye for art and style?"

"I've been listening to my wife. She's really smart in the art world." He nuzzled her neck.

Kris looked at Cassie. "I guess you have a subject." She shook her head.

"Thank you." Cassie sat on the lawn. "Can you tell us what happened? Oh and please, never, ever do a white dagger again. I think you're low on blood. You threw up a lot of it yesterday."

"Just don't tell me I have to eat liver, yuck. Can we wait for everyone, so I only have to tell it once?" Kris asked.

Cassie nodded. "Omar and Marcus are on their way. Omar was frantic half the night. Apparently, Gaspar finagled Cedric's help with the portal. The higher ups are pissed, but considering who got vanquished, they're trying to be decent."

"I wondered how Gaspar's arm got so long and muscular to help me out of the under realm. It must have been Cedric," Kris said.

They sat out in the sunshine for a while, chatted and enjoyed the peace of the morning. Roman helped Kris get dressed and they walked into the rectory kitchen where Fathers Rupert and Greg were getting breakfast prepared. Father Rupert put together a special cup of lemon and honey tea for Kris to help soothe her throat. A mountain of pancakes, sausages and bacon, steaming eggs, and fresh squeezed orange juice, waited on the table.

After Father Rupert said grace, Kris sipped the tea and played with a pancake, but didn't eat much. Her stomach still did somersaults.

Omar and Marcus came in mid-way through the meal and grabbed a couple of plates. Otter played with a piece of toast, and covered himself with crumbs. Since they hadn't brought the high chair, Otter sat in Roman's lap and shared his crumbs with his dad. Every now and then, Otter held a piece of toast up to Roman, who wolfed it down and cause giggles to sprout from their young son.

Kris felt awful, but enjoyed watching her boys. She started to get up to prepare a bottle for Otter, but Lorrie ordered her to sit back down and got it ready. Otter sat with his back to his dad's chest, the bottle balanced between his feet.

As the meal wrapped up, it seemed no one wanted to leave the table. Kris sat back and after she managed to eat the one pancake, looked around the table at these people who meant so much to her. She thanked God for each one of them.

She heard Omar say, "So Kris, tell us."

Looking at him, she smiled. "There's not too much to tell, really. Guillermo wanted to drink wine. Brael Mist, go figure. He left the room where he kept me and I managed to get the poison into the bottle. If I knew he would make me drink, I would have thought of something different. I thought ..." She paused, turned away from them and tried not to focus on death. "When the poison started to affect him, Gee hit me and kicked me in the ribs. He dissolved into a pile of ash and I lay on the floor." She paused again, felt the hairs on her neck rise and knew someone stood behind her. Turning in her chair, she saw Gaspar and Cedric come in the door. "A portal opened in the ceiling and I saw Gaspar's face," she finished and, her voice faded. She smiled at the two.

Turning back around, she looked at Omar again. "Please, no questions right now. We have to figure out how to get rid of the demons surrounding the church," she said. She saw Father Rupert open his mouth to say something, but he got cut off.

"Mrs. Lake, the demons are gone," Gaspar replied. She turned and looked at him. "Don't know when they left, but they're gone for now."

"That's right, Father Rupert told Roman. I thought I might have dreamt it," Kris said.

"I wonder what they were waiting for," Father Greg said and refilled coffee cups.

"I guessed the second coming." Marcus stood up, and offered Gaspar his place at the table.

Everyone looked at Marcus and she thought hard

about his words.

"Ah guys, it's a joke. I think we should lighten up a bit." He arched a brow, took his dishes to the sink and started the hot water. Marcus looked at Kris and winked.

She turned to Cedric who sat across from her. "Cedric, thank you," she said.

He smiled at her and nodded. "We've managed to get all of the demons corralled in Parcel and they've been vanquished. There is some damage, but no lives lost. I heard one of the commanders say that the old Oracle may have been overrun by a demon and turned. The new Oracle is getting settled." He looked at Omar. "I'm in hot water again, Omar, for going off with Gaspar."

"If we can do anything to help, Cedric, please, let us know," Roman said. "They need to understand your gift helped save a very important life." He looked at Kris and leaned over to take her hand.

"Yes, Cedric, we would happily step up for you," Kris said.

"I don't believe there will be any problems once Marcus and I put in our reports," Omar commented and sipped from his coffee cup. "The administrators knew what Cedric would be doing and approved it, but the reports will help."

"I'd gladly help if needs be." Kris looked at the young Guardian.

"Thank you, Mrs. Lake." Cedric seemed embarrassed. He turned his attention to Otter, who grinned around his bottle.

She heard them tell what happened on this side and how the demons followed them out to the church. Kris noticed Roman listen, but he didn't say much and made no comments about his time being beaten.

She didn't say much more about her time in the other realm and didn't want to think about Guillermo anymore. If he'd kept her there, he might have turned her evil. If she hadn't used the poison, Lord only knows what would have happened. She wanted to believe that she would have remained strong and would have fought against him. The vision she'd experienced still haunted her and made her wonder about her strength and loyalties. She need to rebuild her trust in herself. She started to stand and then leaned over to Roman's ear, not wanting to interrupt the conversation.

"Babe, I'm going to go lie down." She kissed his cheek.

"Want me to come?" he whispered.

"Always." She grinned at him. "I'm just tired. I'll be okay."

"I'll check in on you in a little bit." He kissed her again.

As she walked out of the kitchen she heard Roman comment, "She's tired," and she was. She made her way to the guest quarters, crawled onto the bed, and pulled the comforter over her. Her stomach roiled, but she was damned if she'd throw up again.

Kris felt herself slide into a deep sleep and didn't remember many dreams. One that she did remember, felt unsettling. Her mother appeared to her and warned her that Garda was on the warpath. Kris wondered if her mom really told her or had she just dreamt it.

When she did wake up, the sun danced in and out of clouds. She tried to roll onto her back, but found Roman behind her. His arm wound around her and felt warm and close. When she opened her eyes, she looked over her shoulder and saw him watching her.

"Hi, babe," she whispered and wiggled herself around to face him.

"Glad you decided to wake up." He kissed her shoulder.

"How long have I been out?"

"Three days, but you needed it." He touched her lips.

"Where's Otter?" She saw Roman lift his head up and look over her shoulder. She turned over and could see the crib with her son conked out.

"He's still sawing logs, too. Cedric and Gaspar kept him very busy." Roman got his arms around her. "The rest took off back to the lake a couple of days ago. Father Rupert said we could stay as long as we need to." Roman put his head in his hand and looked down at her. "You healed up your eye and ribs two days ago." He ran his hand down her side. "How does it feel?"

"It doesn't hurt anymore. I guess I needed the rest. When I came back to bed, whenever that was, my stomach killed me. I have to go to the bathroom. Keep my spot warm."

She got up and tiptoed into the other room and shut the door. Looking at herself in the mirror, she found her black eye cleared up and the massive bruise on her side gone, too. She felt along her ribs and couldn't detect anything out of line. There was no pain.

When she returned, she snuggled next to Roman. "When did you strip my clothes off?"

"Three days ago, why?" Roman whispered.

"No reason, just curious. I came back only to take a nap," she said and sat up. "You know, other than being really hungry, I feel pretty good. How's your back?"

"Better. I helped the priests clean up the mess outside from the storm. It helped loosen things up in my body." He sat up next to her and kissed her neck.

"I know we have to go home, but could we plan a honeymoon? We could go to Europe, or New York, or even take Otter to Cancun. Anything, really. I suddenly want a honeymoon."

"Your wish is my command, my love. When do you want to go?" he asked.

"Now, of course. Or in a couple of weeks." She put her arms around him and leaned on his shoulder. "I can get things settled a bit at the gallery and leave Lorrie in charge. We still have a couple of months before opening."

"What's nagging at you, babe?" Roman lay back down and pulled her into his arms. He ran his fingers over her forehead.

"Roman, I want Otter to have a childhood, you know? I don't want him to be an angry teenager with hang-ups. I don't want him to feel used for his gifts." She rested her chin on his chest and looked into his eyes.

"I agree," Roman said.

"Good. I want him to get muddy and bring home frogs. If we went somewhere warm with a beach, he could play in the sand, build castles, collect shells, and pee in the water," she said.

Roman laughed. When he settled down, he rolled Kris onto her back and looked down at her. "What happened to you?"

She put her fingers in his hair and listened to him breathe. "When I had the poison in me and thought I might die before ever telling you how very much I love you"— her throat started to tighten—"it was an awakening like no other. I don't want to lose one more minute with you and Otter, because of some stupid evil lurking around. I want to hear every new word he learns and see him walk. I want to wake up with you wrapped around me every morning and just live for only you and Otter. Even though it's going to get around that I took out Guillermo, I know some stupid demons are going to have the balls to try me. I'm ready to fight for my life now and whoever tries to cross me is going to regret it big time."

"That's my girl. I love you, Kris." He kissed her chest and neck, and then brushed his lips over her chin up to her lips.

"I love you, too." She put her hands on his back. "What do you say? I get things with the gallery smoothed out and we leave in two weeks?"

"Deal." Roman put his lips over hers, kissed them and then lifted his head. "You taste great, my love," he said.

Chapter Forty-Two

Two weeks to the day, Kris, Roman, and Otter boarded a flight to Cancun. Roman arranged for two weeks in a private villa on the beach.

They spent the daytime with Otter playing on the beach and found that he loved floating in one of his parent's arms in the warm water, watching the seagulls flying around in the air, and putting sand in a bucket with a small plastic shovel. Splashing became a great diversion and, although he was only six months old, he'd become able to float briefly by himself. Every night, he need to be washed to get the sand off of him. Otter got to be a child and peed in the ocean.

On several of the nights, Roman arranged for a sitter so he and Kris could be alone. They went into town once to go dancing, but spent the rest of their evenings walking and nighttime swimming. They made love in the water and on the beach in the darkness and relished their closeness and willingness to give to one another.

Kris could tell Otter felt happy that she and Roman hadn't fought once.

During the flight back to Seattle, mother and son sat by the window looking out at the clouds as they whizzed by the plane.

Roman dozed off and put his seat back to take a bit of a nap. He dreamed that he ran a maze made of steel and stone. He could hear a voice talk to him in a low, gravelly tone. *He's coming, watch yourself, he's coming,* the voice kept saying. Roman couldn't find his way out of the gray walls.

When he woke up, he looked over at Kris and frowned. She wore a different outfit than she'd had on earlier and read an art magazine.

"Babe, where's Otter?" He straightened in his seat and frowned.

Kris looked up at him with a blank expression on her face. "Are you talking in your sleep?" she asked.

"No, where's Otter?" he said.

"Who on earth are you talking about?" She looked at him with brows creasing. "Who's Otter?"

As he watched he saw her eyes flash black at him.

ABOUT THE AUTHOR LAUREN MARIE

Lauren Marie's first published series - The Men of Haller Lake - originally came out in 2010. She's learned so much over the last seven years and it's been a dream to get the stories re-edited and problems with point of view corrected. With Books to Go, Now's help the dream has become a reality with the release of A Demon Scheme - Book 1 of the Haller Lake series and now, Magicks Pathway - Book 2 of the Haller Lake Series.

She is also the author of Big Mike-Little, Golden Ribbons -

story 4 of the Miss Demeanor Private Detective Agency series, I'm Not What You Think, Love's Embers - book 1 of the Canon City Series, Love on Ice - book 2 of the Canon City Series, One Touch at Cob's Bar and Grill - story 3 of the Montana Ranch Series, Love's Touch - Then and Now, Going to Another Place.

She lives in Western Washington State with four cats, Agamemnon, Tazmania, Jericho and Jasper.

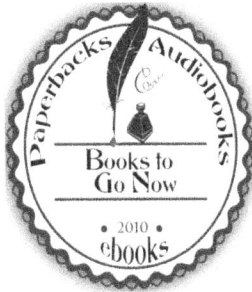

Books to Go Now

You can find more stories such as this at www.bookstogonow.com

If you enjoy this Books to Go Now story please leave a review for the author on a review site which you purchased the eBook. Thanks!

We pride ourselves with representing great stories at low prices. We want to take you into the digital age offering a market that will allow you to grow along with us in our journey through the new frontier of digital publishing.
Some of our favorite award-winning authors have now joined us. We welcome readers and writers into our community.

We want to make sure that as a reader you are supplied with never-ending great stories. As a company, Books to Go Now, wants its readers and writers supplied with positive experience and encouragement so they will return again and again.

We want to hear from you. Our readers and writers are the cornerstone of our company. If there is something you would like to say or a genre that you would like to see, please email us at inquiry@bookstogonow.com

Made in the USA
Monee, IL
01 May 2023

32720348R00184